THE TEARS
OF THE
MADONNA

Also by George Herman

CARNIVAL OF SAINTS
A COMEDY OF MURDERS

THE TEARS
OF THE
MADONNA

George Herman

CARROLL & GRAF PUBLISHERS, INC.
New York

Copyright © 1996 by George Herman

First edition 1996

Carroll & Graf Publishers, Inc.
260 Fifth Avenue
New York, NY 10001

ISBN 0-7867-0243-5

Library of Congress Cataloging-in-Publication Data is available.

Manufactured in the United States of America.

For Eric

striving artist, compassionate clown, dreamer
and second son
whose gift of laughter has lightened my burdens
and blessed my days,
with deep affection and hope for his future.

CONTENTS

ASSASSINS

September 1499

Montagnana

Yes.

This is the man who has been sent to kill me.

Cecco, twenty-five, stocky, with hair the color of autumn wheat, sprawled with a studied indifference behind an isolated table within the small inn and studied the face and figure of the tall, black-cloaked man who had just entered and taken a position near the fire. The realization that he had identified the assassin did not alarm him. There had been other threats over his five years with the Cambio, and he had always succeeded in delivering his burdens without harm.

There was nothing about the newcomer to suggest that he was a professional. Cecco judged the man to be in his mid-forties with chestnut hair and the affectation of a single curl molded against his forehead. He wore a short, trimmed beard and mustache after the style currently popular with the nobility, and a small scar above the bridge of his nose appeared inflamed by the firelight. His thick brows shadowed his eyes. A soft cap with a pheasant's feather anchored to it, also fashionable among the present courts of Italy, was perched on one side of his head.

When the newcomer removed his long cloak, Cecco could see that the man wore a burgundy velvet tunic and the striped hose of an aristocrat. A thick leather belt around the man's waist supported the customary sword, and a dagger was sheathed in a plain leather scabbard in the small of his back and angled to his right. This indicated to Cecco that the man was right-handed and probably adept at fighting in the style of the Venetians, with both weapons simultaneously, but swords and daggers were common necessities for travelers through the Lombardy plains and not necessarily a sign that murder was the man's profession.

A medallion hung from a chain of woven gold around the newcomer's neck, but Cecco, deep in his shadowed corner, could not discern any heraldic crest or impresa, no mark of familial or political loyalty.

But the way the man had filled the doorway and slowly and methodically surveyed everyone in the common room before he glimpsed Cecco, and then that cold smile of recognition although the courier could not remember ever meeting the man, that was enough to make the young Venetian believe that this was the person who had been following him for the past hour and a quarter, perhaps from as far as Mantua.

The courier sipped at his tankard of warmed wine and continued his surveillance of the possible assassin. The newcomer moved fluidly despite his heavy, knee-high leather boots. He made no sound as he crossed to the bench before the fire. He wore no spurs. One of his gloved hands rested on the hilt of his sword, and the other hung by his side, never far from the sheathed dagger. On the middle finger of his right hand he wore a wide golden ring capped by a large emerald, and Cecco imagined that beneath that hollowed jewel a small receptacle would contain a poison.

Although the new arrival seemed to concentrate on the warmth of the fire, something about the way the man sat erect and rigid in the chair suggested he was accustomed to authority and appropriate service, and he was fully aware of everything around him.

Cecco could certainly not leave the inn without the man noticing.

The Venetian watched as the noble received a tankard of the mulled wine from the proprietor. His hand did not tremble. He did not look at the courier.

4

Yes, Cecco told himself. This is the man they sent to kill me.

He assumed that they would dispatch someone, someone who would surely be commissioned to take his life considering what he was transporting for the Cambio this time, but he was an experienced courier, and his horse had been bred for both speed and stamina. Upon leaving Mantua he had felt reasonably confident that he could put enough distance between himself and any pursuer to give him an advantage, but then, where the roads forked above Legnago, he became aware of the soft footfall of a horse some distance behind him, and he immediately decided to break his journey at the Olive Tree just outside Montagnana. It was approaching sunset, and the inn would provide him with an opportunity to study his possible pursuer and formulate a plan.

Cecco turned from his examination of the new arrival and glanced through the small window at the mist beginning to rise from the Adige River. It would be a moonless night, clouded, almost without stars, and he knew that a trained assassin would prefer such a night and the solitude of a country road for his sinister work. Cecco was safe if he remained indoors and among witnesses.

He wondered which of the concerned parties had sent the man after him. Someone from Ferrara possibly, being blood kin, or from Imola, considering the history of what he was transporting. Perhaps someone from one of the courts in sympathy with the now-deposed duke of Milan, Ludovico Sforza. The assassin could also be in service to the Vatican or possibly an agent to an ally of the Borgian pope.

The history of the packet he carried was so entangled in political intrigue and the pursuit of power that such speculation was useless. He began to consider his options. To fight man-to-man would be useless if the newcomer was truly a professional. Cecco had been trained in combat, but he had

5

been chosen for his calm and his cunning. His assignments were always conducted in the deepest secrecy so he traveled without an armed escort, which would draw unwanted attention. He carried only the customary weapons, for a more heavily armed man might invite challenge. His routes between the city-states were never rigidly laid out for him. His knowledge of the countryside and his ability to adapt to threats left him free to change direction at any time. Like all the couriers for the bankers' guild, he was never identified by a family name, thus preventing blackmail or reprisals.

Cecco dressed simply, without elaborate clothing or jewels, so he would appear to be no more than a clerk carrying lengthy and tedious contracts between merchants in Lombardy or the Dolomites.

Of course, this meant that the man by the fire had inside information, knew his description and his probable route.

The courier considered leaving immediately and racing toward Padua.

No.

To leave now would simply put both the killer and his prey back on the darkening road where Cecco would be most vulnerable. It would be another three hours to Padua, then perhaps another two before he reached Venice. Cecco knew that word of his departure from Mantua would precede him, and the Cambio would very likely have their own mercenaries watching and waiting on the outskirts of Venice to escort him safely to their chambers. Consequently, an assassin would have to intercept him before Padua or somewhere between Padua and Venice, and, if it should come down to a race, Cecco reasoned that it would be better if his horse was rested.

Yes, he thought, his best chance was to stay here tonight and attempt to leave before his pursuer in the early morning. He would take a room, bar his door, and see if the man in the cloak was still about at dawning.

The courier knew that the Olive Tree had no accommodations for an overnight guest other than the small room at the top of the stairs. There was another small room below these stairs, but these were the living quarters for the proprietor, his wife and young daughter. This meant that the newcomer, should he also choose to stay the night, would have to either sleep in the stench of the barn or on the hard, short bench near the fire, both unpleasant alternatives for a man so well-dressed and apparently accustomed to comfort. If the assassin believed that the courier would not leave the Olive Tree until midday, he might just choose to ride on a little farther, perhaps to where the road forks toward Terme and where there was a larger inn with private accommodations and good food. The autumn evenings were not cold, and although the sky was clouding, there was no sign of imminent rain or snow. The assassin could be at the second inn in three-quarters of an hour, just as the dark descended, sleep well, and then rise early and wait to ambush the courier on the road.

Cecco picked at what the fat, perspiring proprietor called a tournedo, a small mound of undercooked veal and kidneys, while he continued surveying the man by the fire.

Cecco took a deep draught of the lukewarm Muscadine and loudly summoned the proprietor by name. He had acquainted himself with every inn along the roads of Lombardy and the Piedmont, and the young man wanted to suggest a familiarity with the place and the proprietor in the hope that the assassin might feel this was a poor place for murder.

"I will stay the night, Signore Pepoli," he announced so that most of the guests in the common room could hear. "See to it that my horse is fed and brushed and given water and oats. I will depart tomorrow at midday."

Cecco rose and placed four soldi tornesi, coins of base silver and copper, on the wooden tabletop. The other currency Cecco carried with him were of higher value but would most certainly attract attention.

At the sight of the silver and copper, the corpulent proprietor smiled broadly at Cecco through his blackened and broken teeth, nodded, and motioned the young man toward the narrow wooden staircase that led to the small landing and the only door on the second level.

The cloaked man gave no sign of recognition or interest as Cecco passed by him but continued to stare into the flames, one hand on the hilt of his sword, the other holding his tankard of wine.

The other occupants of the inn paid no attention to either the courier or the aristocrat. Two friars in the dark brown robes of the Franciscans sat eating in silence and detachment. Three middle-aged men, presumably bargemen who worked the ferries across the Adige, were angrily trying to divide the day's profits. A drunken farmer and his equally intoxicated woman were bent over the only other table, and neither glanced his way as Cecco ascended the stairs with his saddlebags over one arm.

He felt he should not sleep, but he knew he must.

Cecco threw his saddlebags on the narrow bed and surveyed the room. Drafty. Narrow. Directly beneath the roof. Beams overhead. Only one door, which could be barred. A small window of waxed paper that offered a fragmented view of the stable area. A table beneath the window held a single oil lantern, which Signore Pepoli lit with a taper. A single bed with four corner posts that pretentiously supported a dingy cloth canopy. A washbasin and a cracked pitcher rested on a rickety wooden stand by the window.

He waited until the proprietor had closed the door behind him, and then Cecco crossed and barred it with the heavy section of wood provided for that purpose. He glanced through the window and was not surprised to see the black-cloaked man striding through the twilight toward the stables.

As Cecco watched, the man appeared again, mounted on a grey stallion, and rode away. Cecco smiled. The man had apparently decided to ride to the crossroads farther on and spend the night in a more comfortable inn. The confrontation had been delayed, which was all Cecco could hope for at this point.

The courier sat on the edge of the bed and drew the packet of black velvet from his saddlebags. He fingered the small burden reverently, as if a man's touch would somehow corrupt it. He laid the packet carefully on the stand and prepared to sleep.

Milan

The full-bearded man in the billowing black cloak and the soft, crushed-felt cap leaned wearily against the frame of the doorway and struggled for breath. He was uncommonly tall, with huge hands stained with pigment, the markings of a life spent working with tools and marble and paints. His hair was worn long, in soft curls streaked with silver that clung about his broad shoulders. His nose was thick, drooping slightly toward his thin lips, and most of his face was mantled in the fine mustache and beard that revealed only the high cheekbones and the small pouches beneath his eyes. His brows were thick and shadowed his eyes, and the corners of his mouth were bowed downward as if in infinite anguish.

It was darkening rapidly now, the day resigned to dying, and the bearded man felt as if his own will to live, to persist in the struggle of life, might be draining away with the light of the sun.

Five hours earlier Maestro Leonardo di Ser Piero da Vinci had watched as the last remnants of his huge clay model for the equestrian statue of Francesco Sforza, already mutilated by French gunners, had been encircled by jeering Gascon and Swiss mercenaries and a small horde of the Milanese townspeople. They had flung coils of rope around the model and drawn them taut as they struggled to wrench the horseman from its pedestal. Finally the monumental artifact had trembled, as if frightened at the fury and venom of the mob, and tilted slightly on its pedestal. Then it had fallen, slowly at first and then with alarming speed that scattered some of its tormentors, and shattered against the cobblestones of the piazza.

Having fled through the secret passageway that led to the street from the Castello Sforzesco, Maestro Leonardo had watched the desecration of his work with a bitter resignation, and now he felt as though he, too, might collapse and crumble in the face of such rage and barbarism.

Only a week earlier he had realized that the paint of his fresco, 'The Last Supper,' in the refectory of Santa Maria delle Grazie was beginning to crack and peel away, a consequence of his attempt to formulate a new way of painting on plaster that would allow for a more leisurely application and accommodate repeated changes and alterations. He had spent nearly two years, striding the short distance from the castello to the chapel at least once a day, to dab and revise and dab again at his work. He had been satisfied with it. The completed painting stretched the width of the refectory in an impressive demonstration of forced perspective. The upper room that temporarily housed Christ and the apostles appeared to be exactly the same width as the refectory itself and extended beyond the depicted room until a landscape and a distant horizon became visible through the two windows and the arched portico in the back wall. This attempt to fool the eye by perspective had been mastered by a contemporary, Maestro Andrea Mantegna, now the resident artist in the Gonzaga court at Mantua, and Leonardo had been fascinated by the mathematical laws that had to be applied.

But perspective was not the crowning achievement of this 'Last Supper.' No two figures in the painting were alike. Each had its own story to tell. Each expressed his own feelings. No artist had captured such a variety of emotion and expression.

11

Leonardo had labored at the project with concentration and love. He would come and paint in spurts of feverish activity, and then he would sit and study his fresco in a somber silence for perhaps four or five days at a time, wondering if this figure might be better turned a quarter to the right, if this hand should be raised rather than resting on the table. He would study, and dab, and reflect.

Now he had to concede that the slow disintegration of his painting was irreversible, a result of his refusal to work quickly and absolutely.

In time, like its creator, it would crumble into dust.

Leonardo had also received confirmation that invaders had destroyed his magnificent model city of Vigevano. His engineer's vision of "a perfect and beautiful world" of magnificent fountains and hidden sewers and paved streets and graceful aqueducts had been senselessly destroyed before he had time enough to finish even the Carrera-marbled stables that were to line the north boundary of the central park.

Now the full-scale clay model for the largest equestrian statue in the world had been systematically mutilated and destroyed. He had spent twenty years sketching designs for the work. The statue was to stand as tall as four men mounted on each other's shoulders and would require two hundred thousand pounds of bronze and an entirely new method of casting. If he had only been given time enough to construct the proposed underground system of circular ovens, the weight of the metal horse and rider might have been withstood the mob's attempts to dislodge the statue from its pedestal!

Time. The persistent assassin.

Leonardo could understand, and forgive, the rage of the Milanese populace against his former patron, Duke Ludovico Sforza. The duke, who was known as "Il Moro" because one of his Christian names was Mauro and his complexion was somewhat darker than that of his contemporaries, had been depicted in some circles as a blackberry, but he was not a Nubian.

During his reign, the duke had brought this glorious and once prosperous city of northern Italy under siege and permitted its lucrative armories and reservoirs of salt to pass into the hands of the French invaders. He had alienated some of the oldest and most respected families and been abandoned by bankers, especially by the overlord of the Bank of St. George in Genoa, who had sent his daughter to the Milanese court for "finishing" only to have the girl impregnated while she was a ward of the duke. Then she had been murdered by Il Moro's security chief, Bernardino da Corte, while undergoing interrogation to identify the father of her unborn child.

The people of Milan had been taxed unmercifully to compensate for the subsequent denial of loans from the banks of Genoa and Florence, and their fury and restlessness had erupted into civic disturbances. The duke, apparently oblivious to the poverty of his people, arrogantly paraded his borrowed wealth through the Piazza del Duomo at the head of long columns of the parasitical lords and ladies of his court, all beautifully gowned and gloved and festooned with jewels. The poor had been forced to pay as much as fifteen soldi for a small container of oil while Il Moro bestowed a dowry of hundreds of thousands of gold florins upon a niece. The Milanese groaned as the tax on salt (which Il Moro monopolized) increased twenty times in a single year, and they grew restive when the tax on eggs increased twelve times in the same period.

Leonardo understood the wrath of the popolo against their former duke, but the desecration of his statue was incomprehensible. He had not profited from the taxes on the poor. The duke, like many other self-acclaimed "patrons of the arts," had been reluctant to part with a florin for his artists-in-residence, but there was little Leonardo could do, other than implore the duke by letter and in person for some small portion of the promised commissions.

This destruction of his work, with which he had tried to enrich the lives of the Milanese with paintings and statues of beauty and grace, of engineering accomplishments that could elevate and enhance their lives, now made the tall, bearded man inconsolable.

"Let this be placed in the hand of ingratitude," he murmured to himself. He leaned wearily against the frame of the doorway, feeling older than his forty-seven years, wondering if his old enemy, Time, would ever permit him to leave behind something of value, something that would demonstrate his skill and knowledge, his dedication, his love for God and humanity.

As he remembered the sight of the broken portions of his great statue being ground to dust under the hooves of the Swiss horsemen, he thought, "There is more than one way to kill a man."

Trumpets announced the arrival of the conquerors, and Leonardo drew back even further into the shadows to avoid being seen.

The procession was headed, of course, by Louis of France under a canopy of golden cloth, his wardrobe richly embroidered with golden bees and beehives. Behind him came the principal ally of the French, the darkly handsome Cesare Borgia, son of the present pope, Alexander VI, and a man of ambition who wished to rule the Romagna. Cesare preferred a black wardrobe, but unlike Leonardo, he did not hold simplicity to be an element of beauty, so his soft cap featured an overwhelming diamond clip. His ermine and gold-embroidered cloak trailed from his shoulders and fell gracefully over the flanks of his white stallion.

He was followed by the other enemies of the deposed Il Moro.

Leonardo recognized the regal and bejeweled woman in virtuous white who followed immediately behind Cesare. Tall and elegant, flame within ice, golden-haired Isabella d'Este rode beside her husband, Gian-Francesco Gonzaga, captain-general of the armies of Venice. His breastplate was emblazoned with the lion icon of that city. Leonardo noted that the lady's lustrous blond hair was braided and worn in a net of heavy golden thread. The elaborate velvet gown was cut low on her shoulders, sleeves gathered and ballooning to below the elbow. The lady's nose was a trifle large for perfection, her thin lips pursed as if in disapproval, the dark eyes puffed and cold, her prominent chin and ivory throat thickened and shadowed.

Leonardo shook his head, knowing that this sister to Il Moro's late wife was reveling in her moment of glory. She had triumphed, with the aid of the French, over the man whom she held responsible for her sister's untimely death.

Leonardo's attention was suddenly drawn by the refraction of light to the exquisite necklace the marquesa wore. Three strands of diamonds gathered the evening light on the lady's breast and sent it back, splintered, in rainbowed reflections.

The play of light fascinated the Maestro more than the obvious value of the necklace. Then his attention was drawn to the excess of rings upon the lady's fingers, to the gold bracelet and the rich ornamentation not only on the marquesa's gown and cloak, but also on the ermine pad and jewelled saddle and harness of her horse.

He reasoned that the lady did not understand that a lovely face arrests the attention of the people, not the rich adornments. The costly gold and silver decoration diminished her resplendent beauty. She had not seen the women of Vinci mantled in rude draperies who revealed far more loveliness than the court women who decked themselves in ornament.

If I were to paint her, he reflected, it would be without jewels and gold, in plain gown and unbraided hair.

His contemplation of the lady's attributes resurrected the image of his portrait of Il Moro's onetime mistress, Cecilia Gallerani, now the Bergamini contessa. He had painted her in three-quarter profile, her hair straight and connected under her chin as if she was wearing a country bonnet. No rings or bracelets. A plain shift. A single strand of beads. Nothing more, save the young woman's natural beauty and youth.

Behind the Gonzaga in the victorious entourage rode the allies of the French: Isabella's brother, Cardinal Ippolito d'Este, arrogant in scarlet and gold; Cardinal d'Amboise and, to Leonardo's surprise, a known enemy of the Borgian family but a man of cunning, ambition, and power, Cardinal Giuliano della Rovere, grim-faced, watching everything.

Waiting, thought the Maestro. For the glory of Peter's throne? Or for the inevitable assassin?

Leonardo's view of the conquerors' parade was suddenly blocked by a large coach and four that stopped directly before him in the archway. The door of the coach was flung open, startling him, and one of the Maestro's apprentices smiled and beckoned to him from the interior. The handsome young man wore the crest of his noble family embroidered on his tunic and his short cape, and he extended a gloved hand to the cloaked man in the shadowed doorway.

"Please come, Maestro," pleaded Giovanni Francesco Melzi. "My father thinks it best if I see you to sanctuary until we can read the humors of the invaders. Too many, I'm afraid, associate you with the court of Il Moro and may attempt to harm or discredit you because of it. My father has bribed a few officials and acquired passes that will see us through the French lines."

"Through the French lines? To where, Francesco?" asked the Maestro.

"Father Abbot is awaiting us at the Certosa. If we hurry we will be there just after nightfall."

The Maestro studied the young man. Such a contrast to my other apprentice, the yellow-haired and incorrigible thief and liar Giacomo Salai, he thought.

But not as beautiful. Never as beautiful.

"Hurry, Maestro!" Melzi insisted.

Leonardo nodded in quiet resignation as he placed one slippered foot on the narrow step and was assisted into the coach by his young apprentice.

"Did Niccolo escape?" Leonardo asked, referring to the young dwarf with the remarkable memory whom he had first met at the Certosa, the friend who had attempted to teach him Latin.

Melzi sat back against the cushions embroidered with his family's arms and nodded. "I saw him fly over the castello walls on your dragon wings, and I think he was picked up by that band of wandering actors. What were they called? I Comici Buffoni?"

Leonardo smiled at the memory of Niccolo leaping from the castello windows on the Maestro's wings to escape the mercenaries who had been sent to capture or kill him, because he and Leonardo had witnessed and recorded a series of murders in the castello. These crimes had been duly annotated in the little red book now in Niccolo's possession, some attributable directly to Il Moro and his military commander, Galeazzo di Sanseverino. The Maestro had noticed that the turncoat captain-general also rode in the victory parade behind the Cardinals, which was only appropriate, because for years he had really served Cardinal Albizzi, Cesare's spy in Milan, who had operated under the name of "The Griffin."[1]

The Maestro could not bring himself to watch the looting of the city by the mercenaries as they passed through the Piazza del Duomo and down the Corso Porta Romana. He found, to his surprise, that he still clutched the small book of Epictetus that Niccolo had given him to help with his Latin studies. He opened it without intending to read it, but something caught his attention.

He read: "Have you not been given powers to endure all? Have you not been given a greatness of heart? Courage? Fortitude? What shall distress or discomfort you? Should you not use these powers to the end for which you received them instead of moaning and wailing over what has come to pass?" The passage made the Maestro pause and reflect. Then, rocked by the gentle sway of the coach as it proceeded south, he fell asleep.

---

[1] As recorded in Niccolo's red book and ultimately transcribed in the earlier text, "A Comedy of Murders" (Carroll & Graf, 1994).

Montagnana

Cecco was awakened from a fitful sleep by heavy thudding against the downstairs door to the inn. It took him some time to orient himself, but then he remembered his assignment, the sense of being followed, his arrival at the Olive Tree, and the man he thought had been sent to kill him.

He threw back the rough woolen blanket and wrapped it around himself as protection against the chill. He did not light his oil lamp but made his way across the bare, cold floor to the solitary window. He judged it to be near midnight. Through the waxed paper he could discern lights in the stables and other lamps moving through the gloominess like fireflies, and he could make out five or six horses being led into the barn by a man he took to be a mercenary. The two Franciscan monks, who had apparently been granted sleeping space in the stables, were now being driven away at swords' point and slowly began a resigned trek up the road in the direction of Padua.

By the flickering light of the torches Cecco could see no crest, no mark of whom the soldiers served, but he did not need a heraldic symbol to tell him why they had been sent after him. He knew he had been right about the man in the black cloak who rode away earlier in the evening.

Now he had returned with mercenaries.

That surprised the courier. It was not the way of the professional. Such murders are committed quietly, with no witnesses nearby, and usually made to resemble an accident, a misjudgment or a sudden loss of attention. But this invasion by armed men was crude and somewhat stupid. There will be too many loose ends, the courier thought. Then he concluded that some power pressed upon these men. They were not afforded time for the customary stealth and ritualistic niceties of assassination. This attack was brash, overt, violent.

The end was inevitable.

They would kill him.

And they would take what they came for.

He quickly slipped on his boots and his tunic, having slept in the rest of his clothes, and seized the saddlebags from the floor beside the bed. He picked up the black velvet packet and glanced around the room.

Bed. Floor. Walls. Roof. Rafters. Washstand. Little space in which to hide something of such value. And so little time.

Downstairs in the common room Signore Pepoli shuffled from the small chamber behind the stairs where he resided with his family. The pounding had an urgency to it. Although in nightdress and cap, he quickly lit a lamp with a taper and crossed to the barred door.

"No room!" he called. "I have no room left, signore!"

"Open the door!" came the imperious command, followed by another series of loud pounding. A cold hand gripped the heart of the fat landlord. He quickly placed the lamp on a nearby table and hastened to remove the stout timber that barred the door.

"Hurry!" a voice thundered.

He removed the bar just as the door was flung open, and the man in the black cloak who had been in the establishment hours earlier brushed him aside and strode into the center of the common room. Behind him came five mercenaries in red-and-yellow livery, all with drawn swords.

"I'm—I'm sorry, maestro," whined Signore Pepoli, "but I

19

have no more rooms available. This is a small inn as you can see, and I . . ."

The man in the cloak paid no attention but strode to the staircase and ascended it. At that moment another light illuminated the common room, and a woman with a blanket thrown over her nightdress appeared with a second lamp. Behind her, a pretty, dark-haired and obviously frightened girl in her teens, also clothed only in nightdress and blanket, clutched her mother's arm and peered over her shoulder.

"If they are to see the dawn," said the man on the stairs coldly, "send them back to their beds!"

Signore Pepoli quickly crossed to the two women and urged them to retreat behind their bedchamber door and to bar it. "I will be all right," he whispered. "Just do as they say. Please."

The women withdrew. The man on the staircase turned and, joined by three of the mercenaries, began kicking at the door until the proprietor heard the leather hinges pull from the frame and saw the wooden portal pivot and collapse. The man in the cloak swept into the room with the captain of the mercenaries.

The others did not follow them, but took up positions on the landing, one on either side of the doorway.

In the common room below, one of the two remaining mercenaries stationed himself outside of the Pepoli bedchamber, and the other forced the perspiring proprietor to sit down by the hearth and then sat opposite him with the blade of his sword across his lap.

"Now, my fat fellow," he whispered, "be silent or die."

The first wild scream came soon after the door to the courier's room had been breached. It startled Signore Pepoli who sat on the bench by the hearth wringing his pudgy and trembling hands, and it aroused some commotion from the landlord's room, but the mercenary standing guard outside quickly rapped on the door of the bedchamber and growled to the women inside, "It's nothing! Go to sleep!"

Then the shattered remnant of the door was pulled aside, and the man in the black cloak appeared, the blade of his sword bloodied. He stepped onto the landing with the mercenary officer behind him and gestured the two sentries to follow them into the room.

For the next hour, the only sounds heard were loud thuds and crashes, an occasional curse, the crack of a shattered basin.

"Sweet Mother of God," Signore Pepoli blessed himself, "what are they doing?"

It was well into the morning before the man in the cloak appeared again. He stepped across the tilted wreckage of the door, followed by the mercenary captain, and both descended into the common room. Behind them two perspiring and obviously weary mercenaries carried something wrapped in the woolen blanket from the bed. Signore Pepoli could see the spreading scarlet blotch that stained it. The man in the cloak had the courier's saddlebags thrown over one arm, and he quickly crossed to where the proprietor watched and trembled, and he dropped a single gold florin on the table.

A florin!

In gold!

"Nothing happened tonight," the man in the black cloak snapped at Signore Pepoli. "Nothing. Do you understand?"

The fat landlord nodded, his eyes still fixed on the gold coin.

"The gentleman who occupied that room stayed the night and departed at dawn, which is true. That money will reimburse you for some small changes we had to make in the bedchamber." The man stood erect, glaring down at the portly proprietor. "Say nothing more," he repeated. "Remember nothing more, and you will live a long and undoubtedly boring life. Speak of what happened here this evening, and I shall return and personally cut out your tongue and slowly slice your wife and daughter into strips before your eyes. If you

21

attempt to hide, you ball of stinking blubber, I will find you. If you run, I will follow until I've killed all of you. Is that perfectly clear?"

He suddenly removed one of his gloves and raised the back of his hand before the proprietor's eyes. Inscribed on the bare skin, between the thumb and the forefinger, were two half-arcs with a line between them. Signore Pepoli had never seen the sign before, but he had heard the stories.

"Do you know this mark?" the assassin asked the proprietor.

Signore Pepoli nodded, barely able to keep from collapsing, and the dark man replaced his glove.

"Then you know that it is a mark that I keep my promises!"

The proprietor watched silently as the two mercenaries passed out into the night with their burden, and the other two followed. The man in the cloak was the last to leave, but once he had warned Signore Pepoli, he sheathed his dagger, wheeled, and strode through the door without looking back.

The proprietor heard the hoofbeats of their horses as the band of mercenaries and the man in the cloak raced down the narrow lane and away. He quickly crossed to the open door in time to see that the mercenaries had also taken the horse of the man who had rented the room. The bundle wrapped in the stained woolen blanket had been thrown over the saddle and lashed down.

"Sweet Mother of God," he murmured again.

It was nearly half an hour before Signore Pepoli was able to calm himself and then his wife and daughter. He showed them the florin, which his wife quickly snatched and deposited in the shadowy vault between her breasts.

Then he forced himself to climb the stairs to the room.

It was a scene of total destruction.

Deep holes had been gouged into the walls. The mattress, now mostly crimson, had been mutilated and its goose feathers spread across the floor. The bed frame itself was broken, and several loops of rope around one of the canopy poles suggested that once someone had been lashed to it. The support beams for the canopy had been pricked with daggers as if hungry woodpeckers had dined on them. The pitcher and the bowl had been shattered, and the stand itself had been destroyed. The lamp had been reduced to crystal on a sea of oil, and the proprietor silently thanked his angels that there had not been a fire.

Nothing in the room was untouched. Everything was scarred.

There was no sign of the courier, and Signore Pepoli now knew with certainty what the rolled blanket had contained. The scarlet stains, on the walls, on the floor, on the wooden frame of the bed and what remained of the washstand, silently spoke of the horror that had occurred in this room.

"Sweet savior," he prayed to himself, "how could any human do this to another?"

Padua

The following afternoon the black-cloaked man who had returned with the mercenaries to the inn urged his grey stallion along the wide Corso del Popolo. It was evident that he had been riding for some time and quickly. The flanks and chest of his horse were flecked with froth, and his long cloak was peppered with the grey dust of the road.

The horseman crossed the narrow bridge that spanned the Bacchiglione, nodded to a passing Dominican monk, and paused before the Cappella Scrovegni. He tied his mount to the heavy iron ring set in the stone wall and entered the small chapel, picking dead leaves from his cloak and his velvet tunic as he walked. Inside the doors he stomped his feet to dislodge the mud from his boots. This caused an old woman praying in the last pew to turn and glare at him, but the horseman only stared at her, put a finger to his lips as a signal for silence, and walked quietly down the aisle to his left.

He barely glanced at the beautiful Giotto frescoes lining the walls that illustrated scenes from the lives of Mary and Christ. He went directly to a wide metallic framework holding perhaps two dozen candles in tiers, and with his gloved hand he swept away a portion of the sand and charred tapers in one corner of the bottom receptacle and removed a small folded piece of parchment. He read it quickly, frowned, and silently cursed.

This change in the place of their meeting was intolerable and unprofessional! They were playing games! The entire procedure, which had been under strict command from others, reeked of amateurism! He silently cursed as he dipped the message in the warm wax of a burning candle. He watched it flare into flame and then dropped the few blackened ashes in the sand. He glanced around, chose a taper from the receptacle, and lit a candle in penance. Then he stood silently, as if praying. Suddenly he wheeled and stormed from the chapel.

He stood outside for a moment, glancing around the piazza, and then he unhitched his horse, mounted, and nudged the tired animal along a pathway that led through the gardens that used to be part of a Roman arena. He emerged from the gardens before the Ermitani church where he knew the court artist, Maestro Andrea Mantegna, was presently laboring on interior frescoes. He did not wish to encounter the man now, especially under the present conditions, so he urged the horse to a trot, and quickly turned down a side street that took him past the university and into the outdoor marketplace before the Palazzo della Ragione.

The market teemed with merchants and farmers hawking their wares and servants choosing fresh vegetables and fruit, cheese and milk, and long sleeves of crusty bread for their masters' refectories. Butchers offered newly-slaughtered pigs and chickens, fat sausages, and partridges and grouse. Silk merchants displayed and shouted the advantages of the fabrics newly arrived from the east. Whores and young bravi lined the periphery looking for a young and perhaps wealthy student from the university or a visiting merchant looking for diversion.

The sight of the fresh fruit and meat reminded the rider that he was hungry. It took some time for him to work his grey stallion through the throng.

He turned down another dark side street that led into the broad Piazza dei Signori where master masons and architects were busily supervising armies of workmen in the construction of several new palaces. He let the horse pick his own path past the wooden scaffolding, the piles of sheet lead for the roofing, the winding crab used to hoist materials to the upper levels, the basket-hods of mortar and the barrows. The weary horse plodded between small bands of quarreling carpenters, sawyers, joiners, and plasterers, all debating in which order the guilds should do their appropriate work. Finally the rider and his mount arrived at the Roma Ruzzante where they paused in the center of the adjoining piazza before Donatello's huge bronze equestrian statue.

Ahead of the rider loomed the massive basilica of Sant'Antonio. The black-cloaked horseman glanced at the Byzantine domes and the tall towers that suggested mosque minarets and shook his head at the obvious Muslim appearance of the Christian cathedral.

Blasphemous!

He reined in before the basilica and tied the horse to an iron ring set in the side wall. He quickly and momentarily embraced the sweaty neck of the stallion as if to reassure the great horse that he might soon rest, and then he climbed the stone steps and entered the duomo. Again he passed the ornamentation without seeing the marble reliefs by Tullio Lombardo and bronzes by Donatello that honored the namesake saint. On his way down the side aisle to the line of dark confessionals the horseman passed the acclaimed bronze of the Madonna, and he noticed that the flickering light from the candles placed around the base of the statue cast deep fluttering shadows of sorrow over the lady's countenance.

The Madonna, he thought, appeared to be weeping.

And that thought amused him.

The horseman stalked to the third confessional. He swept aside the curtain of the penitent's closet, entered, and knelt in silence and shadow until he heard the small door behind the screen slide open.

The whispered conversation was brief. Hardly more than three minutes after he had entered, the now obviously angry man exited the confessional, went to the center aisle before the great doors of the basilica, turned to face the high altar, genuflected, blessed himself, and departed.

Outside the church the man mounted the grey stallion and again turned its head toward the Piazza dei Signori. He directed the mount down the side street into the Piazza della Ragione and worked his way through the bustling crowds once more until he reached a small shop on the corner.

The shop, which offered both carpentry and funeral services, was small and was operated by one grey-bearded skeleton of a man who seemed to be a walking advertisement for his trade. The horseman had to wait while the old man tended to other customers, which further irritated him. Finally, after he had told the proprietor what he wanted and a price was agreed upon, he threw two ducats on the wooden board that served as a counter, and strode from the establishment.

The horse and rider passed down a narrow, cobbled passage and found themselves in a small, wooded area bordered by canals that completely encircled it and which flowed directly into a small tributary of the Bacchiglione, creating a verdant island set down in the heart of the city. A black-bearded officer, as weary and dusty as the rider, waited near a dense section of shrubbery. He wore a dark brown tunic with a serpent embroidered on the breast and a short black cape trimmed in silver.

In his hands he held a square wooden chest.

The horseman dismounted and crossed to the officer. "I regret the delay, Captain, but the king rat is playing at god again, and he changed the meeting place at the last moment. You had no difficulty?"

The bearded man shook his head. "I am not comfortable with this damned serpent on my tunic, but no one asked any questions, and no one tried to stop me. Here." He handed the horseman the chest. "Do you want to look at it?"

27

The horseman did not smile. "No. It's not of my choosing. Can't I trust you?"

"I thought you might want to make certain," growled the captain. "I had the devil's own time doing it. Grim business."

"Yes," the horseman acknowledged with no show of emotion. "What of the man's horse?"

"I sold it to the livery. Got a good price."

"His possessions? Clothes? The saddlebags?"

"Burned," the officer grumbled.

"The others?"

"I sent them back to the court. I changed my uniform, as ordered, and brought the dead one here."

"Take the body to the carpenter's shop on the Piazza della Ragione," sighed the black-cloaked man. "I have made all the arrangements. Simply give it over to the proprietor and then return to the court. You may tell Meneghina that I will follow in three or four days to fill in any details, but, under the circumstances, it is best if we do not return together."

"I still don't see why it was necessary for me to wear this."

"Games again," frowned the horseman. "King Rat informed me that a uniformed officer can be traced to his regiment, and we wouldn't want you to be identified, would we?" The horseman placed the wooden chest on the grass and loosened a leather purse from his waist. "You did well, Captain," he said. "I am sorry the final phase of the assignment was so unpleasant for you, but I can assure you it was not the way I would have conducted the affair. I am as embarrassed as you, but we will have our revenge, and our rewards."

He extended the purse toward the bearded officer, and then it slipped from his gloved hand. The captain quickly bent to catch it. As he did, the horseman suddenly slipped his knife from its sheath, stepped behind the man, and pressed the blade against his throat.

"Wha—what—are you doing?" the captain managed to murmur under the pressure of the blade.

"I want you to remember how simple it would have been for me," whispered the chestnut-haired man to the officer's ear.

"This entire operation has been clumsy and unprofessional. I wish it to be forgotten. If you ever betray me, I'll kill you. Remember that."

He stepped aside and permitted the officer to rise. He then recovered the chest from the grass.

"It's been a long day, eh?" he whispered to the closed chest. "Well, we're nearly done."

The horseman mounted the stallion and placed the chest before him on the saddle. He glanced at the captain who glared at him while rubbing his throat, and then the horseman slowly walked the tired animal back to the basilica.

A black coach bearing no identifying crest waited at the foot of the steps.

As he approached, the coachman, who was standing by the entrance to the basilica, saw him, turned, and rapped twice on the door. The portal swung in and from the dark interior waddled a dwarf dressed in the clerical robes of a cardinal.

He was a perfect miniature, from the ring of authority on his gloved left hand, to the scarlet robes and short cape, the soft slippers and the wide-brimmed "barber's bowl" hat. His mustache and goatee joined at the corners of his mouth, and as he saw the horseman approach, he smiled and nodded.

The coachman quickly ran down the steps and took the chest from the horseman. He returned as rapidly and passed it to the dwarf who unhooked the lid, opened it, and glanced inside. Then he slammed it shut, again smiled and nodded to the horseman and let his coachman assist him into the upholstered interior.

The horseman watched the vehicle move across the piazza, circle the statue of the condottiere, and head east. He spat on the cobbles as if trying to rid himself of an unpleasant taste. "You're welcome, King Rat," he murmured.

He patted the neck of his dusty stallion and turned him in the opposite direction. "Now," he sighed, "if we can find an inn with a comfortable stable, oats and fresh water, and perhaps a big-breasted woman and a roast fowl for me, we can enjoy ourselves for a few days, eh, Dragon?"

He gave a small laugh.

"And then, of course, reunion!"

REUNIONS

October 1499

Cremona

The morning was cool, autumnal crisp, and in the shadow of the Torrazo in the central piazza of Cremona the members of the traveling *commedia dell'arte* players known as I Comici Buffoni, the Company of Clowns, gathered behind their colorful wagons to watch their newest member perform.

Centered in the ring framed by the nine players, a tall, big-bellied man in the breastplate, cape, and plumed hat of a condottiere swaggered and strutted. Under his red half-mask which suggested that the owner was sanguine and a lover of wine, the capitano bellowed in a false baritone voice about his many accomplishments in the wars "against the infidels." He boasted of his conquests in boudoir and bordello, of the loves he left behind, usually pregnant, of his victorious exploits that too often went unappreciated. Through all of this, he waved and slashed in all directions with an absurdly long sword that threatened to decapitate the listeners gathered around him.

"My golden chariot dragged the dead body of Achilles around the walls of Pompeii!" he proclaimed.

The other players laughed.

"I believe the body was Hector's!" called Piero Tebaldo, the balding leader of the company who normally played the role of the capitano. "And the city was Troy!"

"That's right!" nodded the mock general as he mimed riding an invisible horse. "I remember now! It was the Trojan sector of Pompeii. Dirty. Dilapidated. Foul smelling, rather like Venice where the sewers empty into the canals! A damnable eyesore on the plains of Philippi!"

"Philippi is nowhere near Troy," jeered Marco Torri, the lanky man who, in his role as the scholarly Doctor Graziano of Bologna, supposedly knew everything.

"Well, not *now* it isn't!" thundered the braggart warrior. "But in those days the world was much much smaller, remember! Hardly larger than a walnut! A thumbnail! Infinitesimal! Ah yes, the good old days! I weep at the memories! Why, in those days, I remember, I could leave Rome after Matins and arrive in Constantinople in time for Vespers!"

"Never!"

"Well, certainly in less than a day and a half!"

"More likely a month and a half."

"Well, yes, of course," the captain acknowledged, "if you travel the Via Emilia during pilgrimage time and then take the left fork at Treviso and stop for some of those delicious mussels in garlic sauce at Monfalcone! But remember! I was riding the famed winged horse, the legendary Icarus!"

"Pegasus!" called Piero.

"It's true I tell you!" roared the captain. "He had wings! And his back was as broad as the deck of a ship! I could sleep upon it fully stretched! I can recall as if it were only yesterday how we circled the Adriatic! Over Corsica I shall never forget looking down on the mighty pyramids!"

The company howled. "The pyramids are in Egypt!" cried Francesco, the handsome young actor who played the lover.

"Not *those* pyramids, imbecile!" thundered the man in the red mask as he twirled the ends of his false waxed mustache. "Those Egyptian pyramids are mere dunghills compared to the great pyramids of Corsica! I mean the really great pyramids! The ninth wonder of the ancient world!"

"Plato described only seven," Prudenza called to him, shaking her scarlet curls.

"Well, yes," agreed the capitano, "if you count the hanging gardens of Ithaca as only one, but they were actually in two sections, you see, so they naturally counted as three. There were the actual hanging gardens, and then there were the ones that were just sort of sagging a little at the corners, and—"

"The hanging gardens were in Babylon!" sneered Marco.

"Why are they always moving those damned hanging gardens?" cried the swaggering officer, and then, suddenly, he took two or three faltering steps forward and began to topple.

Instantly Piero, Marco, and Francesco were on their feet and caught the mock warrior as he began to pitch forward. As he fell, the scarlet half-mask with the bulbous nose and the thick mustache dropped from his face and landed at the feet of the company's Arlecchino, the skeletal Simone Corio, still in his commedia costume of multicolored diamonds.

"Careful, Niccolo," he warned.

"Very good, Niccolo!" cheered Rubini the acrobat, squatting on a keg with his black half-mask of the comic servant perched astride his curly hair. "But take smaller steps, my boy! Remember that the stilts are attached to only your ankles and your calves. They are not like the larger stilts that I use which can be manipulated by legs, ribs, and shoulders. With these smaller models, if your body is not centered correctly, you will fall. You must think of balance always, Niccolo! Balance!"

The prostrate capitano, who without his half-mask had the face of a young boy, was suffering the indignity of having his legs raised and his pantaloons and boots, which were anchored in wooden frames, laughingly removed by the three women of the company.

"I think you did very well, little one," said the portly, red-headed Prudenza of Siena to encourage him.

"Certainly as good as Piero," added the dark songstress, Anna.

"Better," laughed the beautiful ingenue, Isabella.

They whipped away his oversized trousers and began to unstrap the wooden appendages from Niccolo's own short legs, which were encased in scarlet hose. They unfastened the cloak from his padded shoulders and pulled the pillow, which provided the dwarf with a sizable belly, from under his tunic.

"I was doing well, wasn't I?" pleaded Niccolo. "I was! But I got involved in the wordplay, you see, and forgot I was only two-thirds the size I was pretending to be. I started to strut and these legs just wouldn't move as fast as I felt they should."

"The problem of every actor," nodded Piero as he placed a hand on the young man's shoulder. "One must concentrate not only on movement and voice, but also remember the lines and the lazzi, and still be conscious always of the audience and their reaction, but, at the same time, he must still be so involved in the sequence on the stage that the emotion and the dialog seems natural and true."

"You must also be conscious of the degree of laughter," said Simone as he returned the half-mask to the dwarf. "How long the laughter lasts, and *when* they laugh, tells you what sort of mood the audience may be in that afternoon. With some audiences, those who have been harangued by their guild masters or informed of some new tax, it may be the pratfall and the vulgarisms that will most amuse, because the last thing they want to do is to think. With others, the ones who got a good price for their olives or had a quick midmorning fling with their lover and consider themselves to be exceptionally brilliant and immortal, they will enjoy the comic line and the clever turning of the plot. A comic jest requires the listener to think, to get the joke, and a plot with turns asks something of the spectator. You, as an actor, must be able to read the mood of your audience quickly and shift your style of playing to elicit the most laughter and give the greatest pleasure, remembering that no two audiences will ever be alike."

"And, simultaneously, you must try to keep track of the number and denomination of the coins thrown on the stage, so Piero can't later cheat you of your share," Francesco yelled.

"Don't worry, Niccolo," Prudenza assured the dwarf as she folded the trousers. "You did very well for someone who only received the stilts three days ago."

"I felt as though I was back in the Maestro's workshop at the tower's top in the Castello Sforzesco," said the handsome young man as he stood upright on his own two legs. "I always seemed to be the tester of some new and bizarre device that Maestro Leonardo had just invented."

He remembered his first flight from the "madman's tower"

on the great dragon wings, which the Maestro has assured him would carry him grandly around the ducal gardens and land him safely on the soft grass. The second time he used the wings was to flee Il Moro's mercenaries who were coming to kill both himself and the Maestro.

"I wonder," he said quietly. "Do you think Maestro Leonardo was able to escape from the castello?"

"You needn't worry about Maestro Leonardo," said Anna as she took an apple from the fruit barrel and bit into it. "He's far more clever than Il Moro's underlings."

"Maestro Leonardo will live forever," Isabella nodded. "He sees everything, knows everything, and has the good sense not to reveal either of these talents before jealous and arrogant men."

"The Maestro," added Francesco, "is a man for the age. He is perfect."

"Really?" sniffed Marco as he brushed a hand over his long robe. "Well, he doesn't know how to read and write in Latin, now does he?"

"He was improving," snapped Niccolo, rushing to defend his friend and mentor. "There are so many other things that demand his time."

"Perhaps," said Marco with a touch of the pompous character he played in the commedia productions, "but Latin is the language of all princely courts and the church, and not being able to converse well in it will always mark the Maestro as only a country peasant from Vinci who is indulged by true lords and ladies of quality."

Then Isabella screamed.

There was a flurry of activity as eight armed and helmeted men in tunics of chain mail under chasubles of green and gray suddenly burst into the area, shouting commands and prodding the players with their swords until they gathered every one of the players into one small circle. Anna attempted to hide behind Turio, and Francesco ran to Isabella for protection. Prudenza, of course, stood her ground and dared the soldiers to touch her. Rubini, always the calm acrobat, abandoned his perch on the keg and backed into the ring with the others, his attention focused on the mercenaries.

"I trust you know with whom you are dealing," growled the acrobat. "I would hate to be forced to divulge my revered father's name, which would mean instant death for all of you."

"What in hell do you want?" Prudenza bellowed from the opposite side of the ring. "My performance wasn't that bad! If you want your money back, talk to Piero!" She delicately seized the point of a soldier's sword with two fingers as if it were made of lace and gently moved it aside so she could approach the mercenary. "But listen, my handsome young friend, I could teach you a few useful tricks with that thing if you have the time, and the money, and the balls."

She was prevented from further discourse by an officer in a highly polished breastplate bearing an impresa of three trees. The helmeted captain wheeled his horse among the performers, sword drawn, and demanded, "Is one of you known as Master Niccolo da Pavia?"

Piero studied the officer, exchanged rapid glances with the others and then called out, "I am Master Niccolo da Pavia!"

The officer glared at him from under the beak of his helmet. "I am told this Niccolo is a dwarf."

"Well, that was yesterday," Piero explained. "I'm feeling myself today."

Instantly Simone dropped to his knees. "I am Niccolo," he piped in a high and unnatural voice.

"No!" shouted Rubini, dropping on all fours and pointing to Simone. "I am Niccolo the dwarf! That pretender is just short and likes to believe he's a dwarf, but he has none of the graces! He has delusions! See how much smaller I am than he is?"

"Ridiculous!" cried Anna, throwing herself on her back on the grass. "I'm the one you want! Only the name is Niccol-ah! My mother had a terrible time with masculine endings, and members."

Prudenza snickered at the obvious confusion of the mercenaries, but the officer did not smile. He pulled his horse around to face Niccolo who had been lifted onto Marco's shoulders and now straddled his neck, appearing to be seven feet tall.

"Aren't you Niccolo?" asked the officer, pointing his sword at the dwarf.

"Do I look like a dwarf?" growled Niccolo.

"You're sitting on that man's shoulders," thundered the officer.

"Man? What man?" Niccolo pretended to be surprised to find Marco's head between his legs. "Is that a man down there? Thank God! I thought I had an ugly tumor growing on my . . . !"

The officer turned his horse in a tight circle. "If you don't come with me immediately, Master Niccolo, my soldiers will cut the legs from under all of your vagabond friends, and this will be the only company of dwarves in existence."

"A troupe of commedia dwarves?" Rubini pondered. "It has possibilities! We could open in Venice at carnival in five months and . . . !"

"Go with you?" frowned Niccolo as Marco gently lifted him and deposited him on the ground. "Go with you where?"

The officer leaned forward in his saddle to address the young man. "You'll know when you arrive," he said. "In the meantime it is enough for you to know that your immediate presence is requested by my master."

"And whom would your master be?" asked Niccolo trying desperately to think what he might have done that would attract the attention of nobility.

"God," snapped Prudenza. "All nobles want to be God."

"My master is the count, imbecile!" growled the officer.

"Count Imbecile?" Anna frowned at Francesco.

"The bastard son of the Duke of Stupidity," laughed Rubini. "I remember him well."

"Probably French," sniffed Francesco. "They have no sense of decorum."

"That's true enough," nodded Mario, trying not to laugh. "They leave their corum lying all over the place! I remember in Lyons where . . ."

"Silence!" roared the officer, and the command was dutifully echoed from each of the performers in turn. Then the mounted man pointed to Niccolo. "Now climb behind me, young man, and put an end to this nonsense. If I wanted to be amused, I would send for a trio of Neapolitan whores and not a masked band of grubby montebanks who perform only in the streets for the rabble."

"Neapolitan whores won't perform in the streets?" asked Isabella.

"Too narrow," Anna informed her. "Requires standing through most of it. Bad for the back."

"And never for the rabble," Prudenza added. "Just for mounted officers, so their horses can watch."

"And participate," nodded Isabella.

The officer did not smile. Piero could see that he was not amused and to challenge his authority further could bring the wrath of "the count" upon all their heads, and that would prove hazardous. Wandering players enjoyed no rights or privileges. They were stateless persons, dependent upon the kindness of the ruling families in the cities in which they played. He saw, too, that trying to distract the armed men with jests and byplay, a device that had worked to their advantage in the Castello Sforzesco, was obviously not working here. He glanced around at his troupe and sighed. He turned to Niccolo, and gently lifted the dwarf and placed him on the saddle before the officer. "What is all this?" he asked quietly. "What is this young man accused of?"

"I don't know," said the officer. "The count said find him and retrieve him, and I am merely following his orders."

"If the count ordered you to bring your horse to a gallop and plunge off a cliff, would you do it?" Prudenza growled at the officer.

"Not after that last time, he wouldn't," mocked Anna.

Piero crossed to Niccolo and looked up at him. "Don't worry, Niccolo," he whispered. "Montebanks and street performers are always picked up for questioning when there is some local disturbance. A calf is stolen, search for the players! A woman is insulted, interrogate the mummers! They'll release you in a few hours, and we'll wait for you."

"Provided they don't fine you more than ten soldi," Rubini called as the mounted captain and the soldiers began to withdraw. "Any more than that, and we'll have to meet you in Arezzo on the Feast of the Nativity."

"Bring your own wine!" caroled Anna.

Pavia

Leonardo was awakened at dawn in his small, sparse room in the Certosa monastery by the persistent tolling of the morning bell. Upon his arrival nearly a week earlier, he had been assured by the Father Abbot that this was simply a "summons to the brothers for the milking of the cows and goats, the preparation of the ovens for the bread baking and the distribution of the hymn cards for Matins, and it does not concern you." So now the tall, bearded guest turned on his side, attempted to find at least one soft area on the pallet bed, tugged the threadbare woolen blanket around his shoulders and surrendered to a fitful sleep.

The second summons of the bell jarred the Maestro back into the world of the monastics, and he realized, gratefully, that in the interval between the first and second tolling, someone had entered his chamber and renewed the fire in his small fireplace. He sat upright, put his feet over the edge of the bed, and silently thanked the divinity that the faded piece of carpeting supplied for the guest saved him from experiencing the initial shock of the cold stone floor.

He dressed by the fire, donning his usual dark blouse and thick hose, the fur-lined slippers and the long heavy woolen robe that he cinched about his waist with a wide leather belt. He stood before the narrow mirror provided him by Father Abbot and ran a comb through his long hair and beard, noting with dismay the additional threads of silver. He stood for a moment examining the deep furrows of his brow, the liquid eyes that seemed to float in a milk-white substance, the thick mustache and beard. He recalled being somewhat handsome once, of being admired for his beauty and his strength, when he would bend horseshoes with his large hands to amuse his fellow students and when . . .

He tore himself away from the mirror and those memories, and stood by the single window gazing at the long flat Lombardy plains surrounding the monastery. He stared toward that distant point where he knew that the Ticino and the Po rivers embraced one another.

The sky was ashen and depressing, as he studied the transit of the shadows of the clouds across the plains. Then he turned abruptly, sat down at the small table which was one of the few furnishings in his cell, dipped his quill in the clay inkpot, and began to write.

"The shadows and illuminated areas of open country take on the color of their sources," he wrote, "because the darkness caused by the opaque nature of the clouds, combined with the absence of direct sunlight, tints whatever it touches, while the surrounding air, beyond the shadows and the cloudbanks, is exposed and illuminates the location, so that it assumes a blue color."

He paused and studied what he had written. Then, still wrapped in quiet contemplation of the play of light and shadow, he lightly blew on the ink to dry it.

He felt as if he might weep.

The notes were written in Italian and in his own reversed code which could only be read by holding the parchment before a mirror.

This practice of disguising his work was less to protect his discoveries and observations from the eyes of rivals than to protect himself from the prying of suspicious clergy. Twice before such clerics had summoned him before church courts to defend his views and to answer accusations of immorality and sodomy raised against him. There was no proof, and he was twice acquitted, but the memory made him realize that he was now at the mercy of the clergy, in a monastery. He had noted that some of the monks had avoided looking at him upon his arrival, and his old distrust of the Catholic clergy was resurrected.

It had only been three years, he remembered, since the hook-nosed monk, Fra Girolamo Savonarola, had assumed absolute authority in Florence and led his followers over the four Arno bridges and through the streets burning paintings and smashing statues considered "immoral" or "sacrilegious," meaning they did not directly relate to, or inspire devotion for, Christ or the Madonna. These bonfires of the "vanities" increased to the point where Savonarola had denounced the painting of Saint Sebastian by his fellow Dominican, Fra Bartolomeo, and ordered it removed from Savonarola's own church, the San Marco. The reason for this, the monk explained, was that "the friars had found, through the confessionals, that women sinned after looking at the comely and lascivious realism" in it.

Leonardo shook his head in dismay as he recalled that he, too, had to publicly acknowledge that it was possible for a "painter to induce men to fall in love with a picture that does not portray any living woman," citing an instance where a patron so lusted after a Madonna in a sacred painting that he implored the Maestro to remove the sacred symbols in it, so "he might kiss the lady."

Savonarola was now dead of course, having been executed by order of Pope Alexander VI a year earlier after the monk had denounced the orgies and reported debaucheries in the Vatican. Ambassadors to the Milan court had related how the inquisitors had erected a high platform so everyone in the Florentine piazza could see, and then the condemned had their faces and hands shaved before they were hung in chains and

44

their bodies devoured by the fire that also consumed the entire platform. Even after the arms and legs had fallen off the torsos, the executioners threw stones at the remaining trunks of the dead until all portions fell into the flames. Then the ashes were collected and thrown into the Arno lest anyone recover a relic of Savonarola and his two brother clergy for future reverence.

Still, Leonardo knew, the suspicious animosity between the artist and the "good Christian" clergy could not be so easily burned away.

Upon his arrival at the Certosa, the Father Abbot had half-heartedly welcomed the Maestro, and then privately warned Leonardo that some of the monks considered him "the devil's disciple." This, the abbot explained, was not because of the Maestro's art, much of which depicted sacred and biblical events and personages, but because he was one of the few people in Christendom who had been granted ecclesiastical permission to dissect naked human bodies for "study." To many of the monastics this smacked of diabolical work and the blackest of magic.

Leonardo realized at once that he would have to tread softly while in residence at the Certosa, and he assured the Father Abbot that he would depart as soon as possible. In the meantime, he meant to keep to his room, the refectory for meals, and the library.

His initial visits to the library had been difficult, because Brother Pax, the librarian, genuinely believed Leonardo to hold "blasphemous and heretical notions" and had so warned Niccolo when the dwarf departed for the court of Il Moro. Indeed, the book of Epictetus that was now in Leonardo's possession had been given to the foundling by the librarian to "advise and protect" the young man while he was in residence in the same castello as Maestro Leonardo.

It was plain, therefore, that Brother Pax was annoyed and confused when Leonardo showed him the Epictetus and told him how the book had sustained and comforted him during the fall of Milan.

"But Epictetus was a slave," Brother Pax lectured the Maestro, "and a cripple, so I felt the work might prove of more value to a young man, smaller in stature than others of his age, who was about to enter service to the duke. Epictetus had much to say concerning the importance of cultivating personal independence while in the midst of disturbing external circumstances, you see, and he stressed the necessity to find happiness within one's self."

"Those lessons are applicable to all of us as well, Friar," the Maestro smiled. "In a sense, an artist is a slave to his patron, and I most certainly agree that one must cultivate an inner serenity, an independence if you will, in order to survive among the decadence and intrigue of today's princely courts."

"Do you indeed?" said the fat little librarian, making it quite evident that he did not believe much of what Leonardo professed. "Then, perhaps, I have been mistaken about you, Maestro. But, nevertheless, if I were to recommend a specific book to you, for guidance you understand, knowing what I do about you, it would not be Epictetus. It would most likely be the Meditations of Marcus Aurelius."

"Marcus Aurelius? Why?"

"Because he was the last of the pagan moralists."

"Ah," smiled the Maestro, "I see."

"He was also the most noble of all the later emperors of imperial Rome," Brother Pax rambled on hurriedly, "and his reign, in general, was marked by justice and moderation, although he continued the persecution of Christians. He remained conscientious even as the empire was collapsing around him. He had to deal with armies that were now largely mercenary and who refused to fight for anything but gold. He also had to cope with a severe pestilence that raged through the provinces."

"A turbulent time," the Maestro nodded.

"In the face of these calamities, Marcus Aurelius argued that man must endure what he cannot change and that rationality, manifested through discourse, reasoning, and logic, was the ruling principle of the universe. From what Niccolo has written Father Abbot about you, I believe you, too, maintain the same confidence in logic and reasoning, over simple and pious faith, which is what truly sustains man through misfortune."

"I have faith in logic."

"Then this, indeed, is the book for you," Brother Pax said, plainly annoyed, and he handed the Maestro a narrow leatherbound volume. "Though Roman, he wrote in Greek." There was a pause. "Do you read Greek, Maestro?"

The monk noticed the slight flush to the Maestro's cheeks. Leonardo knew that the portly monk must have been informed of his lack of classic languages, and he assumed, therefore, that the monk was deliberately embarrassing him, and the old distrusts were strengthened.

"I regret that I am *omo sanza lettere*," he said softly, "a man without letters, but perhaps I will be able to work my way through it." The Maestro forced himself to smile. "Though I was under the impression that most monastics scorned everything Greek, since the pagan Greeks believed the nude human body was beautiful and should be so represented in statues and paintings."

He saw the monk's cheeks redden, and the corners of his mouth tighten.

"The body is merely the temple of the soul," Brother Pax replied as if enlightening a child. "It is the radiance of the soul which God has breathed into man that is truly beautiful. That is why the poet is superior to the painter, because he can capture and depict the soul of man with words and phrases."

The Maestro bristled. It was an argument he had fought a thousand times. "I yield to you, a master of manuscripts, as a man more acquainted with poetry than I am," said the Maestro, "although I will not concede that writing is superior to painting. Painting presents nature with more truth and accuracy than do words or letters. Words are the invention of man and require interpretation while the glories of the world are conveyed immediately to the eye in painting and sculpture. I also believe the soul is composed of harmony, and that harmony cannot be generated save by proportionality."

The monk, confused by the Maestro's explanation, resorted to a more simplistic logic. "By the magic of his words," he rhapsodized, "the poet may inflame men with love!"

"But the painter can do it better," the Maestro said softly, "because he can present the gentleman with an accurate representation of his beloved, instantly perceived. He may even hold and kiss it. He does not have to know Latin or Greek to immediately appreciate the beauty of the subject. And, miracle of miracles, his beloved will not grow a day older or one jot less beautiful."

"I suppose that is an attribute," sneered Brother Pax, "if one wants to embrace inanimate objects. I would personally frown on kissing a book as I imagine it might harm the binding."

"I wouldn't know," smiled the artist, "having never kissed a book, although I have often seen a priest perform such an act as a part of ritual services."

The monk had been wounded. "Remember, Maestro," he intoned solemnly, "the painting only depicts the external attributes of his beloved. The inner qualities, the spiritual qualities, are what the man loves most in his sweetheart, and *that* cannot be captured in paint. It requires the skillful use of words and phrases."

"It has not been my experience, Brother Pax, that it is the 'spiritual qualities' that most endear women to men," the Maestro said quietly. "At least not in the courts where I have been in attendance."

"That is because the courts are decadent and corrupt."

"True," the Maestro acknowledged, "but even among the peasantry the eye delights less in the hidden 'radiance of the soul' than in the proportional harmony of the beautiful externals."

Brother Pax actually blushed. "Beautiful externals?" He

emitted a deep sigh and shook his head. "I see we are of different worlds, Maestro Leonardo."

"No," smiled the artist. "It is the same world. We only perceive it differently."

"Thank God," sighed the monk.

Cremona

There was little discussion between Niccolo and the stiff-backed officer who transported him from the wagons of the performers to the palazzo just off the Via Palestro. The building was a four-story edifice with the high arched walkways and the broad inner courts that marked most of the palaces in Lombardy. To a young man accustomed to the lavishness of the Castello Sforzesco, it was not impressive.

In the center of one of these courts the dwarf was lowered from the officer's saddle by two servants in uniformed livery who rushed down the steps to assist him. Niccolo searched the keystone of the arch over the main entrance for some sign of a family crest, but except for the impresa of the three trees on the livery of the servants, he had no way of telling to whom the loyalties of the occupants of the palazzo were assigned. They could easily be allied to the exiled Sforza since Cremona was a fief of Milan. They could just as easily be a family personally and quietly bound to enemies of Il Moro through marriage or mutual interests, perhaps the Orsini or the Vitelli.

Although considered to be a subject of the exiled duke, Niccolo felt that if he was charged with being an ally as a former resident member of Il Moro's court, he could argue that he became Il Moro's enemy by his possession of the red book that documented his crimes.

Provided he would be given the opportunity to answer any charges.

Niccolo was led down a long corridor by the two servants who had to pace themselves so they did not get too far ahead of him. The corridors were lined with frescoes and paintings, some of which seemed familiar. That Masaccio, where had he seen it before? And the della Francesca? Surely that was Crivelli's 'Annunciation' in the alcove to his right, softly illuminated by well-placed candelabra.

No matter who the occupant of the palazzo might prove to be, there was no doubting his very good taste and his wealth.

And then Niccolo saw it. On the wall directly facing him, bathed in the soft light of a suspended lantern, hung a portrait of a strikingly beautiful young woman, her long and delicate fingers embracing a symbol of purity, an ermine. Her face was turned as if to look at someone beyond and to the right of the viewer. It was most certainly the Maestro's painting of Madonna Cecilia Gallerani when she was mistress to Il Moro, the portrait of the woman who was now the Contessa Bergamini, the elegant lady who had temporarily abducted him on his way to serve Il Moro and for whom Niccolo had spied on certain members of the Milanese court.

"Ah, my little master of intrigue and deception" came the soft, warm voice through the open doorway to his right, the voice of the woman waiting in the antechamber, "why did it take you so long to come to me?"

Pavia

The two Franciscan monks seemed weary but calm and resigned. They tucked their hands deep within the folds of the wide sleeves of their robes and nodded to Maestro Leonardo, and he, in turn, gestured them into his small cell.

"With your indulgence, Maestro," said the taller of the two, a monk with a deep voice and a thick curly beard, "when my companion, Fra Martino, and I learned you were here at the Certosa, we asked Father Abbot's permission to meet with you and to express our admiration for your 'Adoration of the Magi' which we had the pleasure of viewing at the San Donato a Scopeto. We were told you had agreed to this meeting."

"Of course," the bearded painter nodded. "I am honored, Friars." The monks sat on the edge of the bed. "How is the situation in Florence?" asked Leonardo as he sat in the only chair.

"Volatile, I'm afraid," said Fra Martino. "Fra Angelo and I were there nearly a year after the execution of Fra Savonarola, and the city was in turmoil. Those who exiled the Medici to establish their 'city of God,' as they called it, were still active and powerful, and Piero de Medici seems content to waste his time and money in Rome. Nevertheless, his followers maneuver behind the scenes with the Priorate. It is the Priorate who supposedly runs the city now."

"I am sorry to hear that," Leonardo said softly, his thick

brows forming dark shadows over his eyes. "I thought perhaps I might return to Florence."

"It would be ill advised, Maestro," said Fra Martino.

"How did you come to be in Scopeto?"

"Fra Martino and I are on pilgrimage through the major shrines of Italy," explained the taller monk, "in petition to God that He may move the hearts of the people to successfully mount a crusade against the Turks and avenge the defeat of the Christian fleet at Sapienza."

"You make a religious pilgrimage to advocate a war?"

The taller monk nodded. "We believe the Holy Father will impose a tithe to pay for the crusade."

"I'm certain he will," sighed Leonardo.

"We began at Assisi, of course, where our chapter house is located, and then to the monastery of Sant'Ubaldo in Gubbio for the Festival of the Candles, then to the house of the Virgin in Loreto, and so up the peninsula."

"I trust your pilgrimage has been relatively comfortable?"

"Oh, we have been the guests in most of the noble palaces and castelli," smiled Fra Angelo, "and most innkeepers, while less generous, have at least given us food and a night's shelter in the stables."

"The stables?"

"Our Savior was born in a stable," Fra Martino smiled.

"I remember," Leonardo replied dryly.

"The only time we were denied was at Montagnana about two weeks ago," sighed Fra Angelo. "And, even then, it was not the fault of the innkeeper."

"Montagnana?"

"We were en route from the Santa Giustina in Padua and stopped at a small inn to the south, the Olive Tree, I believe it was called. The proprietor, an unhappy man with a wife and daughter, halfheartedly offered us some plain food and accommodations in the stables, but near the midnight hour, we were shaken from sleep by a small band of mercenaries who forced us from the stables and sent us down the road on foot. We pleaded for compassion, because we were very tired, but the officer in command spoke to the noble traveling with the mercenaries, and we were forced to leave."

Fra Martino broke in. "One of the mercenaries whispered to me, 'It is for the best, friar. You will not want to see what will happen here tonight.' And then we were driven off."

"Indeed?" asked Leonardo. "And what did happen there that night?"

The taller monk shrugged. "I have no idea, but I suspect it had something to do with the other well-dressed young man in the inn that evening."

"Not elaborately dressed, mind," Fra Martino interjected. "But obviously of better quality than the local populace. Though he was certainly not as ornamented as the noble in the red velvet tunic and the heavy black cloak."

"Is this the same noble with whom the mercenary captain spoke later? Was he wearing arms? An impresa?"

"None that we could see. No arms. No crests."

"Unusual, don't you think?" frowned Leonardo as he rested his chin on his hands and stared at the two friars. "A nobleman on a remote road in an obscure inn without arms or an impresa? One would think he did not wish to be identified."

Again Fra Martino shrugged. "Perhaps. Just after we had settled into the stables for the evening, he came, saddled his horse, and rode away."

"I thought you said he was with the mercenaries?"

"He returned with them."

The Maestro combed his long fingers through his beard. "Curious," he said.

"Later, we had found a relatively comfortable sleeping place in a small cave just off the road, and the entire mercenary detachment came racing by us. They had an extra horse with them, and something was wrapped in a heavy blanket and lashed across its saddle."

The Maestro frowned. "I think, my brothers, you were very fortunate that night."

Three days after the Franciscans departed the Certosa, still extolling the wonders of the Maestro's 'Adoration of the Magi,' that Leonardo was summoned to the Father Abbot's office."

Waiting for him there was Francesco Melzi.

The young man leaned forward in his chair. "The time has come to speak of your future plans," the apprentice said quietly. "Where would you prefer to go, Maestro?"

Leonardo shifted uneasily in the uncushioned chair. "I would prefer to return to Florence, of course, Francesco," he said. "I consider it to be my home. My formative days, some of my happiest, were spent there."

Francesco shook his head. "I do not think that practical, Maestro," he said.

"The French have promised to restore Pisa to the Florentines in exchange for certain concessions, but from day to day no one is certain that the streets might not again ring with the cry of 'Palle' and the Medici supporters declare war against the Signori. Until things are settled one way or another, Maestro, I would not recommend returning to Florence."

"Well, where then?" asked Leonardo wearily. "I cannot return to Milan even though many of my inventions, including the war machines and most of my own library and supplies, remain locked in my former workshop." He sighed. "The entire country is like a string of webs stretching from one city-state to the next. The Spanish rule in Naples. The French in Lombardy and the Piedmont. Florence is a republic. The Venetians covet everything, and the pope shifts allegiances with the wind. With so many spiders, where can a poor fly find sanctuary?"

"Don't you have it here, Maestro?"

The Maestro glanced around to make certain he had privacy, and he lowered his voice to a whisper. "I am grateful for the Father Abbot's kindness, of course, but my welcome, and my own patience, is wearing thin here, Francesco. Half of the monks regard me as some sort of black magician, because I have authorization to dissect corpses for study, and the other half feel I am just a simple heretic seeking to lead the innocent into lust by depicting beautiful women realistically. I have even heard rumors resurrecting the charges made against me as a sodomite. Father Abbot has even been forced, by vote of the community apparently, to outlaw any communication between the young postulants and myself."

"Surely they know those charges were unfounded."

"They believe what they choose to believe," shrugged Leonardo. "They look at you with your dark, handsome features and your opposite, the blond Salai, and they think: 'If these are the ones he has chosen for his apprentices, surely he is a wicked old man.'" He ran his fingers through his beard. "To allay some of their fears I have spent an inordinate amount of time in one of the side chapels, where they assume I have been praying. Actually I have been examining Alberti's stations of the cross. Interesting. I am especially intrigued by the final stations, where the Christus is removed from the cross and the body given to the Madonna. It is the subject of all Pieti, of course, but Alberti has managed to convey the Madonna's pain without the use of the obvious device, her tears."

"You have the library here," Francesco smiled. "Could you not pass the time more profitably among the manuscripts?"

"There have been some compensations," the Maestro admitted. "Brother Pax has begrudgingly located some Latin translations from the Arabic of Euclid's theorems on mathematics. I am fascinated, fascinated, but I hunger for more, and, well, the Latin. I now have a list of nine thousand words, but unfortunately it is a language in which I still stutter and stop. It would be convenient if Niccolo was here to continue guiding me through the frustrating maze of tenses and verb endings."

Francesco smiled, rose, and crossed to the Maestro, removing a small folded parchment from the wide expanse of his glove. "Then perhaps this will be an answer to our mutual problem," he said.

"What is it?" asked the Maestro as he took the parchment from the young man and broke the wax seal.

"It is an invitation from Cremona," smiled Francesco, "for you to come and be in residence with the Count and Countess

Ludovico Bergamini. The French have granted them amnesty and promised protection as long as they affirm their loyalty to Louis of France. The count and countess, in turn, now promise to protect you, should you decide to accept their offer and come to Cremona. "

Leonardo scanned the letter. "What are they doing in Cremona? The last I heard of Madonna Cecilia, she and her husband were fleeing to Bologna as guests of the Bentivoglio."

"Cremona is the count's own fief," Francesco explained. "And I understand that Ercole Bentivoglio now commands an army for Cesare Borgia, so I doubt if the count and countess would be welcomed in their cities."

"But what would I do in Cremona?"

"Study."

"But . . . ?"

The dark young man leaned forward and lowered his voice. "You would find it much less complicated, Maestro," he said. "And she tells me that Niccolo will soon be there. He has been traveling with the players since he escaped from the castello. The countess plans to have him abducted."

The Maestro smiled. "Again?"

Cremona

"Are you surprised, Niccolo?"

The contessa smiled at him from a high-backed chair in the small antechamber off the corridor where the dwarf had spied the portrait. She was radiant in a loose-fitting scarlet gown that revealed her throat and shoulders. Around her forehead and her hair, which was worn straight and bound behind and under the chin as in the portrait, was her customary velvet band with a small ruby embedded in it. The middle finger of her right hand still bore the ring with the Bergamini crest in cameo, and the forefinger on the right was decorated with the diamond that Niccolo knew was a gift from Il Moro upon the occasion of the birth of their bastard son, Cesare.

She gestured him into the chamber, and a servant closed the doors behind him. "Come here and kiss my hand," she commanded. "Aren't you happy to see me again?"

The dwarf smiled as he approached her. "I am delighted," he said. "But surprised. Shouldn't you be in Bologna with the Bentivoglio?"

"A subterfuge, Niccolo," she sighed as the dwarf kissed the offered hand. She gestured him to a chair opposite her across a small table laden with a carafe of wine, two glasses, and a silver platter of small cuts of meat and cheeses and delicate pastries. "My lord and I had no intention of going to Bologna. The Palazzo del Verme had ears. I could trust no one. I told you we were going to Bologna, so if you were caught or tortured, you would not be able to reveal our true destination, and if you divulged our destination as Bologna, it would make our enemies believe we had sided with the Borgia fraction and the French. But Cremona is my husband's own domain. The city is vulnerable, of course, especially to pressures from Milan to the west or Venice to the east, but we were fortunate that, how shall I put it? The lie about going to Bologna led the French spies to believe we were sympathetic to their claims. Further, they could not believe I had any great love for the man who seduced me and by whom I had a child. Especially since he married me off to an aristocrat of no great distinction. The Bergamini are honorable, you understand, and of proud lineage, and I am devoted to my husband, but the family is hardly on the same political or social level as the duke of Milan or the doge of Venice, eh?"

Niccolo had mounted the small footstool which enabled him to seat himself in the chair, and was now devouring the pastries, silently noting that the members of the commedia troupe did not eat as well as a contessa. "But how did you find me?" asked the dwarf.

"I never lost sight of you," she laughed at him. "My agents reported that you escaped the castello on the Maestro's wings and that the players picked you up and carried you to the south and east. My spies also told me that the Maestro had been whisked away to the Certosa by an apprentice. What was his name?"

"Salai?"

"No, the decent one."

"Francesco Melzi?"

"Yes! Melzi took the Maestro to the Certosa. But I am certain that the monastic schedules and their plain fare will soon prove intolerable for Maestro Leonardo, so I have sent an invitation, by way of this Melzi, for the Maestro to come and reside with us, at least until the temper of the time cools enough to provide us with a clear picture of which family is allied to whom and where our own allegiances should be placed."

GEORGE HERMAN

"The Maestro is coming here?" cried Niccolo in delight.

"I have invited him, and I think he will come," the contessa said, "especially since I mentioned that you also would be in residence here."

"The Maestro and I together again!" Niccolo beamed. "That is the most wonderful reunion imaginable!"

The voice that came from behind him was just a trifle shrill and quite familiar.

"Fickle boy!" the voice cried.

Niccolo turned to see Ellie, the small, pretty servant girl who had become his lover at the Castello Sforzesco. No longer dressed in the scullery clothes she wore when he first met her, Niccolo now saw his love radiant in satins and silks, her long hair neatly curled and held in place by a black ribbon around her forehead. He instantly slid from the chair with a wide smile and ran to embrace her.

The kiss was, at first, salutary, but it soon became heated as the two young people clung to one another.

"Now, now, children," laughed the contessa. "Not in this chamber please. The carpets are foreign, made for my husband and of incalculable worth."

Mantua

Madonna Isabella d'Este, twenty-six and the celebrated marquesa of Mantua, sat enthroned in the high-backed chair in the center of the head table under a gold canopy in the great hall. Strands of lustrous pearls were wound in her blond curls, and the milky whiteness of her throat was enhanced by the sable band that encircled it and supported a two-carat emerald. Always voluptuous since her early teens, her figure was apparent under her camora that exposed both shoulders and the tops of her breasts. Loops of gold were woven into the pile of her velvet gown, and captured and fractured the light from the thousands of candles and torches.

Her blue eyes scanned the huge, galleried hall festooned with banners and heraldic shields that now served as a refectory for the formal dinner to honor her guests. She glanced over the faces of the two hundred men and women who were seated at long tables placed diagonally to that of the head table, which was also mounted on a dais as if to remind the diners that the marquesa's position was above and apart from them. She forced a smile upon what she considered to be a small army of elegantly dressed and chattering parasites who fed upon her generosity and her goodwill. She placed her right hand on the damask cloth, instinctively reaching for the hand of her husband, Gian-Francesco Gonzaga, but, as usual, his chair was empty. He had been summoned to Venice to consider a response to the latest threat. That threat, as perceived by the doge, was the very man whose triumphant visit to Milan had commanded their presence, Cesare Borgia. The marquesa despaired of understanding these sudden shifts in the sands of politics, but she managed to maintain a listing of both friends and enemies, even as they themselves changed loyalties.

She quickly determined that most of the feast had been consumed. The great saddles of venison, the coveys of partridges and gaggles of geese, the baskets of lobster, trout, and salmon, all had been reduced to skeletons. The wild strawberries once nestled in the castles of citron were now only sparse beds of crumbs and stems. The perfumes emanating from the kindled wads in the beaks of the stuffed white peacocks that graced every table had slowly melded with the dusky smoke from the great portable firepots. The crystal carafes of spiced Pauillac, the Malvesian, the Corsican, and the Nerac wines had long been emptied.

She glanced down at her own empty platter, a three-tiered plate of glazed majolica that depicted an array of mythical creatures and intertwined flowered vines surrounding an idyllic scene of Adam and Eve contemplating the apple in the garden of Eden. She picked up her heavy silver fork whose twin tines were modeled to suggest bird bills and whose handle was shaped to resemble a Greek goddess emerging from a cocoon of grape vines, naked to just below her navel. Rudely seizing the lady, she lightly tapped the fork against the crystal goblet and was pleased at the delicate tone produced by the Murano glass.

Instantly the musicians and the two choirs serenading the diners from the side galleries stopped and turned their attention to the lady. A courtier by the archway to her left slammed his heavy wooden staff of authority against the floor with a resounding boom, and the lords and ladies slowly ceased their conversations. Someone, possibly the belled fool in motley who sat on the floor at the far end of one of the tables, pulled the string through the hide covering of his ca-

carella making a vulgar sound that set those in the vicinity to tittering.

Finally there was silence throughout the great hall.

"My most illustrious lords and ladies," the marquesa began, her voice barely echoing from the stone walls covered with tapestries, "tonight is a threefold cause for celebration." She gestured with one delicate hand weighted with an enormous emerald ring to the bearded, dark-haired young man seated on the opposite side of her husband's empty chair. "We have with us tonight my lord Guglielmo Gaetani to whom we have offered sanctuary. He brings us word from my lord duke of Ferrara and kinsman, Ercole d'Este, that Cesare Borgia has now been named the duke of Valentinois by the French. Of course this means he is no longer a cardinal, by God's good grace." There was a small ripple of laughter, and the marquesa smiled at the scarlet-robed cardinal seated directly to her left. "I trust you will not report that small jest to His Holiness, your most Reverend Highness?"

Ippolito d'Este, plainly intoxicated and with one arm cinched about the waist of the lady to his left while the fingers of his other hand toyed with her bodice, shook his head. "I am not in the confidence of His Holiness, dear sister," he said softly.

"Understandable," the marquesa said, "since we are told that Cesare has designs upon our kinsman's city and, indeed, for most of the Romagna, and since we have been given to understand that his ambitions are being encouraged by His Holiness, the bastard's father."

There was a rustling among the diners who, though accustomed to the marquesa's blunt speech and frequent use of profanity, did not expect such an outburst on a public occasion. Although the statement was correct, the reference to Cesare Borgia's bastardy was startling.

The marquesa seemed not to notice the response. "We have also learned that Duke Cesare seeks a titled wife." There was another nervous ripple of laughter among the ladies of the court. "But we have been told that the Valentinois has been refused by the Princess Carlotta of Taranto, Carlotta of Aragon, and the daughter of the King of Navarre. We trust, then, that this obvious disapproval of him by the nobility might give the Borgia pause, and by offering our hospitality and protection to my lord Gaetani, His Holiness must surely come to realize that Venice, whose armies are under the command of my husband, and the republic of Florence are among those states defiantly opposed to any usurpation of Ferrara." She gave a small nod of her head in the direction of Guglielmo. "On behalf of my most illustrious lord and absent husband, I welcome you, signore."

Gaetani rose and saluted the lady with his goblet. "I thank you, your Excellency."

Isabella smiled indulgently and continued. "We also celebrate tonight the return to our court of our beloved Ser Ottaviano Cristani who has been apart from us for some time on a mission of some delicacy and has now returned. We are grateful for your loyalty and your diligence, and we welcome you home, Ottaviano."

She nodded toward the chestnut-haired, middle-aged gentleman seated to her left at the far end of the table. The man, dressed entirely in black, lightly brushed his hand over the small scar above the bridge of his nose, rose, and also saluted the marquesa with his goblet. "My heart and hand are always yours, Excellency," he said without emotion.

The marquesa smiled. "Pity then that the first seems occupied this evening with thoughts only of Madonna Louisa, and the other holds only an empty goblet."

The mild scolding aroused a wave of laughter throughout the hall, but Ottaviano only glared at those around him and again ran a finger over the scar above the bridge of his nose. He attempted a smile, bowed his head smartly in salute, and intoned, "Such as they are, your Excellency, they are yours."

The marquesa smiled again as she studied Ottaviano. After he was once again seated beside the blushing Madonna Louisa, she turned to face the guests.

"We also welcome to our court Ser Johannes Vendramm, the

young nephew of our respected and generous Belgian friend
and a master of the Hanseatic League, Ser Bruno Vendramm."
She gestured to her left where a handsome young man with
hair as golden as the marquesa's smiled and stood. "Ser Bruno
has sent his nephew to us with a letter in which he commends
him for 'seasoning.'" There was another wave of laughter
throughout the hall and the galleries, and the marquesa turned
to face the young man who seemed uncomfortable. "Judging
from his choice of words, Ser Johannes, your uncle seems to
equate you with a flank of mutton."

The Belgian grinned nervously and somewhat shyly and replied, "Due undoubtedly, your Excellency, because I come to
your court as innocent as a lamb and as submissive and obedi-
ent to your will as any sheep to a benevolent and beautiful
shepherdess."

There was a surge of "ohs" and polite applause from the
diners, and the young man, encouraged, continued. "On behalf
of my uncle and myself, I am delighted and honored to be in
residence in this, the most respected and the most noble of all
courts in Italy, and to be so honored by the presence of the
most illustrious, excellent, and singular lady of the age."

Now the hall erupted with cries of "Bravo!" and a rising tide
of murmured commentary. After a moment the marquesa
smiled again, nodded to Johannes and said, "Well spoken,
signore, and your first duty will be to prepare something for
the Magi Gifts, an annual custom of this court in which our
lords and ladies create small benevolences to be distributed
among our abbeys, monasteries, convents, and churches near
Twelfth Night. The items themselves may be of no great value
save for the fact that they are created in love, humility and
Christian charity."

The blond young man frowned. "I don't think I understand,
your Excellency."

"It is simply a matter of preparing something from our own
hands and limited skills as gifts to the Church, signore. A
gesture that affirms our humility and subservience to the spiritual leaders on the feastday of His nativity. Since many of our
court have been working on their projects for some time, we

will have to find one for you, Johannes, that can be completed in the time left you. Perhaps I can assign a lady to assist you. Would that please you, sir?"

The young man flushed. "Any assistance would be most welcome, your Excellency."

"Then, let us see," said the marquesa as she quickly surveyed the young women seated on both sides of her table. Finally her gaze rested on a beautiful young woman with long red hair that cascaded down nearly to her waist. "Madonna Maddalena d'Oggiono, I believe you are preparing a damask altar cloth with lace edging. Is that project far enough along that you may spare some time to assist Ser Johannes?"

The lady replied softly, eyes averted, "Yes, your Excellency."

"Then be so kind as to assist our young guest in choosing a suitable project for the Magi Gifts."

"If it please you, Excellency."

"Then done and done!" proclaimed the marquesa. She turned again to the young man on the opposite side. "Johannes, Madonna Maddalena will assist you in choosing something appropriate for your gift. Since your illustrious uncle has sent you to us to learn what life is like in the court of the Gonzaga, it is only appropriate that you begin your residency with this singular act of charity and tribute."

"I will give the assignment my complete dedication, your Excellency."

"I am certain you will perform your duties with talent and industry while at our court, signore."

She made a small gesture with her left hand that permitted Johannes to again seat himself. She glanced at the tall man in elegant silver who stood by an archway halfway down the hall.

He nodded.

"And now our evening's entertainment is prepared," the marquesa announced. "My illustrious lords and ladies, respected guests, my brother Eminence, for your entertainment, I give you the irrepressible Nanino!"

The solemn procession of miniature maidens, two lady dwarves each dressed in elaborate but revealing costumes of silks and gauze, entered the great hall. The bottom half of their faces were more or less hidden under diaphanous veils after the imagined fashion of the Turks, and their fingers and bare toes were painted and adorned with tiny bells. They came intoning a mock Latin chant that actually seemed to be in praise of the breasts of the goddess Venus, swinging small bronze censers from which perfumed and multicolored smoke billowed and clouded the great hall, and as they approached the head table, they turned and looked to the rear of the room.

The papal pretender sat erect on a throne chair that rested on twin poles carried on the shoulders of two small men in the scarlet robes of the cardinalate. The dwarf seated on the throne was garbed in the traditional white robes of the pope, and a triple tiara that was far too large for his small head nearly covered his eyes. His dark mustache and goatee joined at the corners of his mouth which seemed to be suppressing a laugh. In each hand he held a large golden key which were crossed upon his chest.

The marquesa glanced at her brother and was pleased to see him roar with delight and then resume toying with the laces on the bodice of Madonna Teresa, who giggled.

She was suddenly conscious of the presence of the tall man in the silver tunic, and she turned to see her chamberlain, Andrea Meneghina, standing motionless behind her chair.

"Yes?" she whispered as she turned her attention back to the antics of the dwarves.

The chamberlain had a shaven face and hollowed cheeks with a narrow, hooked nose like a bird's beak and wide owl's eyes. He leaned around the side of the chair like a pet cockatoo anxious for a morsel from his lady's plate, and whispered at the marquesa's ear. "His rooms have been searched, your Excellency, but we found nothing."

"You believe, then, that Ottaviano told the truth? He did not recover the packet?"

The chamberlain shook his head. "I cannot say that, your Excellency," he whispered. "I merely report that we found nothing among his possessions or in his room that would contradict his story. He may have hidden the packet elsewhere. But I have learned that one of the mercenaries who accompanied him, Captain D'Angennes, has been unusually agitated and impatient since his return and is drinking heavily."

"Is he? Well. Keep vigilant eyes upon the good captain."

"I have already attended to it, your Excellency."

Their whispered exchange was interrupted by a thunderous wave of laughter as the dwarf pope pretended to be conferring the Catholic sacrament of Confirmation on a hapless courtier. Instead of applying the ritual slap, he was actually boxing the man's ears. The put-upon nobleman glanced quickly at the cardinal as if expecting him to put a stop to this blasphemy, but seeing that Ippolito had now worked the laces of Madonna Teresa's bodice loose and had inserted his hand inside to stroke her breast, he realized he must endure the insult. He smiled through clenched teeth and pretended to be enjoying the jest.

At his table Ottaviano Cristani watched the dwarf's mockery of the courtier with obvious displeasure.

"Isn't he amusing?" laughed Madonna Louisa.

"I find the King Rat about as amusing as the plague," snapped the nobleman as he raised his goblet. The large emerald ring on the middle finger of his right hand caught the light. "I wonder if he would be as difficult to eradicate."

"We have also received a message from Fra Pietro da Novellara that Maestro Leonardo di Ser Piero da Vinci has sought sanctuary in the Certosa," Meneghina whispered to the marquesa.

"Has he?"

"May I remind your Excellency that Maestro Leonardo has been in residence at the Castello Sforzesco for more than a decade? There are rumors that he has annotated certain indiscretions of the duke of Bari in a red book that he has taken with him to the monastery."

"Indeed?" The marquesa smiled. "That is of some interest."

"Rumor has it that if the Emperor Maximilian were to be

made privy to the information in that book, he would turn against the duke who is presently under his protection in Germany."

"I would enjoy that," the marquesa said softly, "if only for a way to avenge my sister's treatment by that damned black-berry. For that, and for this present unpleasantness with the Tears, I can never forgive him." She turned from the entertainment to look at her chamberlain. "Could this book pass into our possession, think you, Andrea?"

"I think so, your Excellency," the chamberlain whispered. "If we could get the Maestro here. Your reputation as a patroness of the arts is well established. With your indulgence, may I suggest you offer Maestro Leonardo a commission to paint your portrait? With the duke of Bari in exile, he must want for money. If you would offer a commission of such weight that he could not refuse, then, after the Maestro is in the court, we may search his belongings for the book or we could elicit the information from him or from his associates."

"Associates?"

"Maestro Leonardo has two apprentices, Giovanni Francesco Melzi and Giacomo Salai. He also has at least two pupils, and wherever he has established himself, there are usually a number of individuals who associate themselves with him. He is a frequent correspondent with Ser Benedetto Dei, something of a world traveler, who often visits with him for extended periods. In his last years at the castello, the Maestro also cultivated friendship with a foundling dwarf named Niccolo who instructed him in Latin."

"A dwarf?" The surprise was obvious in the Marquesa's tone.

"I am told this young man differs somewhat from your Excellency's own dwarves," Andrea whispered. "He is perfectly proportioned, not short-legged as Nanino, and he possesses a remarkable memory that enables him to recall anything that he hears or reads."

The marquesa turned to stare at him. "He reads Latin?"

"A result of his education at the hands of the monks in the

Certosa, your Excellency. At nineteen, he can read and write in Latin, Greek, and the vulgar tongue."

The Marquesa was plainly intrigued. "Remarkable. I would like to see this literate dwarf. Perhaps he could be an addition to our own assembly. It would do Nanino a world of good to have some competition. He is becoming a spiteful little bore." She shook her blond curls. "But I am in no position to offer residency to an army of the Maestro's devotees. Gian-Francesco constantly complains of the vast number of courtiers already in attendance."

"None of his apprentices or pupils are with him at the Certosa. Perhaps your Excellency can stipulate that he come only with this literate dwarf. He is in no position to negotiate. A patronless artist cannot provide shelter or nourishment for followers. If the commission offered is generous I feel certain he would accept the terms."

"I cannot afford a 'generous' commission," she snapped. "You know that, Andrea."

"Maestro Leonardo does not know that, Excellency," replied Meneghina. "And it is unlikely you will ever have to honor the contract. Your Excellency may impose a specific date for the commission to be fulfilled. Maestro Leonardo is notorious for not finishing commissions. He is easily distracted. If the portrait is not finished on the day for which he is contracted, your Excellency may simply give the man a small stipend for his effort and send him on his way. By that time, if the book is in his possession, we shall have it."

The marquesa nodded. "Possible. Of course he may receive other commissions. Is there anything else we might dangle before his eyes to entice him to our court?"

"Your Excellency might mention some of the scholars presently in residence," the chamberlain advised. "Pietro Bembo. Baldasar Castiglione and Niccolo Panizatto. I understand that he also respects our court painter, Maestro Andrea Mantegna whose 'Dead Christ' he admired in the Brera in Milan. Maestro Leonardo has an appetite for knowledge, and he relishes discourse with learned men. Perhaps that might help to persuade him."

"Then see to it!" The marquesa ran a delicate hand across her forehead. "I suppose I will have to justify the expense for my husband, but I shall tell him that I intend the portrait to be a present to him upon our anniversary."

In the center of the room, the mock pope was announcing the new names for the recently confirmed noble, which included several obscenities and vulgar references to the gentleman's sexual shortcomings.

"You think he will come?" asked the marquesa.

"I believe he will, your Excellency," the chamberlain said as he stood erect beside her chair. "No artist in Italy would refuse a commission from the illustrious and revered Marquesa of Mantua."

Isabella toyed with her two-tined fork. "Then," she smiled, "upon his arrival perhaps we shall have some small amusements."

AMUSEMENTS

November 1499

Pavia

Maestro Leonardo's decision to abandon the Certosa and take up residency with the Bergamini in Cremona was met with mixed emotions by some of the clerics.

Brother Antonius, imperial overlord of the scullery, silently mourned Leonardo's departure. During the Maestro's stay, the Father Abbot had given the chef permission to prepare special meals for Leonardo, meals more elaborate than the simple fare of the monastics. The kitchen master, whose physical appearance suggested a round onion topped by an albino prune, had then imagined himself to be the overlord of one of the vast sculleries in some palazzo of the nobility, and he had created for the Maestro such rarities as trionfi, a succulent and miniature masterpiece sculpted from sugar. He had soaked the Maestro's share of the meat in wine and basted it with a sauce of quince and pear and orange. He had manufactured a delicate lace of brill and turbot, smothered seafood in a rich broth of garlic and mushrooms, and embellished everything with small bouquets of parsley and basil.

Not that the Maestro himself had ever shown a preference for anything beyond plain fare. Dining, the culmination of the master chef's art, seemed to be viewed by the Florentine as something required for sustenance with no further value. That was most disappointing for Brother Antonius, because an artist thrives on recognition by other artists whom he respects.

With Leonardo leaving, the maestro of the scullery would have to return to the frustration of dark bread baked with the poor-quality grain from the monastery's own fields and the butter churned from ass's milk and the limited variety of vegetables and fruit that the monks enticed from the Lombardy soil.

Not that the quality of the meals would be noticed, because the Certosa, like all religious houses, ordained that all meals would be accompanied by a reader of sacred scripture, so the attention of the diners should remain steadfastly focused upon God and not on the watery consistency of the stew.

Father Abbot was visibly relieved to be rid of the Maestro. The necessary disciplines of monastic life did not allow for residencies of worldly and reputedly "sacrilegious" artists. He personally had no objections to Leonardo, although he secretly wished that the Maestro might be a monk himself, like Fra Bartolomeo. Then his more offensive or questionable artifacts could be reviewed and, if necessary, censored or altered by direct command. As far as the Father Abbot was concerned, Leonardo represented a source of infection for the evils from which Father Abbot had always strived to protect his brothers in Christ, new and secular ideas on the makeup of the world and its origins. Consequently, when the Maestro informed the head of the Certosa that he would go into residency with the Contessa Bergamini, the Father Abbot seized one of the painter's huge hands, pumped it enthusiastically, and then went straightaway to the chapel to offer four decades of the rosary in thanksgiving.

Brother Pax, surprisingly, was a little reluctant to see "the devil's disciple" leave, because he had come to believe that, due to their several discussions in which the good monk demonstrated his mastery of philosophical and spiritual texts available only in Greek, the Maestro was about be converted from his immoral practice of dissecting human bodies. To encourage any such turn of heart, Brother Pax snuck a copy of a Latin translation of the Meditations of Marcus Aurelius into the Maestro's luggage and left the ribbon bookmark on a specific passage, hoping it would attract his attention and praying that Leonardo had mastered enough Latin to translate it.

It read: "No longer distract yourself . . . but, as if you were about to die, despise the flesh. It is only blood and bones and a network of nerves, veins and arteries . . . Consider this: you are an old man . . . Remember . . . how often you have received an opportunity from the gods, and yet did not take it. You must now at last perceive of what universe you are a part . . . and that a limit of time is fixed upon you, which, if you do not use it to clear away the clouds from your mind, it will pass, and you will pass, and the opportunity will never return."

Brother Pax felt very pleased with himself.

On the day that the Maestro departed, in a coach sent to bring him to Cremona, the wide sky over the Certosa was grey as ashes and accompanied by a cold rain. Leonardo, depressed by the fact that he was about to impose himself upon the charity of the Bergamini, opened the Epictetus. He paused on a page where Niccolo had made notes in the margins in the vulgar tongue to speed the translation process.

He read: "Behold me! I have neither city nor house nor possessions nor servants . . . I have no wife, no children, no shelter . . . but what do I lack? I am untouched by sorrow or fear, because I am free."

Leonardo was not consoled.

Cremona

Niccolo and Ellie, having reveled in the enthusiastic revival of their relationship for nearly two weeks, amused themselves at the last afternoon performance of I Comici Buffoni before the troupe was to leave Cremona and travel south to reach the warmer climates before winter delivered her promise of snow. Even now, as they huddled together among the small assembly of peasants, workers, clerics, and children, the cold wind licked at their noses and ears.

The sogetto was typically *commedia dell'arte*, an absurd plot in which Isabella and Francesco in order to keep the girl's father busy while they eloped, convinced Pantalone that he was pregnant. The cunning servant, Arlecchino, assisted the young lovers by assuring the old miser that babies frequently supplied wombs to those who lacked them, especially to the rich who could afford anything. When Pantalone argued that he had not slept with a woman for over a year, Arlecchino offered the view of the Church that children were "gifts from God" and noted that copulation was not only unnecessary but also exhausting for a man Pantalone's age. Finally the learned Doctor Graziano himself, paid in silver ducats for his contribution to the lovers, performed a brief and somewhat bizarre examination in which he compared what was supposedly a pail of Pantalone's urine to a bottle of cheap Neapolitan wine. Doctor Graziano announced that the old man would, indeed, deliver a child, and within a matter of moments. To speed the normal process of gestation, the good doctor produced a huge syringe from his black bag, and poor Pantalone was forced to drop his pantaloons and receive the injection while Anna as Lesbino and Prudenza as Colombina offered outlandish and vulgar advice on how to survive pregnancy with an intact sense of humor. A few moments later Pantalone delivered, from under his cloak, a full-grown Scapino who began instantly to wail. Under a barrage of commands from the old miser, Arlecchino was put to picking lice from the "infant's" hair, and Colombina was forced to rock the "baby" at an ever increasing tempo while Lesbino mocked them. Lesbino's laughter died quickly, however, when Scapino demanded to be suckled by her, and Pantalone threatened the distraught servant girl with immediate unemployment if she refused. Finally the old miser negotiated an agreement by which Colombina offered one teat and Lesbino the other at alternate feedings.

The sogetto ended, as did most performances by I Comici Buffoni, with a mad chase over and around the furniture, the battes of the black-masked clowns slapping against backsides, and the capitano's sword being employed to lift the women's skirts as they raced by.

"What a stupid and ridiculous plot," Ellie whispered to Niccolo. "Imagine! A pregnant man!"

"Farce does not demand credibility," Niccolo advised her. "You might be surprised how many normally intelligent people would consider a pregnant man a fitting source for laughter."

"If they knew what it is like to actually endure pregnancy, they wouldn't find it so hilarious," she snarled.

It was only much much later that Niccolo wondered if Ellie had been trying to tell him something he should have suspected.

The young couple watched as a few lira rained upon the stage, and then Niccolo took two gold coins from his tunic and tossed them to the players. Simone caught one, saw that it was one of the newer coins called scudi del sole because it depicted a sun over the armorial shield, and he smiled and bowed elaborately to Niccolo and Ellie with his beaked cap dusting the stage. Prudenza caught the other, tested it with her teeth to make certain it was not merely base metal under a gilded exterior, and then, satisfied with its worth, she deposited it between her breasts and blew Niccolo a kiss.

The young man and woman left immediately and hurried up the narrow roadway to the palazzo.

"Won't they be upset that you did not say good-bye?" asked Ellie.

"Only two things upset an actor," Niccolo replied, "missing a meal and being upstaged. Besides, I don't consider it good-bye. We'll meet again, I'm sure. Just yesterday Rubini sent me the pair of stilts he had constructed especially to my size. The stilts were his way of saying 'Til we meet again!' I said the same by throwing the contessa's gold."

They walked a little in silence, and then Ellie asked softly, "Are you bored here at court, Niccolo?"

"No," the young man frowned. "Why would you ask that?"

"Because I know you found the intrigue at the Castello Sforzesco, what? Invigorating? Amusing?" she said. "Here you have no such dangerous games to occupy your time."

"I have you," Niccolo smiled at her. "That's enough of an invigorating amusement." He studied the deep brown eyes of the young girl and the pouting lips. "And twice as dangerous."

Mantua

Andrea Meneghina, the dark Gonzaga chamberlain elaborately adorned in scarlet velvet trimmed in gold, strode quickly down the long corridor of the marquis' palace, glanced from the window at the Piazza Sordello and the dome of San Sebastiano to the south, hurried past the wing housing the dwarves' apartments, and threw open the great doors that opened onto the Camera degli Sposi. He expected to find the marquesa in the reception hall, but when he found the room empty and unattended, he crossed quickly into the smaller antechamber adjoining it. Here he discovered the leader of the dwarf community, Nanino, posturing before the life-sized portrait of Federigo Gonzaga, the father of the marquis. The dwarf was attempting to mimic the pose of the man in the painting. He was dressed in a miniature copy of the tunic and hose, the high boots and the short cape depicted in the portrait, complete even to a small copy of Federigo's ring on the dwarf's right middle finger and the jeweled scabbard for his small dagger at his waist.

The dwarf barely glanced at the chamberlain as he entered. "I know something you do not," he taunted him.

Meneghina swiftly drew his stiletto from its scabbard, and the dwarf glared at him while trying to conceal his momentary shock and alarm. The chamberlain smiled, crossed to a credenza, and speared an apple from the bowl of fruit placed there.

"It may not be prudent to know too much in this court, you obnoxious little maggot," he said coldly.

"Knowledge is power, you diseased dog's ass," Nanino snarled as he broke his pose and impudently snatched the apple from the stiletto's point.

The chamberlain wanted to strike the dwarf, but he and Nanino both knew that such an action would bring a reprimand from the marquesa who indulged the perversions of her pet. Meneghina merely smiled at the miniature man, sheathed his stiletto, and took a clump of grapes from the sideboard's dish.

"If knowledge is power, then no one need fear you, you insignificant little turd," the chamberlain snapped. He tore a grape from the stem and popped it into his mouth. "With that twisted, tiny substitute for a brain, there can't be much room left in its dark corners for genuine knowledge, not among the grotesque obscenities and the blasphemous mockeries you nurture there."

The dwarf bit into the apple. "I say again: I know something you do not, you pig's behind," he sneered.

"I doubt it," the chamberlain replied.

"I know the marquesa has sent an invitation for Maestro Leonardo di Ser Piero da Vinci to come to our court and paint the lady's portrait."

"I prepared the commission myself," Meneghina informed him. "And why should a matter of art and culture concern you, you malevolent toad? In your circle, art is a fart ignited by a flame, and your culture could be summed up in a scroll of illustrated pornography."

The dwarf hurled the apple at him, but Meneghina ducked, and the fruit splattered against the wall. "It concerns me, you arrogant bastard, because they say the Maestro has a dwarf with him, an unusual dwarf with a keen mind. Perhaps he and I can pool our superior intellects and bring you down a step or two, shitface!"

Meneghina smiled at the dwarf's frustration. "You have an

array of little pimpled asses around you already, you poisonous spittle, and, with all their combined talents of spying and assassination, I still have the marquesa's ear."

Nanino glared at the chamberlain and shrieked, "But I have her heart!"

The dwarf suddenly performed a cartwheel into the center of the room, and then he squatted on the thick carpet and crowed, "And I know what is happening that concerns Captain D'Angennes!"

Meneghina's temper flared. He was annoyed that the dwarf might possess information concerning the security of the court which was his responsibility. He despaired when any of his activities on behalf of the marquesa became openly discussed among the courtiers and the servants. He knew that the dwarves of the Gonzaga maintained a pipeline through their constant spying throughout the fortress that resulted in a flow of supposedly confidential information. To protect himself he had slipped an agent of his own among the little men and women, so he did not wish to jeopardize that personal connection by suggesting to the marquesa that the activities of the dwarves be curtailed. Like all security men, he felt that what could not be stopped completely could be controlled and manipulated through infiltration and misinformation.

The chamberlain tore another grape from the stem. "Do you indeed?" he asked. "And what do you know of the good captain, eh?"

"Do you like riddles?" inquired the dwarf with a small laugh as he began to perform a little dance around Meneghina. "Beyond the walls, beneath the moat, there is a ship that cannot float. There is a cage, but the bird's abed with a toasty fire at his feet and head."

"I haven't time for riddles, you insignificant worm," Meneghina replied. He started toward the door, turned, smiled at the dwarf, and said, "but if you are trying to tell me that a good friend and companion of Captain D'Angennes has been conducted to the torture chambers below the moat, then I hasten to inform you that I was the one who ordered him taken there."

"But I know what they have done to him," trumpeted the little man as he advanced toward the chamberlain. "You give commands and never know what follows!" His grin was sinister. "They dressed him in his armor, helmet, greaves and everything, and they passed the iron rings in the back of the breastplate through a metal rod and suspended him over the fires until his screams almost deafened his tormentors." His smile was twisted. "Did you envision that, Meneghina? Is that your concept of amusement?"

"Be careful that no one bakes *you* like an apple, you little abomination," the chamberlain threatened. "I happen to know that the marquesa is wearying of you, Nanino, and who knows? In time, perhaps, I may have the pleasure of turning *you* on a spit until you sing for me."

"Is that what this young officer is doing, Meneghina?" the dwarf scowled. "Is he singing prettily? Does he know if Ottaviano has the Tears?"

"Everything he knows and does not know he will soon warble for me," said the chamberlain coldly. "And I will be present to transcribe every note."

He laughed and quickly closed the door behind him, as the dwarf wheeled, and pointed his small backside at the departed chamberlain.

"Cacapensieri!" screamed Nanino in the vulgar tongue.

Cremona

Leonardo was both amused and a bit puzzled by the apparition that suddenly formed to welcome him in the reception chamber of the Bergamini palazzo. It certainly had Niccolo's face and voice, but his head was nearly level with the Maestro's own.

"I see they have been feeding you well, Niccolo," smiled the Maestro.

Niccolo beamed and took one or two tentative steps toward the artist. "Welcome to the Palazzo Bergamini, Maestro!" he trumpeted. "The very air here is invigorating. See how I've grown?"

"Very skilful, Niccolo," the Maestro nodded, and then he said quietly, "An excellent demonstration of compound balance."

Niccolo frowned at the analysis. "What?"

"I assume you are wearing some sort of extensions on your legs that require balance," Leonardo observed with a smile. "I have observed that if a man balances on one foot the shoulder on the side on which he rests is always lower than the other, and the pit of the throat will be above the middle of the leg on which he rests. The navel, of course, always lies on the central line of the weight that is located above it, and . . ."

"Yes, yes, Maestro. I understand," said the dwarf as he carefully lowered himself to the top of a table and gestured to Ellie to help him remove the stilts. "I should have expected a lecture rather than a burst of applause."

The Maestro could see that the dwarf was annoyed. "I am impressed by the skill, Niccolo. Truly. I am only pointing out to you, my young friend, that there are laws, mathematical laws that govern . . ."

"Yes, Maestro," Niccolo nodded, plainly irritated that Leonardo had so quickly seen through his charade. "I understand!"

Leonardo studied the young man and shook his head. "You are no longer interested in my observations, Niccolo?"

"Engulfed would perhaps be a better word," said the dwarf as Ellie removed the long pantaloons and proceeded to unfasten the belts that bound the wooden appendages to his legs. "So much information, Maestro. So many details."

Niccolo saw the Maestro stiffen, and he knew Leonardo was now annoyed with him. "Whether it be painting, sculpture or walking on extensions, young man, the essence of any art is in the details."

After the stilts were removed, Niccolo quickly crossed to the Maestro and stood at his side, his head just below Leonardo's chest. Suddenly all annoyances, all petty differences were washed away in the joy of reunion. "It is good to see you again, Maestro," he said quietly.

Leonardo's frown also dissolved into that gentle smile with which Niccolo had become so familiar. "It is good to be reunited with you, my friend." His voice lowered, and he glanced at Ellie as if he were unsure about their privacy. "The invaders used my clay model of the Sforza for gunnery practice, Niccolo," he said softly, "and then they pulled what was left from the pedestal and crushed it into gravel. And Vigevano, that beautiful city of my vision, they tell me is in ruins."

Niccolo shrugged. "Aren't you the man who pointed out to me that 'the blind cannot judge colors'? What did you expect of barbarians but barbarism? Have you accomplished all that you told me you wished to accomplish when we departed the castello in such haste?" His face broadened into that wide grin that the Maestro always found disarming and enchanting. "Did you learn from Jean de Paris how to color *a secco*? Or the white salt method? Have you mastered the technique of *cornage tempera* that so fascinated you? Have you learned how to dissolve gum lac?"

The tall, bearded man studied the younger man whose clean-shaven face reflected his optimism and boyish enthusiasm. "You remember all those things that I mentioned only in passing?" he said softly. "You never cease to amaze me, Niccolo. As for my ambitions, I had to abandon all my equipment: easels, palettes, pigments, my collection of medicinal herbs and powders, my own small library, the models of my war machines, everything."

"Well, you have no need for them at present, do you? Here we are, safe and secure, for the time!" cried the dwarf. "So let us continue to amaze one another!" He gave a small laugh. "I will scheme and plot and steal from the sculleries, and you can handle the details!"

The Maestro could not resist. A smile formed, and then he chuckled.

"We have enough amusements to last the winter," added the dwarf.

Mantua

"The original proposals were promising," the marquesa commented to her chamberlain as she examined the music on the clavichord before her in her private apartments which were referred to by the entire court as "Paradise." "But it is the details that determine the quality of the projects," she continued. "I will not have something come from this court that does not represent the very highest of standards, even something as relatively unimportant as the Magi Gifts. This is not to be considered some idle amusement. It is an exposition of the works by the very talented and distinguished members of our court and reflects upon our own prestige."

The lady's smile did not waver. She extended her right hand, and Meneghina, who stood by her chair, instantly placed a rolled parchment in it. The marquesa unrolled it and said quietly, "Now look you! Ser Girolamo has forged a pair of fire tongs. Now that undoubtedly has a useful purpose, but does it reflect the grandeur of the Gonzaga? Hardly. Perhaps if it were cast in bronze and engraved with some suitable commentary in Greek, but plain tongs? Pitiful. And Madonna Francesca has spent four weeks working a vestito in shaved velvet! Now I ask you, Andrea, who will wear it? The Mother Superior of Santa Maria de Gaino? An overgown! Imagine! As a Magi Gift!" She scanned the listing. "What is this? Ottaviano is preparing what?"

"Requiem candles, Excellency," replied the chamberlain. "Black. But the decorative figures and scenes from the life of our Savior that he has envisioned have not yet been inscribed upon them in colored waxes. He says he is awaiting the return of Maestro Andrea to sketch the figures for him. You may remember that Maestro Andrea is finishing the frescoes in the Ermitani in Padua."

"Maestro Andrea may not return for some time," the marquesa snapped, passing the parchment back to Meneghina. "Ottaviano should make some effort to complete the project himself."

"May I suggest, Excellency, that this part of the process might be given to someone else, perhaps Maestro Leonardo, as his contribution to the Magi Gifts?"

"I have seen no indication that the Maestro is in receipt of our commission much less accepted it. But should he agree to come in residence, he will be far too involved in painting my portrait to assist Ottaviano with requiem candles."

"But if we were to request the Maestro's assistance in such small matters as finishing the candles or perhaps designing the costumes and decor for one of the spring festivals, it might guarantee that your portrait would not be completed on time, which would nullify your agreement. His fee could be renegotiated."

The marquesa sounded a chord on the keyboard. "Ah, my dearest Andrea, you are *astuto*! You are indeed!" She sighed and added, "But I will give the matter some consideration." Suddenly she stood and faced her chamberlain. "Nanino tells me that one of my garrisoned officers has been taken to the dungeons. Is that correct?"

"Yes, Excellency," nodded Meneghina, inwardly seething at the dwarf.

"By whose command?"

"Mine, Excellency," the chamberlain shrugged. "But with your implied permission of course." He lowered his head to indicate his subservience. "Was I mistaken, Excellency? I had reason to believe he had something to tell us. You may remember that I reported that Captain D'Angennes has been

89

drinking heavily? This officer was his constant companion. I would not presume to accuse D'Angennes directly, but if testimony could be elicited . . . !"

"Indeed?" frowned the marquesa. "And have you 'elicited' any information from this officer?"

"We shall, Excellency." Meneghina bowed his head.

The Marquesa returned to her chair before the clavichord. She made a few runs along the keyboard with her long, delicate fingers, and then she paused again. "Should you succeed, bring the information to me directly, and I will act upon it. It may appear presumptuous of you to have ordered this officer to the dungeons without first consulting me." She resumed her fingering. "However I know you had our interests at heart, Andrea, and I cannot assign someone responsibility without also allocating some degree of authority."

"Thank you, Excellency," said the chamberlain as he bowed again.

"But I will assume command of this situation now," she said softly. "If Ottaviano has been lying, something I find difficult to accept considering his personal and professional standard of ethics, I would have to adjust what I told the Cambio." She stroked a chord that resonated through the antechamber. "Still," she smiled, "that might even prove amusing."

Cremona

The Maestro and Niccolo stood side by side before Leonardo's portrait of the contessa, which was displayed at the end of the corridor. Both admired the youthful beauty of the lady who was now their hostess.

"The ermine was inspired, Maestro," said Niccolo. "But it surprises me a little, considering that many at the time regarded the lady as grossly immoral because she was mistress to Il Moro."

"I did not add the ermine to symbolize purity," replied the Maestro, reexamining the portrait. Niccolo knew he was pondering what he might have done to improve it. "Don't you see? It is a form of a visual jest."

"A jest?"

"It is a play upon the lady's name at the time, Gallerani. Galee is Greek for ermine," the Maestro said, turning to smile at the young man. "I would think you'd know that. Perhaps you need to devote a little more of your time to your studies in the classical languages, my dear Niccolo, and perhaps less with Madonna Elenora."

"A jest?" Niccolo repeated.

"A play on words."

"You surprise me, Maestro," Niccolo said. "A jest in painting? And from you?"

Leonardo frowned. "Why not me? When I studied with Mae-

91

stro Andrea del Verrocchio I was considered quite amusing by some. I was very young then of course and frivolous." He paused as if remembering. "Let us say I found much in those years in Florence that amused me."

Niccolo's smile stretched from ear to ear. "Forgive me, Maestro, but it's just that one doesn't always associate you with jests. Your demeanor is usually quite serious."

"Oh? Well, Il Moro found the little puzzles and games I created for him to be amusing. Yes, Niccolo, forgive me, but I am frequently amused. I may not reveal it as readily as you, but there are times when I most certainly have to laugh." He paused and seemed to reflect on the statement. "Otherwise," he added, "I would doubtless weep." The Maestro turned from the portrait, lowered his head and stroked his beard, and Niccolo sensed a sudden melancholy descending upon his friend. "There are times, Niccolo, when I think perhaps I am one of God's little jests. I believe He must be watching, shaking his head and laughing at me."

"I assure you, Maestro, no one, not even God himself, laughs at you."

"I can understand if the people do," Leonardo murmured. "I must appear foolish at times, and I do not really mind the laughter. I certainly do not wish to be regarded as some sacred ornament before the high altar."

"You are the consummate artist, Maestro," Niccolo replied softly. "Only genius could create such beauty as this." He gestured to the portrait of the contessa.

"God created that beauty, not I," Leonardo said, turning again to face the painting. "I was given only the skill to reproduce it. The lady is one of the few with perfect features."

"What do you mean by that? What is perfection?"

"Precise proportionality," Leonardo instructed him. "There are absolutes in the structure of the human face. For example, the space between the mouth opening and the base of the nose should always be one-seventh of the entire face."

"Always?"

"Always. And the space from the mouth to beneath the chin should be a quarter of the face, and the space between the chin and the base of the nose a third of the face. The space between the top of the nose to below the chin will normally be one half of the face, and the thickness of the neck one and three-quarters of the space from the eyebrows to the nape of the neck."

"I am astounded," smiled the dwarf.

"It is fact!" The Maestro frowned at him. "Furthermore, the greatest width of the face at eye level should be equal to the area between the hairline at the top of the forehead and the mouth whereas the width of the nose is half the length of the space between the tip of the nose and the start of the eyebrows."

"And this is true in every case?"

"In any face that is not deformed. It is mathematical."

"Yes, I know," laughed Niccolo as he imitated the Maestro's intonation and voice pattern. " 'Art, life, war, politics, they are all derived from mathematical laws, and such laws allow no exceptions. None. Absolute truth. Nothing, nothing is true unless it can be proven by mathematics.' "

Leonardo turned to face him. "Is that what I said?"

"Word for word."

"I have no reason to doubt you," nodded the Maestro. "That memory of yours! But there! Don't you find my obsessions amusing? My dedication to painting and engineering and mathematics and everything?"

"No," sighed the dwarf.

The invitation from the Marquesa Isabella d'Este with a commission for Leonardo to paint her portrait arrived two days later, and the contessa brought the document to the Maestro herself. She found him with Niccolo in the library where the dwarf was testing Leonardo's translation of Caesar's history of the wars.

"I have heard many stories of the lavish court of Mantua," murmured the Maestro as he examined the commission, "and I have met both the Marquesa Isabella and the Marquis Gian-Francesco Gonzaga. At that time the marquesa occasionally came to the Milan court to visit her sister, Beatrice." He looked up from the parchment. "She offers me a substantial amount of money."

"Indeed," said the contessa softly. "But, if you will forgive me, Maestro, I would advise against accepting this commission."

"Why?"

"Because I know the lady well. Isabella d'Este, at only twenty and six, has a fiery temper and an arrogant disregard for human life," she said intently. "She continues to wage a genteel vendetta against Il Moro. She insists, for example, that her court always refer to him only as 'the duke of Bari' rather than by his title as duke of Milan."

"Surely she does that only because Il Moro is, in point of fact, no longer the duke of Milan," replied Leonardo.

"She does it to deny his legitimacy for the dukedom," the contessa persisted. She seated herself in a high-backed chair of dark wood. "Perhaps you do not know that Isabella d'Este was Il Moro's first choice for a wife, but she turned from him when I became his mistress."

"I did not know that, contessa," said the Maestro.

"Then she quickly engaged herself to the Gonzaga. Later, when Isabella learned that her sister was to be Il Moro's substitute bride, she lectured Beatrice against marrying into the family, and she so strenuously pressed the lady's case against me that poor Ludovico had no choice but to marry me to the Count Bergamini. He was even forced to remove me, and our son, from the castello. Now I have heard that she holds Il Moro personally responsible for her sister's early death because of his continuing affairs. She was reportedly livid when, almost immediately following his wife's death, he fell directly into the bed of that putana, Madonna Crivelli."

"We should not judge the poor man," Niccolo said quietly, glancing at Ellie seated across from him. "Perhaps the duke had need of, well, consolation. Men frequently seek that in women."

Ellie glanced at him and shook her head in dismay. "I know what men seek in women, Master Niccolo," she snapped. "And we should not discuss it in proper company."

Leonardo drew a hand across his forehead, and Niccolo knew that once again he had said too much, but the contessa continued to smile at him, shook her head and replied softly, "The alternative, I believe, is abstinence, Niccolo. At least for a proper period in which to adequately mourn one's wife." She shrugged. "Then it would largely be a matter of taste."

Niccolo gave a small laugh, and the lady turned to face the Maestro. "I also believe that Isabella wants to get you to her court, Maestro, so she can elicit information from you about Il Moro, information that might discredit him with his only remaining ally, the Hapsburg Emperor."

"Me? What sort of information could she possibly elicit from me?" asked the Maestro.

"Perhaps the red book?" she said softly. The Maestro and Niccolo exchanged quick glances. "It is no longer a secret, Maestro. Everyone knows, or thinks they know, what it contains and how it could destroy Il Moro's reputation with the emperor."

"Ah!" Leonardo nodded.

"And I assure you, Maestro, that Isabella is not as she may have appeared on her visits to Milan. She is a true virago, a woman who erupts with vulgar gutter language when angry. And she has surrounded herself with a regiment of fawning sybarites and assassins."

"That may be true," Leonardo nodded, "but I cannot continue to accept your hospitality forever, contessa, and a commission, especially one of this magnitude, is the lifeblood of the artist. We rely on commissions and subsidies in order to practice and develop our art. Charity is fine, and you have been generous, but I must honor commissions. The only thing I have attempted since I fled Milan was a chalk study of the Madonna with Saint Anne and the two children."

"Perhaps the Madonna with Saint Anne will prove a superior work, because it was not commissioned."

Leonardo shook his head. "Artists have always been subsidized, contessa. From the days of the Greeks, artists have always relied on patrons or state subsidies to support their work."

"With every commission there are restrictions, Maestro. Doesn't that restrain the freedom of the artist?"

"Not as much as poverty, contessa." She laughed, and Leonardo continued. "I must admit that I am also intrigued by the assembly of gifted scholars reportedly in residence in Mantua." He referred to the document before him. "Pietro Bembo is there with Baldasar Castiglione and Niccolo Panizatto, the young scholar in classical literature. The commission also points out that the Mantuan court possesses one of the largest and most diversified libraries in Italy. I know that they possess copies of three texts with which Niccolo and I were working in Milan, John Pecham's *Perspectiva Communis*, Pliny's *Historia Naturalis*, and Sallust's *Bellum Iugurthinum*."

"I understand," the contessa nodded.

Leonardo looked up from the document and glanced at Niccolo and then at the contessa. "But, knowing my weakness in Latin in which most of these texts are written, and apparently aware of my relationship with Niccolo, the marquesa has generously suggested that, well, that he accompany me."

The suggestion seemed to startle Ellie, but the contessa did not look at her handmaiden. She turned her attention to Niccolo. "That would be entirely up to our young friend. What say you, Niccolo? Do you wish to accompany the Maestro to Mantua?"

The young man lowered his head, knowing what Ellie must be thinking. He did not wish to hurt her, but he said softly, "I have been a trifle useless at the court, contessa, haven't I? I mean: I really have little or nothing to do here, and, despite your generous hospitality, I, ah, I sometimes feel as if I have been indulged as, well, as something of a toy or a pet."

"You think I look upon you as a pet, Niccolo?" frowned the contessa. "I am disappointed in you, young sir! I assure you that I respect and love you as I would a son. And I must warn you that in the court at Mantua, Isabella maintains five dwarves who are indeed treated as her personal playthings. They have their own quarters where everything is scaled to their size. They are dressed in fine clothes and jewels, and she occasionally employs them as couriers and, according to rumors, when necessary, as assassins." She shook her head again, rose suddenly, and said, "Well, give the lady's commission some careful consideration. I warn you, Maestro. But I will accede to whatever you wish."

She swept from the room.

Ellie glared at Niccolo and trailed after her.

Mantua

Captain D'Angennes returned to his rooms in the garrison wing of the Gonzaga palace both agitated and dismayed, and more than a little drunk from the potent burgundy that the marquesa had been given from the Hospices de Beaune and had generously passed on to the resident garrison. The agitation was a result of the persistent rumors passed among his fellow officers that a friend and companion had been taken to the dungeons and was being tortured without anyone knowing why.

The captain knew why.

The black-bearded officer was surprised to find his room in relative darkness, although he customarily left at least one of the lamps lit at sundown. He picked his way carefully across the wooden floor by the light of the full moon that flooded the room from the balconied window. As he groped for a lamp, he heard a sound as if someone or something had coughed or grunted from somewhere on the balcony, and he crossed to see what it might be.

Just inside the open windows, he suddenly felt the rope encircle his neck and tighten with lightning speed. The bearded officer quickly raised his gloved hands to his throat, but he could not find a way to work his fingers beneath the coils that were slowly choking the breath from him. He tried to scream or to shout the name of his attacker, whom he knew, but it was impossible. He felt the heavy pressure against his back, and was propelled forward. He struggled to maintain his balance, but his momentum carried him through the open windows, and the railing of the balcony struck him at the belly. He struggled to grasp the railing, but his gloves slipped against the marble. He tried to turn, but the attacker remained behind him, wheeling as his prey twisted in his grasp.

D'Angennes was suddenly bent backward over the railing. He reached out to seize something, anything, and the dark cloak of the man in front of him came away in his hands. He toppled over the edge, still clinging to the mantle. He felt himself falling, falling, but suddenly the rope was stretched taut, and his head was nearly severed by the broken fall. He dangled at the end of the noose, and the cloak slipped from his hands to the cobbled courtyard below.

The body swung gently in the cold night air, suspended from the rope wrapped around the balcony railing.

Ottaviano Cristani left the darkened room and descended the staircase without being seen. He recovered his cloak from the stones of the garrison courtyard, checked the broken clasp, and then he became one with the shadows.

The tower bells tolled the hour.

Cremona

Niccolo had been aroused from sleep by a distant bell sounding the hour. He slowly realized that Ellie was pounding on his shoulders. He thought at first that she was upset about his decision to go to Mantua and had come to lecture him on it, but when he rolled over, he saw that she was accompanied by two male servants carrying candelabra. She told him, "Dress, and come to the contessa's bedchamber, Niccolo. She has someone she wants you to meet."

Niccolo wondered why he was being summoned in the dark hours of the morning. It had been four days since the Maestro and Niccolo had informed the contessa, after several long and awkward discussions, that they thought it best to accept the commission. Their departure was scheduled for the day after tomorrow.

"Now what did I do wrong?" Niccolo wondered in the dark as he quickly dressed. He accompanied Ellie and the two male servants to the contessa's suite of rooms.

When he entered her antechamber, he was surprised to find the small area in shadowed light from one candelabrum. The contessa was dressed for sleep in a loose-fitting turca of white lace over a diaphanous chemise. He wondered why the lamps

100

were not lit, and then saw a fat gentleman with a thin grey beard and dusty traveling cloak seated at the lady's right.

"Niccolo," said the contessa, gesturing the dwarf to an empty chair facing that of the portly man, "I want you to meet Ser Agnolo Marinoni. Ser Agnolo has just arrived from Venice in response to an urgent letter I sent him. He is the grand master of the Cambio, the bankers guild of Venice. His time is very important, and he will return immediately following the breaking of the fast tomorrow, so this is the only time I could bring you together."

Niccolo nodded to the banker in salute and accepted the chair offered by the contessa. He mounted the footstool, seated himself, and heard the door close behind him, and he knew that Ellie and the escorting servants had been instructed to leave the trio alone.

"Ser Agnolo will explain why I summoned you so late at night, and why we are meeting in such secrecy."

Remembering that the contessa had once abducted him to her palazzo in Milan when Niccolo was on his way to the court of Il Moro, the dwarf smiled and shrugged as if this was precisely what he would expect of the lady.

"My young friend," the banker began softly in a low-pitched and somewhat gravelly voice, "I must begin by telling you, in strictest confidence, that Venice has been the victim of recent unfortunate economic trends. In the past few years many of our major banks have been shaken or gone under. Thirty-five Venetian nobles now have their entire fortunes tied up in trade and reside in Constantinople or Brussels while the others continue to spend lavishly and foolishly, going deeper into debt, as they persist in giving feasts and festivals and build themselves elaborate palaces."

Niccolo, confused as to why anyone might think him interested in Venetian economics, struggled to stay awake and appear absorbed. He glanced at the contessa who smiled at him.

"A substantial deal of Venetian money is involved with the conditions at the Mantuan court of the Marquis Gian-Francesco Gonzaga who is the captain-general of our armies."

"Why is that?" grumbled the dwarf. "I don't understand."

"What I am about to tell you is confidential information," said the banker, lowering his voice. "I will relate it to you only, because the contessa believes you may be of some assistance to my guild in uncovering the truth."

It was a moment of enlightenment. A smile played across Niccolo's lips as he glanced at the contessa again who continued to smile. "Intrigue, contessa?"

"I understand you are accustomed to such things," said Ser Agnolo.

"I have performed some services of a secret nature," Niccolo declared somewhat pompously. "I think I became rather adept at it. Don't you agree, contessa?"

She nodded. "Most certainly, my dear. You were superb. That's why I have brought you together with Ser Agnolo."

"So," the banker said to Niccolo, "will you swear to keep what I tell you now in the strictest confidence?"

"Yes. Of course."

He studied Niccolo for a moment, and then he began. "Well, some years ago Ludovico Sforza, when he was the duke of Milan, lavished an enormous dowry on his niece when she married the German emperor. He could ill afford it, but appearances must be maintained, you understand? Later he found it necessary to borrow fifty thousand ducats from the Cambio. A loan of such relative magnitude, especially in light of Il Moro's continued extravagances and the prospect of war which always drains treasuries, required some sort of security. His duchess, Beatrice d'Este, appealed to her sister, Isabella. That gracious lady, the marquesa of Mantua, in deference to her sister, offered as collateral for the loan a magnificent three-strand necklace of perfectly-matched but unusually shaped diamonds. The necklace is known as the Tears of the Madonna."

Niccolo struggled to follow the story. He was not far removed from sleep, and even the prospect of spying again did not seem to stimulate him enough to completely clear the cobwebs from his brain.

"When Il Moro fled to Germany," the banker droned on, "he defaulted on the loan. Now the Cambio, at the urgent request of the doge and the Council, had to call for an impounding of the Tears. Even though the marquesa now despised the duke, she realized that she must honor the commitment or risk a scandal that would mean a loss of respect and position for herself and her husband."

Niccolo nodded to show he was still attentive, but he began to wonder where this narrative was leading.

"The marquesa secretly handed the Tears to a special courier whom we utilize in such circumstances. We know this transfer was made, because the courier, following our customary procedure, reported by pigeon that the necklace was in his possession when he departed Mantua to return to Venice. This courier, we know him as Signore Cecco, was experienced in transporting items of great worth for our guild."

"Yes. I understand," Niccolo said softly, trying not to yawn.

"As is our custom, we deliberately do not send armed escorts with such a courier, because it attracts the very attention we wish to avoid. Gangs of bravi and thieves would most certainly attempt to rob such a courier and would be more than a match for any armed escort. Unfortunately in this case the courier and the Tears of the Madonna disappeared in transit."

Niccolo was suddenly awake and interested. Disappeared? A courier and a valued necklace?

"Our agents, backtracking the route, discovered that the courier's last stop was apparently at a small inn at Montagnana, the Olive Tree. The proprietor of the place was questioned and appeared very distraught and agitated. Nevertheless he admitted that our courier had indeed spent the night there and then had departed at daylight."

"And nothing was heard of your courier after that?"

"Nothing. When we informed the marquesa that we had not received the necklace, she suggested that the courier had been secretly in the employ of Il Moro, and that he had probably carried the jewels to him in the German court to refinance the duke's planned return to Milan. Now *that* is a distinct possibility. And the lady *is* the wife of our captain-general. Under these circumstances, and without proof to the contrary, the Cambio had no choice but to accept her explanation and absorb the loss. A serious matter considering the recent losses sustained by the defeat of the Venetian naval forces at the hands of the Turks."

"You said the transfer of the necklace from the marquesa to your courier was made secretly?" asked Niccolo, leaning forward in the chair. "Why was that? Discretion?"

"Quite perceptive, my young friend. The Gonzaga were never really friends with the Sforzas. And if the marquis had been consulted about establishing collateral for a loan to Il Moro, the marquesa felt he would most certainly forbid it, so she did it quietly, in deference to her sister whom she adored. If the marquis learned of this, he would be humiliated. A wife does not arrange such things without consulting her husband, and it might result in the dissolution of their marriage. That could prove somewhat difficult, of course, because the marquesa's brother is a cardinal member of the Curia. In any case, the Cambio does not wish to embarrass the marquesa or the Gonzaga family further, especially in light of our confirmation that she *did* give the Tears of the Madonna to the courier. So, you see, we feel we cannot press the matter beyond this present circumstance."

"Is it not possible, then, that the courier did, as the marquesa suggests, take the necklace to Il Moro in Germany?"

"Unlikely considering the young man's exemplary record. Our agents in Germany report neither the appearance of the courier nor the necklace. Someone would surely have seen one or the other. Signore Cecco is well known in banking circles and could be instantly identified. The necklace is unique and could also be easily recognized, and our guild has connections with all the capitals of Europe, including the Hanseatic league."

Niccolo leaned back in the chair. "But what can I do?"

"I understand that you are to be a guest at the court," whispered the banker. "The Cambio needs eyes and ears in the Gonzaga court. Not just planted agents, but someone beyond suspicion of being an agent. A guest. Simply watch and listen. Try to determine if the Tears of the Madonna might not have, how shall I put this? Might not have found its way *back* to the lady."

"You think she has retained the necklace? But I thought you said she gave it to the courier, and that was verified by his message to you."

"That she gave Signore Cecco the Tears is not disputed. We wonder if the courier might have been waylaid by the marquesa's agents after leaving Mantua, and the necklace then returned surreptitiously to her."

"You question the lady?"

"We are bankers, young man. We would interrogate God himself if we thought Him a party to deception and fraud. But we bankers deal in hard currencies and written contracts. We cannot rely on hearsay or conjecture. It is a possibility that the Tears were somehow diverted back to Mantua. We would like to employ you, young signore, to listen and watch, and determine, if you can, whether the marquesa might still be in possession of the necklace."

"Surely she has no pressing need for funds?" asked Niccolo. "The marquesa is wealthy. She has recently offered the Maestro a sizable commission to come to Mantua and paint her portrait!"

"She *appears* wealthy, young signore," the banker murmured. "So did Il Moro much of the time. So do most of the old and noble families of Ferrara, Naples, Bologna, Rome and Florence, but I can assure you, from my position in the Cambio, that a river of gold is slowly draining from the reservoirs of the nobility and into the private depositories of the merchants, the guilds, and the ship owners. There are universities in Padua and Bologna that now flourish only from the tuitions paid by the new lords of the mercantile. The economic sands are slowly but certainly shifting beneath our feet, Master Niccolo, and the nobles' source of revenue, new taxes, will only be tolerated to a point. I believe it is only a matter of time before you will see some of these grand lords coming, sable caps clenched tightly in their delicate hands, to either plead for credit from their merchants or to beg for admission of their sons into their guilds."

The banker poked around under his cloak for a moment and then withdrew a leather purse that clinked promisingly. "If you honor our little request, we are prepared to pay you well for your trouble." He slipped the purse into Niccolo's small hands, and the weight of it was encouraging. "We would also provide you with a wicker cage of messenger pigeons, but I understand your Maestro has a habit of purchasing pigeons and then releasing them for no apparent reason, so that is out of the question. We will find other ways of communicating with you, perhaps by rerouted epistles. You can tell everyone that your letters are from your young friend, what is her name? Madonna Elenora? So you may keep in contact with her. What say you, Master Niccolo?"

Niccolo glanced at the contessa who was still smiling, and he knew that she knew he would accept just as he had agreed to spying on the court of Il Moro for her. "How will I recognize this necklace? Describe it to me."

The banker smiled and handed the dwarf a small piece of parchment on which a sketch had been rendered in ink. As Niccolo studied it, the banker described what had been drawn.

"It is composed of three strands of diamonds: eight on the first, seven on the second strand, and six on the third. Twenty-one in all. Each of the diamonds is shaped as a tear and each weighs between three and four carats. They are almost identical, perfect matches, which makes the necklace even more valuable. At the top of each Tear is a gold filigree that vaguely suggests a crown of thorns. These hold the diamonds to the strands themselves which are of woven gold. The clasp is in the form of a cross."

"Fine," smiled Niccolo as he folded the parchment and slipped it up the sleeve of his tunic. "I will accept the commission."

"However," the contessa said quietly, "we agree that it would be prudent if we do not involve the Maestro in this little arrangement."

"Why?" asked Niccolo. "Is there some danger involved? Are you willing to sacrifice a dwarf but not a master?"

The contessa laughed. "Not at all." She smiled at Niccolo. "But if there were no danger involved, you'd be less attracted to it, wouldn't you, my little love?"

She stood suddenly and looked down at the dwarf. "No," she said softly, the smile vanishing. "This little arrangement will involve something of which the Maestro is totally ignorant."

"A painter, an engineer, a sculptor, a student of anatomy, mathematics, and logic!" cried Niccolo. "Of what, pray, is the Maestro ignorant?"

The smile returned. "Of something which devours painters, engineers, and sculptors as a hawk devours a mouse; of something that often appears to act contrary to logic or mathematical laws. If the Maestro studied anatomy for a thousand years and dissected a thousand bodies, he would remain ignorant of the driving force behind the courts of Italy."

"What?" frowned Niccolo.

"Women," she whispered.

WOMEN

December 1499

Cremona

The day before the departure of the Maestro and Niccolo for Mantua, the contessa again summoned the dwarf to her chambers, and this time he found the lovely lady seated at a small table filled with platters of food, a carafe of wine, and two crystal goblets. Next to the table waited a chair whose cushions would elevate Niccolo above the level of the table. After he was guided to the chair, climbed the footstool, and seated himself, the contessa signalled the retainers to leave, and the door was closed behind them.

"I thought we should have one last meal together, Niccolo," the contessa smiled as she poured some wine into his goblet, "and, perhaps, a little discussion about the new assignment you have agreed to undertake for the Cambio."

Niccolo scanned the platters of ham, the pasties of pheasant, the roe of mullet and sturgeon, the tureen of soup, the basket of pastries, and the new beans cooked in milk, and he began to fill his plate.

"I must apologize for the poor selection," the contessa said softly, "but I am fasting, that a generous God may assist you in your mission and bring it to a successful conclusion."

Niccolo nodded as if it were perfectly obvious that such an abundant repast could be considered "fasting." In deference to the lady's noble sacrifice, he took only small portions of the chestnut tarts and the prugnoli mushrooms and completely bypassed the soup of pigeons and almond paste.

"You must keep me informed of everything, Niccolo," she said as she heaped ham and pheasant on her own plate. "Everything. I may be able to be of some assistance to you." She poured some wine into her own goblet, sipped a little of it and then, apparently satisfied with its quality and body, took a deep swallow. She dabbed at her lips with the damask napkin and said, "You know what brought Il Moro to his present state, of course?"

Niccolo shrugged as he forked a sliver of the ham into his mouth. "I'm not certain," he said, savoring the honey in which the ham had apparently been marinated for some time. "The principal lesson I learned from our last days in the Castello Sforzesco concerned the futility of vendettas. The warring families were slaughtering each other's relatives at the rate of two a day and seemed to be in competition for new ways of killing one another." He took a swallow of the wine and was pleased to find that it had the flavor of ripe fruit. "No. It was more than futility," he added. "It was murder elevated to an absurdity, a result of that gross irrationality that motivates revenge, what the Maestro calls 'a bestial madness.' Everyone, the entire court, the world, seemed to go a little insane."

The contessa shook her head and sipped at the small cup of soup. "Yes, I understand about the vendettas, but the blood feuds in the castello had nothing to do with Il Moro's exile, of course." She took another swallow of the wine. "The duke lost his power because he did not understand women."

The caviar suddenly lodged in Niccolo's throat. "Women again?" he sighed.

"Yes. Of course," the contessa insisted, as if the explanation was obvious and self-evident. "For example, he saw his marriage to Beatrice d'Este as a profitable union of two prominent families that could reinforce his own ambitions and refurbish his treasury, but any woman could have warned him that one does not marry the sister of a lady who has already rejected the gentleman as unsuitable for herself."

"Ah!" said Niccolo, as if he were suddenly enlightened.

"Then," Bergamini continued, "compounding his stupidity, the duke of Milan actually paraded his mistress, me, through his court as a token of his power and his masculinity, totally unaware that to both the mistress and the wife, I was only a sign of his vulnerability. From that moment on every woman in court knew the duke could be impaled by dark eyes and a slender hand where no sword or lance could penetrate." Her voice softened, and her eyes seemed to be misting. "Nevertheless, Niccolo, it was that very vulnerability that touched me, and that is why I worked so diligently to protect him from his enemies, even after I, myself, was driven from the castello and into a loveless marriage."

Niccolo wondered where this conversation might be heading. He wanted to say something to comfort her, but he was uncertain whether she required consolation. In the meantime he reveled in the excellent food and drink and nodded when he felt it was expected of him.

"You are about to become involved with one of the three most powerful women in Italy," the contessa lectured him softly. "They are a distinct breed, these women, and they are all lethal. They are beautiful, cultured, well-educated, but they are also highly devious and self-serving."

"Three?" Niccolo mumbled through a mouthful of pheasant.

The contessa nodded. "Isabella d'Este is a legitimate daughter of a prince, Duke Ercole of Ferrara, and her mother was Eleonora of Aragon, which aligns her with the ruling house of Spain and with the lords of Naples." The hostess speared a section of rolled ham with her fork and delicately bit off a section. "She is also the wife of a Gonzaga, the marquis of Mantua, who is actually in control of northern Italy from the Milanese border in the west to beyond Venice in the east. You must always bear in mind, too, that her husband permits Isabella to administer this fief while he indulges himself in the two favorite games of Italian men: war, which keeps them away from home, and women of distant cities, who are the awards of power."

"The marquis is unfaithful?" Niccolo asked. If this is true, he thought, the disappearance of the Tears of the Madonna might be even more complicated. Suppose Gonzaga had learned of his wife's collateral, intercepted the necklace, and passed it to a mistress!

"All I know for a certainty," whispered the contessa, "is that the marquis is presently, and secretly, being treated for syphilis."

"My god!" Niccolo quickly emptied his goblet, and the contessa refilled it.

"You also have to understand," the contessa continued, "that while the hot blood of her father has been tempered with the more genteel blood of her mother, the marquesa frequently demonstrates all the vices of her grandfather who peopled half of his province with bastards, acknowledging twenty, and who was reputedly the most cruel man in all Italy. You might also bear in mind that Isabella's brother is notorious for walking naked through the streets of Ferrara and once set a wild bull into a cathedral's piazza, injuring scores of people, while he watched and laughed from his balcony."

"What is your point?"

"It is a warning," smiled the lady, "that while the Mantuan court may appear the most elegant and sophisticated in the world, there is a current of deception and decadence running beneath it. Be careful, but do not be surprised by what you see or hear there."

Niccolo was confused, but he nodded. "You mentioned three women. Who are the other two?"

The contessa refilled her own goblet. "Much of the Emilia-Romagna is actually controlled by Caterina Sforza, Countess of Forli and Imola, a licentious bastard daughter of the second duke of Milan." She shook her head. "This gives her connections to the house of Savoy, you see, and her half-sister is married to the Emperor, which gives her ties to the Germans. She rules her fief from Imola and has already outlived three husbands."

"Poisoned?" asked Niccolo. Because of the lectures on the nobility from the Certosa monks and his experiences in the

Castello Sforzesco, he assumed all marital arguments were terminated by sinister and criminal acts.

"No," the contessa shook her head again. "Not poisoned, although two were murdered. Caterina's first, a Riario, left her a son when he was killed." She paused as though weighing whether she should proceed. Finally she said softly, "The contessa later avenged his death in a manner too cruel to specify, especially over a meal."

Niccolo nodded and was pleased to be spared the details.

"She then married her lover, who was also murdered. Her third husband, Giovanni de Medici, aligned her power with the ruling family of Florence before he too died."

"Ah!" cried Niccolo. "*He* was poisoned!"

"Niccolo!" squealed the contessa. "You have spent too much time among the Sforza. I assure you there are more assassinations in Italy by stiletto than by poison!" She lowered her voice. "As for Giovanni de Medici, it was rumored that the gentleman died from, well, from sheer exhaustion in trying to satisfy Caterina's lusts."

The information surprised Niccolo. "Did he? Well!" He quickly took another deep swallow from his goblet. "And the third woman?"

"Ah!" sighed the contessa. "Possibly the most dangerous, and the most interesting of them all, is Madonna Lucrezia Borgia, younger sister to Cesare and bastard daughter to the pope. She is intoxicatingly beautiful and impetuous and totally devoid of morals. She possesses hair the color of sunlight and a magnificent figure. At eleven she was betrothed to a lord of Valencia and then to Don Gaspare of Naples. This last arrangement was quietly annulled, but not until *after* her first marriage, at thirteen, to Il Moro's brother, Giovanni da Pesaro Sforza. That marriage recently ended when Giovanni was forced by the pope to sign a paper confessing to impotency."

Niccolo snickered at the accusation. "Yes," he said, "I remember the jests about that which circulated through the court in Milan."

"They had every right to laugh," the contessa told him. "Giovanni's first wife had died in childbirth. During the nego-

115

tiations between her husband and her father in the Vatican, Lucrezia was placed in confinement in the convent of San Sisto, where she miraculously managed to get herself impregnated by a Spanish chamberlain."

"In a convent?!"

"Apparently there were entrances that were known only to certain libertine nobles and, I presume, some priests of dubious character."

Niccolo laughed again, and the contessa, studying the young man's reaction, took another long swallow of her wine, and continued. "Consequently the lady appeared at the signing of the annulment papers in her sixth month where she heard the cardinals proclaim her, supposedly after a physical examination, to be *intacta!* A virgin!"

"An immaculate deception!" cried Niccolo as he refilled his own goblet.

"Possibly," nodded the contessa coldly. "In any case, Lucrezia secretly delivered a male child in the Vatican which was later legitimized by no less than two papal bulls, the first claiming Cesare was the father by an unknown mother, and the second claiming that the pope himself was the father."

"I'm more confused than ever, contessa," said Niccolo.

"So was Lucrezia," replied the contessa. "To solidify yet another alliance, the poor girl was then immediately married to Alfonso of Aragon, prince of Bisceglie, and soon miscarried. Now she is rumored to be pregnant again and on her way to Rome, back to the Vatican and her father, which would seem to indicate that Alfonso's days are numbered." She leaned across the table and whispered, "If the rumors are true, His Holiness has still another husband in mind for his daughter. Unhappily it appears to be Isabella d'Este's own brother Alfonso, the one who likes to dance naked through the streets. He is heir to the duchy of Ferrara."

"It sounds as though he's qualified," the dwarf smiled. He brushed a hand across his forehead, hoping to clear some of the webbing that was beginning to entangle his brain. "But what does all this have to do with my assignment, contessa? Do you think one of these ladies has the Tears of the Madonna?"

The contessa shrugged and resumed sipping her soup. "Oh, any one of these ladies might have the necklace. Each of their histories are entwined with it. "

"Indeed? How?"

"Ah!" she smiled. "Now *that* is a story!"

The contessa poured more wine into each of their goblets. "The necklace's origins are somewhat shrouded," the contessa began. "Some say it was designed by the Dominican saint, Vicente Ferrer, and crafted by monastic goldsmiths with three-to-four-carat diamonds that were part of a treasure taken from the Moors after the fall of Jativa. In any case the necklace first appeared as part of the wealth of Senor Juan Domingo de Borja, a Spanish grandee and then transported to Spain's Italian fief, Naples, by Juan's son. That son was Alonso de Borja, Bishop of Valencia and later Pope Calixtus III. And that is how the Borgias, the Italian version of the Spanish name, come into the picture. The Borgias have always believed the Tears to be a family heirloom."

"I see," said Niccolo, sipping his wine.

"Then the necklace, somehow, fell into the hands of King Alfonso of Naples who gave it as a wedding gift to his bride, Ippolita Sforza, and she then willed it to her niece, Caterina, upon her death."

"It passed from Pope Calixtus III to the king of Naples?"

"Apparently."

Niccolo emitted a deep sigh. The simple assignment of spying on the marquesa to find the whereabouts of the Tears was now developing into a series of loans, thefts and gifts between three noble families. "So the necklace was passed to the Sforzas?"

"Yes," smiled the contessa. "Temporarily with Caterina, but she needed money, you see, to prepare to defend her fiefs against Cesare Borgia. It is said she passed the necklace to her kinsman, Il Moro, in return for a loan to pay her mercenaries."

"So the necklace passed to Il Moro?"

"And then to his wife, Beatrice. She, in turn, decided to give the necklace as a present to her sister, Isabella d'Este, on the birth of the marquesa's son. That, you see, is the *real* reason Isabella offered the Tears in promissory to the Cambio to support the loan to Il Moro. It was not only to assist her sister, as the bankers think. She saw herself as repaying a debt to her sister with her sister's own gift."

"So the Tears pass to the marquesa, which is where the Cambio comes into the picture," said Niccolo, attempting to straighten the path a little. "From the Borgian pope to the king of Spain to his wife, Isabella Sforza, to her niece, the Contessa Caterina, to Il Moro, to *his* wife Beatrice d'Este, to *her* sister, the marquesa!"

The contessa speared another roll of ham. "It becomes even more complicated. As I said, the Borgias always considered the Tears as their own. When a marriage was arranged between Giovanni Sforza and Lucrezia Borgia, the present pope, also a Borgian, remember, insisted that as part of the arrangement the Tears be returned as a bridal 'gift.' However, the Tears did not belong to Giovanni, but to his brother, Il Moro. Nevertheless, unaware that his wife had already planned to give the necklace as a gift to *her* sister, Il Moro promised the necklace to *his* brother."

"This *is* becoming very complex," said Niccolo as he ran a hand over his forehead to stop the dull ache beginning there.

"Wait," the contessa sighed again. "Before Il Moro could pass the necklace to his brother to complete the wedding arrangements, Beatrice dispatched the necklace to Isabella. Some say this was the real reason the Borgias sought an annulment of the marriage between Lucrezia and Giovanni. They considered the contract forfeit, because the Tears were not returned to them as promised."

"Then you think Lucrezia had Borgian agents murder the courier and steal the Tears?"

The contessa shook her head. "Unlikely. A pregnant woman has more immediate concerns. But her father, His Holiness, has nothing else to occupy his mind but the ambitions of his bastards. I think it is quite likely that Rodrigo or his son Cesare sent assassins to steal the Tears. The pontiff would consider it the promised property of his daughter and part of her heritage."

"So you think perhaps the Borgias have it?"

"Not necessarily," the contessa said quietly. "There is still another twist to the story."

"Of course," sighed the dwarf as he shook his head like a shaggy dog drying itself. "I keep remembering one of the first lessons the Maestro taught me."

"Which was?"

"There is always another possibility."

The contessa laughed. "Well," she continued, "just before Il Moro's flight, it is rumored that the Contessa Caterina begged him for a return of the necklace. Through her last marriage with the Medici, who were bankers themselves, the Florentines had agreed to provide additional money to finance Caterina's resistance to the Borgias, plus a few thousand ducats in interest to Il Moro, who needed the money, in promise for the necklace. Il Moro, of course, had to tell her he no longer had the necklace in his possession, that it was now the property of the marquesa of Mantua and pledged against another loan to the Cambio."

"So?"

"So, it is conceivable that the contessa, in desperation, had *her* agents ambush and kill the courier and then had the Tears of the Madonna brought to her in Imola."

Niccolo frowned. "Then you believe that the courier was definitely murdered, and that he did not defect to Germany as the marquesa suggests."

"Yes. I think that much is certain. I think the courier was killed."

"But you do not know if the murderers were agents of the Borgias, the Sforza or the Gonzaga?"

"No."

"But if the courier was murdered, why has his body not surfaced? Ser Agnolo said that the Cambio has contacts everywhere, and the identity of the courier was well known and easily recognizable among the banking circles."

"I don't know," the contessa shrugged, "but the fact that the courier has *not* reappeared somewhere would seem to discredit the marquesa's explanation that the man defected. If he surfaced in Germany, or anywhere, someone would have seen and recognized him and reported his presence to the Cambio."

"Of course his body could be quietly buried anywhere in the countryside."

"Possibly," nodded the contessa again.

Niccolo shook his head. "Well, there we have it." He gave a low, small whistle. "You realize that this is madness. All this turmoil and destruction over a diamond necklace worth, what? Perhaps fifty or sixty thousand ducats? Seventy? Eighty?"

"Oh, you foolish young man!" the contessa suddenly exclaimed. "You see? You have missed the point entirely! That is what I mean about not understanding women!" She leaned across the table once more, using her fork to emphasize a point, and Niccolo wisely placed his hands under the table. "The necklace is valuable, but that value cannot be measured in mere ducats or florins. Isabella has enough wealth in her treasury to sustain her in the appropriate fashion of an Este and a Gonzaga for the rest of her life, even if the good do, in fact, die young. And all the wealth in the world cannot save the Contessa Caterina from the Borgias," she said. "That unfortunate lady is doomed. As for Madonna Lucrezia, she is the pope's daughter and can siphon away whatever she needs from the Vatican treasury. It is what the Tears symbolize, my young love. Absolute power!" She stabbed her fork into the pheasant to emphasize her point. "The power to control lives and kingdoms! The power to take what you feel is rightfully yours or anything you covet! The Borgias claim the Tears have always been theirs! The Contessa Caterina says it is the rightful property of the Sforza by direct inheritance from King Alfonso of Naples through his wife! The marquesa also uses this same argument to support her claim that the necklace is now a possession of the Este and can be promised against a loan from the Cambio!"

"Power?" Niccolo murmured. Suddenly he saw his assignment as less that of a gallant and romantic adventurer than a lowly pawn in someone else's game. "Are you saying the Tears is some sort of trophy to demonstrate a woman's power?"

"Why not?" shrugged the contessa, sitting back in her chair. "Men test their strength in the lists or on the battlefields. Women test theirs in the secret corridors of their palazzi and in their bedchambers. The principal weapons of men are swords and lances, and their trophies are shields and armor. The weapons of women are beauty, intelligence, and cunning, and very often their trophies are jewels or kingdoms." She smiled at him and again dabbed at her lips with the napkin. "I promise you, when next the Tears of the Madonna glitter on the ivory breast of one of those three women, it will be a great social and political victory. The message will be quite clear: what you cannot hold is not really yours." She studied the young man for what seemed a long time before she whispered, "And that is why I am warning you, Niccolo. God Himself cannot save the man who comes between any of those three women and the Tears of the Madonna."

"Thank you," sighed Niccolo as he finished the last of the wine. "I find that very comforting."

The departure the following day was a melancholic affair with Ellie trying not to weep or throw things in anger at her lover, the contessa constantly warning of the dangers ahead, and Niccolo trying to untangle both the history of the Tears and the problems connected with his new assignment. Only the Maestro seemed to concentrate not upon what he was leaving behind, but upon what was ahead of him. Despite the assurances in the commission that the Mantuan court would supply him with anything he needed or desired, he nevertheless arranged for a selection of special pigments, brushes, and oils to be purchased and packed for the journey, promising to reimburse the Bergamini upon receipt of his commission.

The only person who seemed genuinely relieved to see the dwarf and the Maestro leave was Count Ludovico Bergamini who appeared from his self-imposed solitude just hours before the departure. During the residency of Leonardo and Niccolo, the count had sequestered himself in one wing of the palazzo with the child, Cesare, the bastard son of Il Moro, for whom the count had developed a warm and reciprocal devotion. This was a customary procedure whenever guests were in residence who were considered to be friends principally of his wife. It was a continuation of the practice begun in Milan where discretion and simple prudence demanded that the husband look away while the wife "entertained." This practice had continued despite the contessa's constant affirmations that she had remained faithful to him from the moment they exchanged vows, and that the frequent visits of Il Moro to the contessa after her marriage always ended in a rejection of the duke's attempts to rekindle the passion once shared by the two lovers.

The present temporary exile, however, was also a product of the count's discomfort when conversing with artists and scholars. His was more a world of hawks and horses, of court presentations and protocol. The artifacts that graced the palazzo in Cremona were entirely of his wife's choosing. The horses stabled beyond the courtyard, rare crossbreeds of Arabian and the thick-necked Bashkir stock, were the count's contribution to their collective wealth.

As the elaborate coach-and-four that had been sent to convey Niccolo and Leonardo to Mantua rattled past the Palazzo del Commune, there was a mixture of relief and anxiety among the well-wishers.

As an omen of some sort, depending on how one interprets seasonal occurrences, it began to snow.

Mantua

The coach ride between Cremona and Mantua was only a matter of hours. The road to the east was a major route that took the coach through only one relatively large village, Bozzolo, and then across the Oglio River. The snowfall was light and did not impede the travelers. While still some distance from the city, the spires of the twin churches of Sant'Andrea and San Sebastiano loomed over the rooftops and the city's walls. Challenging them were the crenellated towers of the Gonzaga palace, which had obviously taken centuries to build.

Even the magnitude of the Castello Sforzesco had not prepared Niccolo and Leonardo for their first sight of the palazzo, which seemed to contain at least five hundred rooms and occupied one complete side of the Piazza Sordello. Both fortress and castle, the palazzo repeatedly displayed the emblem of a lion, the animal-symbol of Venice whose armies were under the command of the marquis, Gian-Francesco Gonzaga, in stone and on banner.

As the coach slowed to a stop in the central courtyard, the newcomers were instantly and lavishly welcomed by the chamberlain, Andrea Meneghina, who came dancing down the wide staircase. He also apologized for the absence of the marquis, who was "in Venice conferring with the doge," and the marquesa, who had "pressing matters that required her presence elsewhere." Meneghina assured the Maestro that the court was "entirely enraptured" that Leonardo has accepted the commission, and that a fitting and more formal reception by the marquesa would be arranged as quickly as possible. In the meantime, the chamberlain was to escort the guests to their quarters and see to their comforts.

Meneghina was apparently surprised at the scarcity of luggage Leonardo and Niccolo had brought with them. He immediately found himself in the somewhat awkward position of asking Niccolo if he would prefer being quartered in the "appartamento dei Nani," the scaled-down wing of rooms that housed the Gonzaga dwarves. Leonardo requested that Niccolo be assigned rooms adjacent to his own, because "the young man is my tutor, and I may require his services at any hour of the night or the day." Further, the Maestro noted, Niccolo was not precisely a dwarf, being perfectly proportioned, with neither the bowed stumpy legs or the large heads common to the little people. This difference, Leonardo argued, might cause some confusion and discomfort among the others.

The chamberlain nodded, but was plainly confused and a trifle annoyed that the young man, whom he continued to identify as a "dwarf," would require additional space.

He escorted Leonardo and Niccolo in silence through long corridors, past innumerable doors. Some of bronze displayed scenes from the lives of the saints, others, panelled in ivory, were carved with figures depicting the Fall of Troy and the Labors of Hercules.

"It seems the marquesa, an Este, enjoys a jest in art, too," Niccolo whispered to the Maestro. "Her father's name is Ercole, Hercules, and, judging from his portrait that we passed in the last corridor, those panels depict that same noble gentleman performing the heroic feats of mythology."

They were next ushered through the massive Camera degli Sposi, the reception hall which Meneghina described as "once a mere bridal chamber."

The room was incredible.

The walls had been painted by Mantegna over a nine-year period and were filled with trompe l'oeil effects that were designed to "fool the eye." It was an extension of the idea suggested by the forced perspective in Leonardo's own doomed fresco, 'The Last Supper,' but this was clearly the work of a man who had mastered the art. Archways appeared to be three-dimensional and to lead into gardens or long arcades that did not exist, save as a painting. Columned decorations of cherubs and flowers seemed solid and shadowed but were entirely flat. Shelves of books and varied instruments used in navigation and surveying appeared real enough to be used and opened. Here and there were figures of masked courtiers and ladies who appeared to be conversing with one another as they might at a formal ball, and Niccolo had to touch the painting to verify that they were not real people. On one wall full-length portraits of the Gonzaga family members, complete with a small dwarfish woman, stared at the viewer or conversed with one another. Overhead, set into a domed ceiling that did not exist, painted groups of courtiers and their ladies smiled down at the viewer from nonexistent balconies, and above and beyond these figures a bright blue sky was continually visible through an opening in the imaginary dome.

"Incredible," Leonardo whispered. "The Maestro has mastered both natural and accidental perspective. He has realized that the human eye can be radically deceived through forced perspective."

"It is wonderful," murmured Niccolo.

The visual trickery was extraordinary. Niccolo was slowly revolving, his attention focused on the painted figures looking down on him. Losing his balance, he struck the wall, brushing against a bouquet of painted flowers mounted on a nonexistent column. To his astonishment, a panel slid open revealing a small recess in the wall, about half the height of an average man.

"What is that?" asked the dwarf, instantly backing away.

Meneghina quickly crossed, touched the flowers, and the panel slid closed. Niccolo could barely discern its borders. "It is a door to the adjoining room," snapped the chamberlain, even more annoyed.

"But it is so small," said Niccolo.

"Yes," Meneghina nodded, unsmiling.

And I know why, Niccolo thought to himself. It's a door for dwarves, for small spies.

"There are other novelties," said the chamberlain, "but I am not at liberty to divulge where they are hidden."

"It is obvious," Leonardo whispered to Niccolo, "that in the Mantuan court, nothing is really what it appears to be."

The four rooms assigned to Leonardo and Niccolo were spacious and well furnished with velvet-upholstered chairs, tapestries, canopied beds, and large fireplaces. To the east their latticed windows opened on a courtyard that contained an expansive garden surrounding a magnificent marble fountain, now slowly being mantled in the immaculate snow that continued to fall.

Meneghina drew their attention to the relatively low height of the balcony railings. "One of our garrisoned captains had an unfortunate accident here," Meneghina informed them. "The gentleman apparently had too much to drink, got himself entangled in a rope and fell over a railing such as this, hanging himself. The court was in mourning for two days."

Niccolo nodded, but wondered how a man could get himself "entangled in a rope."

To the west their suite opened into a fifth and much larger room lined with floor-to-ceiling windows and furnished with upholstered chairs and stools, glass-doored cabinets and walls of shelving, mirrors, chandeliers with rings of candles, and four, new, stoutly constructed worktables.

"We trust this will be suitable for your uses, Maestro?" asked Meneghina.

Leonardo surveyed the room, mentally positioning his three easels and noting the abundance of natural light that flooded the interior. Facing west, the room would offer that rare twilight of the setting sun that he favored for portraiture. The large worktables seemed to indicate that his practice of dissecting bodies of accident victims or mercenaries slain in tourneys would be tolerated if not encouraged.

"This will be more than adequate," the Maestro replied softly. "It answers all my needs. Please express my thanks to the marquesa."

The chamberlain was obviously pleased by the response.

"Where, pray, is the library?" asked Niccolo.

"Down the corridor and to your left," the chamberlain smiled. "But you need not trouble yourself. Any texts you require can be requested through one of the servants who will bring them directly to you." He turned again to address the Maestro. "These rooms are directly over the appartamento del Paradiso, the living quarters of the marquesa, where she would prefer to pose for her portrait."

Leonardo nodded. "As Her Excellency wishes."

"You may rest now if you wish," said the chamberlain. "I will return to escort you to dinner in the great hall. I am sorry to inform you that neither the marquis nor the marquesa will be in attendance. However, with your permission, I will be delighted to introduce you to the other masters in residence and to the many distinguished guests of the court with whom you may wish to be acquainted." He paused suddenly, and he frowned. "Of course, if there is someone you would rather *not* know, a simple sign, such as this, will enable me to steer you in another direction." He touched his breast with an open hand.

Leonardo could not imagine what sort of courtier or master he might not wish to know, but he nodded again, and the chamberlain, satisfied, bowed and backed from the room.

"Well," sighed the Maestro looking at the tapestries that lined the walls, "here we are, my friend."

"Yes," said Niccolo quietly. "But with Paradise below us, where would you say we are?"

Half hidden in the shadows of one of the archways leading to the living quarters of Leonardo and Niccolo, Ottaviano Cristani watched the newcomers with uncommon interest. He held his breath until Meneghina passed, and then he stepped into the wintry light, gathered his dark cloak about his neck and shoulders, and coughed with such force and for such a long time that he had to lean against a pillar and gasp for air.

When he recovered enough to stand erect, Ottaviano raised the hood of his cloak, and silently melted into the shadows.

That night the two new guests at the palazzo dined in the great hall with the courtiers, the artists in residence and Cardinal Ippolito. Both the dwarf and the Maestro had to admire the abundance of food prepared by masters, the variety of wines, the small ensemble in one gallery who played music for the first half of the meal and the choir in an opposite gallery who sang through the remainder. The two chairs in the center of the head table remained unoccupied although the presence of the lord and lady of the manor were still acknowledged by the courtiers who bowed or curtsied to the empty chairs as they took their places at the tables below.

At this head table, Leonardo found himself seated directly to the left of the marquesa's empty chair with a young and seemingly uncomfortable lady in red between the Maestro and Niccolo. The Cardinal and the lady of his attentions for the evening were seated on the opposite side, to the right of the marquis' chair. The newcomers were introduced to the young Belgian, Johannes Vendramm, who then seated himself beside Madonna Maddalena, a lovely but unsmiling woman with long red hair that cascaded nearly to her waist. They were also introduced to Guglielmo Gaetani who wore a black mourning band on his left sleeve.

Leonardo was disappointed to learn from Meneghina that one of the men he had come to see, Niccolo Panizatto, had been sent home, because "unhappily the marquesa is far too busy at this time to resume her studies." Later he was to learn from Pietro Bembo that that gentleman, too, would soon depart the court, because "the marquesa can no longer afford my services."

Leonardo's confidence in the terms of his commission was shaken.

The five dwarves of the Gonzaga court were attired in beautiful satins and silks and dined at a special table erected on a dais at the far end of the room. Their table reflected the head table at the opposite end, as if the dwarves were distorted mirror images of the nobility opposite. Niccolo noticed two young woman among that assembly of little people. One of the three small men was dressed much more opulently than the others with a lavish display of jewels on his fingers and an enormous gem in each ear. Niccolo noted that this over-dressed dwarf seemed to be observing him, and that made him uncomfortable.

One of the dwarves, an attractive young woman with mid-night-black hair and a warm smile, glanced at Niccolo from time to time. Once when he caught her glance, she lowered her eyes behind an ivory fan and laughed to her companion.

After the meal, a fool in belled costume and cap amused the court with ribald songs that he accompanied on a lute. Fire-eaters and jugglers entertained, and a half dozen young women in diaphanous gowns leaped and lunged and twirled to the music of the ensemble in the gallery.

Following the evening's diversion, Niccolo saw that the dwarves withdrew quickly in procession behind the bejeweled one, and that the Cardinal slipped through an archway to the left with his beautiful dinner companion. One of the last to rise and leave was a dark man in a burgundy tunic who paused in the center of the room, seemed to study Niccolo, and then, abruptly, began to cough. After a moment the man recovered, dabbed at his lips with a lace-edged handkerchief, and swept from the room.

Several members of the court found their way to the head table and engaged the Maestro in conversation. Leonardo exchanged views with Baldasar Castiglione concerning the sudden abundance of books on "genteel behavior," during which Castiglione admitted that he himself was preparing a text on protocol and procedures at court.

Niccolo was about to find his own way back to their quarters when he found the attractive young woman with the midnight-black hair at his elbow. She was only slightly less tall than he, with skin the color of ripe peaches and a small and delicate mouth. Her fingers, encased in satin gloves trimmed with an elaborate lace, were long and slender. Her nose was a button set between glowing cheeks that suggested the gentle blush of pink roses. Her hair gleamed under a thin veil sprinkled with tiny spangles that glittered like stars against a cloudless sky.

"You were watching me, signore," she said softly.

"As you were watching me, Madonna," Niccolo smiled.

"You are not one of us, are you?" she asked, her slim, finely-drawn eyebrows arched upon her forehead. "We are similar in height, but you are quite different."

"No. Well, not precisely. I will grow no taller. Ever."

"*Bien.* You are tall enough."

"You are French?" he asked.

"*Mais oui,*" she said as she brought the ivory fan to her lips. "My name is Lizette Fourget."

"I am Niccolo."

"Just Niccolo?"

"I am called Niccolo da Pavia. I was a foundling at the Certosa near Pavia. I have no family name."

"Again a blessing," she laughed. "You do not have to bear the sins of your ancestors."

Her laughter was high-pitched but not shrill. It reminded Niccolo of the warm trilling of a bird. He was about to respond when he suddenly saw fear in her eyes. Niccolo turned to see the black-bearded dwarf scowling at them from the open doorway.

"I must go," she whispered quickly. "On Tuesday, after the

noon meal when everyone retires, I will come and visit your workshop if I may."

Without waiting for his permission Lizette quickly glided toward the black-bearded dwarf, past him, and through the doorway. The other dwarf glared and suddenly raised his gloved hand to his mouth and bit his thumb in a gesture of insult that Niccolo instantly recognized. To his own surprise, Niccolo merely smiled, snapped his heels together in a mock-military salute and bowed smartly from the waist. When he looked up, the dwarf was gone.

He turned and nearly collided with Guglielmo Gaetani, and in an attempt to make conversation, he made reference to the black silk band around the man's arm.

"Ah! I see, Signore Gaetani, that you are in mourning for the garrisoned officer who died in the tragic accident," said Niccolo.

The aristocratic young man studied the dwarf and frowned. "I understood it to be a suicide," he said. "At least that is what I have heard whispered about the court. But in any case, signore, I did not really know the captain, so I have no cause to mourn the gentleman." He lowered his eyes and his voice. "I am in mourning for members of my family. We have received reports that Cesare Borgia lured my brother, Giacomo, to Rome where the damned pope had him thrown into prison. At the same time I have learned that my nephew was caught and strangled to death in Sermoneta by Cesare, or by his companion-killer Michelotto Corella."

Niccolo was embarrassed by his lack of current information. "But why?"

"Partly in response to my sanctuary here. Cesare is obliquely warning the marquesa that she risks the enmity of the Vatican and the Borgias if she continues to shelter me."

"Is it actual war then?" asked the dwarf.

"It is armed ambition certainly," replied Gaetani. "The Borgian bastard has an army marching south through the Romagna. We have received reports that he laid siege to Imola which has since capitulated, but the Contessa Caterina Sforza apparently remains defiant in her fortress of La Rocca."

Niccolo made a mental note that one of the three women who might have an interest in the Tears was now under siege. "Isn't it surprising," Niccolo suggested, "that the two principal opponents of the Borgias are women? The marquesa who offers you sanctuary, and the Contessa Caterina Sforza who has actually sent armies against them?"

Gaetani shrugged. "Even more surprising is that the Borgias' principal weapon is also a woman, a lady who now administers the business of the Vatican even as she prepares to deliver a child."

"You mean . . . ?"

"Madonna Lucrezia of course. Haven't you heard? His Holiness is indulging his bastard daughter, and now, for the first time since the legendary Pope Joan, the church has a woman on the throne of Peter!"

Rome

In the Sala dei Pontifici in the Vatican, Lucrezia Borgia, heavy with child, gowned in gold velvet, and attended by four ladies of her court, perched on the edge of the papal throne and smiled at the two gentleman standing like statues before her. Bartolomeo Martini, the pontifical majordomo, was a stately figure in browns and light green, and Juan di Castro, governor of the Castel Sant'Angelo, stood erect and formal in his scarlet and yellow uniform.

"My illustrious lords," the lady began in perfect Latin, "it is imperative that we construct a new street between the Castel Sant'Angelo and the Vatican to accommodate all the pilgrims who will be coming to Rome for the Jubilee celebrating the Holy Year. My father wishes the street to be called the Via Alessandrina."

Martini nodded and then said softly, "When His Holiness speaks in consistory, Madonna, a cardinal usually takes down the proposals in writing. Should we not have a cardinal in attendance?"

"Madonna Laura da Gonzaga will record what is spoken," replied Lucrezia. "She has a lovely hand and writes well in both Latin and Greek."

"Really, Madonna?" Juan broke in with a leer at the lady-in-waiting. "And where, may I ask, is her pen?"

The question was posed in Latin, and Lucrezia immediately burst into laughter, recognizing the play on the word *penna* which had a second meaning as "penis." Madonna Laura flushed.

"You are wicked, my lord," she reprimanded him with a smile. "My lady's instruments remain tucked safely away from lascivious eyes." Her eyes flashed and she added with just the proper touch of warning, "But should we have need of an extra pen, my lord, I suppose we could pluck one from any number of the ganders at court." The governor quickly caught the implied threat behind the statement and nodded. Then Lucrezia turned to Martini. "To the matter at hand, my father estimates that hundreds of thousands might kneel before the loggia of Santo Pietro to receive his blessing of Urbi et Orbi. We must prepare for such multitudes."

Martini nodded again, and Lucrezia smiled at both men. "The duke of Sagan," she said, "is easily ninety and one and coming all the way from Silesia. Maestro Copernicus will be coming from the pontifical university, La Sapienza, and must be duly honored. And a very special reception must be given to welcome His Majesty Jean d'Albret, king of Navarre."

"Of course," said the majordomo.

"I also think the bodies of the eighteen criminals presently hanging on the Sant'Angelo bridge should be cut down."

"I shall see to it immediately!" Juan responded.

"I think it might even be wise if all Corsicans were expelled from papal territory during the Jubilee."

The governor frowned. "Corsicans, Madonna?"

"They are avowed thieves and cutpurses, and we do not want our guests robbed or murdered in transit."

Both men nodded, and then, realizing that no more instructions would be forthcoming, each bowed smartly from the waist, wheeled sharply, and left the room.

The brown-haired, somewhat effeminate man in silks and laces who had been seated to one side watching the proceedings now came forward, bowed, climbed the dais, and kissed the offered hand of the lady.

"I am pleased to see you again, Ser Tebaldeo," the blond young woman greeted him. "And how did you find things at the court of Mantua?"

"Deplorable," sniffed the courtier. "I wasted my time correcting the marquesa's terrible rhymes and writing sonnets to which she affixed her name as if they were her own."

"Indeed?"

"Yes, Madonna," he sighed and sat at her feet. "We, all of the artisans and poets, were frequently served rotted meat and absolutely vile wines and treated worse than the dogs in the marquesa's kennels." He sighed again. "That is why I elected to enter the service of Cardinal Ippolito and was dispatched here to Rome to prepare rooms for his arrival."

"I am fascinated," laughed Lucrezia. "You must tell me more."

That evening, in her private room in the Vatican, Madonna Laura da Gonzaga, lady-in-waiting to Madonna Lucrezia, reported all that had transpired in a letter to her kinsman's wife, Isabella d'Este.

"I was initially received by Madonna Lucrezia and her favorite, Nicola, fresh from the bath and wearing Moorish peignoirs," she wrote. "Can you imagine? The lady's hair was dressed in the usual simple way, bound in a snood, with a small green cap, and she offered me some of her Spanish blouses, which I accepted but will never wear, because they are badly designed and impractical for most events. She entertained us at a buffet this afternoon, all with gold and silver utensils and plate, silver flasks and exquisite saltcellars decorated with the papal arms and the Borgian device of bulls. The words 'Alexander Sextus Pontifex Maximus' seemed to be engraved or embossed on everything, presumably to deter any of us from stealing one of them."

She dipped her pen in the ink and resumed writing. "And I was surprised to see a necklace at the lady's throat with which neither of us are unfamiliar. You will recognize it by my description: three strands of diamonds shaped like tears, each matched tear attached to a thinly-woven chain of gold by tiny thorns."

Mantua

The letter both alarmed and infuriated the marquesa who immediately summoned her chamberlain and issued a stream of invectives and commands. Throughout the Gonzaga Palace there was a marked increase in the comings and goings of the garrisoned mercenaries, and occasionally one or another of the members of the court disappeared for a day or two.

An unusual surprise awaited the Maestro. A crate arrived from the Castello Sforzesco in Milan, and in it, Leonardo discovered his irreplaceable and extensive collection of jars and small glass urns containing a variety of medical herbs and powders that the Maestro had spent years collecting. Attached to the crate was a simple note:

"My compliments. I felt you might have need of these. Your most devoted servant and admirer, Cesare Borgia, duke of Valentinois."

Niccolo was surprised and pleased when Lizette Fourget appeared at Leonardo's workshop as promised, saying she had heard a great deal about Maestro Leonardo and the young dwarf who was instructing him in Latin. She said she could only stay for a brief period, because the ostentatious dwarf, Nanino, ruled their small kingdom like a petty tyrant, and

137

knew where every dwarf went and what they did every hour of the day.

Niccolo told her that she would certainly be welcomed at the workshops whenever she chose to come. He escorted Lizette through the rooms, explaining how the Maestro preferred natural light, where he placed his easels, the notebooks with the mirror script and some sketches including the anatomical studies which once again brought the ivory fan to the lady's mouth and eyes. He introduced her to the Maestro's collection of herbs and pigments in small bottles and containers that now lined the shelves like columns of colorful soldiers. He described how the various elements were ground by mortar and pestle, which explained why physicians and painters shared the same guild. He demonstrated how pigments were combined for specific colors and hues, and uncovered a faceless clay bust which, he explained, would be used by the Maestro to make a model of the marquesa's head and shoulders so he might continue to work on her portrait on those days when she chose not to pose in person.

They discussed other things then: her birth in Lyons, the rejection by her parents when they realized she was deformed, the years of her "seclusion" in a convent in Venice in which she grew into adult womanhood, the day the convent was visited by Ercole d'Este who "purchased" her from the nuns and took her to his court in Ferrara, and how he then entrusted the young girl to his sister, Isabella, who had just been married to the marquis of Mantua.

"But how old are you?" he asked.

"Twenty and five," she said quietly.

"I am barely twenty," he informed her.

"You appear older."

"It is a consequence of my condition," he told her, uncomfortable with the discussion. "Dwarves of my type are called 'little men with old faces.'"

Suddenly she reached forward and touched his cheek with her gloved hand. He felt as if he had been branded.

"I like your face," she said.

They met nearly every day after that, always in some remote section of the palazzo where Nanino could not find her, or in the workshop. No one else called or presented themselves to the Maestro, which was unusual for a congregation of scholars and artisans. It was nearly a week before Isabella herself finally found time to formally greet the Maestro and Niccolo.

"I am dismayed, Maestro," the young woman said softly, "that the fall of the duke of Bari has forced you from your workshop for the past eighteen years. I will not be hypocritical and pretend that I am not pleased that the Moor has been deposed, but I can sympathize with you, my friend, at the loss of your inventions and works in progress and your personal library which, I understand, remain in the Castello Sforzesco."

"Thank you, Your Excellency, for your compassion."

The marquesa smiled and nodded slightly to indicate that Leonardo had responded properly. "I presume the conditions of the commission are clear and satisfactory? I regret having to impose a date when the portrait must be completed, but, you see, I intend it as an anniversary gift to my husband."

"I will honor the agreement, Excellency."

"I am pleased," she smiled. "I would hope, Maestro, that you may assist me in one or two other small matters."

"I would be honored."

"Excellent!" She sat erect in the high-backed chair and absentmindedly toyed with a huge jeweled ring on her left hand. "I am planning a costumed festival for the spring. I would be delighted if you could design appropriate costumes. Persephone. Orpheus. Pluto. You understand. And, could you, perhaps, stage the pageant? I recall with great delight the festival you designed to celebrate the completion of the palazzo of Galeazzo Sanseverino in Milan."

"I was not entirely pleased with those festivities," the Maestro said softly. "That festival resulted in the murders of Cardinal Albizzi and a pastry cook, the first by an overdose of an aphrodisiac and the other torn by falcons. I had promised myself that I would never again perform such a service, but . . ."

"I would never presume to impose my will upon such a celebrated and honored guest, Maestro Leonardo," the marquesa said without smiling. "But do give the request some consideration."

"I will, your Excellency."

"Splendid." She placed both her arms on the arms of the chair, her wrists dangling over the ends and her rings glistening under the light of the lamps and candles. "One other small matter. We have a tradition in the court that we call the Magi Gifts. By their own hands, our lords and ladies prepare items to be distributed among the monasteries and abbeys of our marquisate. It is an expression of humility and subservience to God and His church. One of my courtiers, Ser Ottaviano Cristani, has prepared some requiem candles that now require ornamentation. As I understand it, the candles are to be decorated in colored waxes with scenes depicting the passion and death of our Lord, but, being more of a warrior than an artist, he finds the completion of the project somewhat taxing. If you would be so kind as to merely sketch the events he wishes depicted, I know it would hasten his completion of the project. I hesitate to ask you, but it is apparent that our own court painter, Maestro Andrea, will have to remain in Padua for a time to complete the frescoes for which he had been commissioned."

"As you wish, Excellency," Leonardo nodded. "I had hoped to meet with Maestro Andrea. His work on this room is remarkable."

"I am certain he will return before the completion of your own commission!" The marquesa beamed. "And then you shall have days and days to discuss your mutual interests. I would be honored to overhear your conversations. It would be fascinating to hear two such masters discuss their art and their convictions."

"As you will, Excellency," Leonardo nodded again.

"Ah, Maestro, you have as generous a soul as you possess remarkable talents. I know I will enjoy your residency with us, and I shall be pleased to commend you to the lords and ladies of my family. In a camerino on the ground floor I eventually desire to have several pictures with a story by the excellent painters we now have in Italy: our own Mantegna, Bellini and yourself, of course. And we must see to it that these talents and generosity do not go unrewarded."

"Again I thank you, Excellency."

"Now! What should I wear for my portrait, think you?"

A week later, during the period known as Christmastide, the marquesa announced the annual Feast of Fools. The names of all male courtiers were inscribed on strips of parchment and placed in a helmet. One of the ladies of the court, appointed by the marquesa, placed one of her delicate white hands into the helmet and drew one of the strips. The name written on it would be the man chosen as *dominus festi* or Lord of the Revels.

The man chosen was Ser Johannes Vendramm.

Niccolo and Leonardo had survived several festivals in the Castello Sforezco including the one to which Leonardo had referred when speaking with the marquesa. That festival, which celebrated the completion of the Palazzo Sanseverino, had featured fourteen *"chambres separes"* placed around the central ballroom of the palace like spokes around an axle. These were used for discreet dalliances between the guests and the ladies of the court. They had even witnessed one or two Feasts of Fools that had included the usual mockery of the Church rituals at Christmastide.

But none of these prepared the Maestro and Niccolo for the orgy of "self-indulgence, debauchery, and blasphemy" of the Gonzaga court. Discretion was totally abandoned, and the "current of deception and decadence" that the Contessa Bergamini had warned Niccolo against, suddenly overflowed the corridors of the castello.

141

The "ritual" began with Leonardo and Niccolo watching in dismay as Johannes, the "chosen" one, was led into the great hall, seated on a wine keg, stripped of most of his clothing, and then was forced to submit, smilingly, to having his head shaven in a monk's tonsurial fringe by the five dwarves. Lizette, Niccolo noted, seemed embarrassed and had little to do other than hold the "barber's dish" while Nanino, with apparent relish, did the actual shearing. The young Belgian was then dressed in priestly vestments turned inside out, to the apparent delight of the diners who shouted obscene comments or insults.

The men of the court attended the dinner in the masks of beasts with loose-flowing robes that suggested the coloring and texture of the beasts depicted. The Maestro and Niccolo were assigned half-masks and robes that suggested a bear and a fox respectively. Niccolo also noted that some males dressed as women and formed a choir that howled and jingled fools' bells following ritual "confessions."

These confessions were at the heart of an "amusement" in which the ladies of the court, dressed as harlots with breasts and thighs openly exposed, knelt one by one before Vendramm who "ruled" from atop his wine-keg throne that sat on a dais erected in the center of the hall. The "harlots" had to loudly and publicly "confess" their most wicked and salacious "sins" to the Lord of the Revels. These confessions had to be shocking and explicit. They ranged from imaginative multiple sexual experiments with a quartet of stinking stablehands to anatomical absurdities with a young stallion.

Johannes, plainly uncomfortable but determined to prove himself a proper courtier, continued to smile even as he was forced to listen to the graphic tales with mock solemnity. Then he had to decide whether the penitent was "truly remorseful" and should be granted absolution.

The absolution was always given, and, in turn, the Lord of the Revels was rewarded for his clemency with long wet kisses and quick gropings, to the bestial howls of the men and the raucous laughter of the women. Following each absolution, Johannes was then expected to pronounce a "penance" which usually followed the shouted instructions of the drunken revelers, especially the thundering commands of Cardinal Ippolito.

The Maestro and Niccolo watched in embarrassment from behind their animal masks as this lady was required to dance totally nude on a table to the music from the galleries or another was assigned to spend the night with a courtier chosen by Vendramm. To this end the Lord of the Revels was bombarded with small packets of gold florins or jewels or rings, bribes from the courtiers for having a specific lady assigned to him.

The marquesa, her own breasts revealed over a low-cut camora and her face hidden behind an elaborate, jewelled, and plumed mask suggesting a great silver-beaked bird, seemed delighted with the ceremonies although she sat at the head table and distanced herself from the proceedings. The dwarves, Niccolo noted, had little to do with the ritualized humiliation once the Lord of the Revels had his head shaved. Lizette disappeared from the great hall soon after the confessions began.

But Nanino and the other two male dwarves, in dominoes and donkeys' ears, remained.

There were others who seemed apart from the proceedings.

Ottaviano Cristani, clad in the mask and robe of a lion, said and did little, and his presence was marked only by an occasional coughing spell. Guglielmo Gaetani, still in black, wore the headdress of a rhinoceros and seemed morose and melancholy. At the head table only Cardinal Ippolito in the half-mask of a serpent and a gaudy cloak of gold and silver scales seemed engrossed in the festivities, being the first to proclaim a specific "penance" for the young ladies and to hiss at the details of a specific "confession."

After one of the penitents had completed her penance of kissing the genitals of a courtier robed as a hyena, to the apparent delight and outcries of the revelers, the marquesa suddenly stood and announced that the time had come for the Lord to choose his queen for the evening.

It now became clear to the Maestro and Niccolo that the ladies had actually been competing, through their bizarre stories and their physical pawings, for the privilege of winning this "honor" as Queen of the Revels for the remainder of the evening. Niccolo, sensing the embarrassment of the Belgian, glanced at the Maestro, but the mask failed to reveal what Leonardo might have been thinking.

Ultimately Vendramm had no choice. He had to select a woman for his bed companion. To everyone's surprise he chose Madonna Maddalena, although that red-haired woman had appeared to be both annoyed and embarrassed throughout the entire proceedings and had seemed so uninspired in her confession that Cardinal Ippolito had called for a penance of scandalous sexual byplay, a penance that Vendramm had the courage to countermand. He then assigned the lady the burden of a single kiss to his cheek.

The marquesa stepped down from the dais to crown the Lord of the Revels and bestow the rod of authority, shaped like an erect penis, on Johannes. This signal sent the members of the court off to their respective chambers for "a continuance of the revels of love and ribaldry," although several couples had abandoned the great hall earlier and were already chasing one another down the corridors.

Suddenly there was an explosion of cannon fire from the towers that shook the great hall. This salute was followed almost immediately by a blare of trumpets. Niccolo noticed that Ottaviano was one of the first on his feet, his gloved hand groping beneath the costumed robe for the hilt of his sword. Gaetani whipped away his mask and paled.

The marquesa was removing her elaborate mask as a guard ran into the great hall and whispered something to Meneghina. The chamberlain snatched off his beast face and wheeled to face the marquesa, but any pronoucement he was to make came too late.

Striding rapidly into the great hall, in full armor and obviously livid, was the Marquis of Mantua, captain-general of the armies of Venice, Gian-Francesco Gonzaga.

The Maestro leaned toward Niccolo and whispered through his bear mask, "The lord has returned home unexpectedly and found his garrisons drunken and disheveled, with masked courtiers racing down the corridors with naked ladies of the court and the entire place in bedlam."

"He does not appear pleased, does he?"

The tall, bearded lord stood erect, hands on hips. Behind him servants and soldiers carrying torches and standards blocked the entrance. Niccolo glanced at the pale face of the marquesa who slowly descended into an extremely low curtsy of welcome that served to hide her naked breasts and melted with the long and overpowering shadow of her husband towering above her.

"Clear the hall" came the terse command, "and close the doors!"

DOORS

January 1500

Mantua

Soon after the Feast of Fools, some of the resident scholars in the Gonzaga court assured Leonardo and Niccolo that this specific event had been "unusual," and Baldasar Castiglione suggested that the entire proceedings were planned and supervised by Cardinal Ippolito d'Este to break what he considered to be the boredom of the Christmastide.

"However," Leonardo told Niccolo later the next day in his workshop, "I believe it is apparent that the marquesa used the festival for some purpose of her own."

"I don't understand," Niccolo frowned. "What purpose?"

"It was obvious, wasn't it, that two members of the court were especially embarrassed by the rituals?" Leonardo explained. "It was certainly clear to me that our young Belgian friend, Vendramm, and the lady he chose to be his queen, Madonna Maddalena, were deliberately singled out by the marquesa for the ridicule of the court. The cutting of the hair, the winekeg enthronement, these were more than amusing mock rituals. There was malice behind them."

"Why would the marquesa wish to embarrass Vendramm and Madonna Maddalena?"

"Perhaps it was like a wind rising prior to the storm, a warning." The Maestro shrugged. "And since you seem to like answering questions with questions, why, pray, is our host so angry?"

The return of the Marquis Gian-Francesco Gonzaga immediately brought changes throughout the court. The afternoon following the Feast of Fools, Cardinal Ippolito hurriedly left Mantua, supposedly to be in Rome for the ceremonies of the Jubilee Year being sponsored by the pope. That same afternoon Leonardo watched from a third-story loggia as Ser Guglielmo Gaetani quickly mounted a black stallion and, leading a mule laden with his possessions, fled to the east.

The following day Maestro Andrea Mantegna, sixty-eight, the official court painter, was summoned from his frescoes in the Ermitani in Padua and given a new commission at Mantua. This provided a welcome change for Leonardo who was now able to spend some time with the elder artist discussing such things as the rising cost of lapis lazuli and the mathematical basis for forced perspective.

For an entire week, there was little sign of merriment or mischief in the corridors or the garrison of the palazzo, and Lizette, when she could slip away to visit with Niccolo, reported that for the first few days following his reunion with his wife the marquis dined alone with the marquesa in Paradise, but there were repeated sounds of loud quarrelling and anguished weeping from behind the doors to the lady's chambers.

"What does all this mean?" Niccolo asked the Maestro that evening as he watched Leonardo preparing a clay head of the marquesa from his chalk sketches so "the lady does not have to sacrifice as much of her time in posing for me."
     The Maestro studied his work, then stepped back, stretched and replied, "It means, Niccolo, that one door has been closed, and another opened." He pressed the thumb and forefinger of

his left hand against the bridge of his nose and closed his eyes. "Apparently the winds of politics have shifted again, possibly due to Cesare Borgia's victories in Forli. It has now become expedient for the marquis to realign himself and his court with the Borgias. With Venice at war with the Turks, and with Cesare obviously eyeing Ferrara, the marquis has probably been instructed to avoid antagonizing the pope or his children. In any case, Gian-Francesco has considered it prudent to send poor Gaetani elsewhere, and Maestro Mantegna informs me that he has been suddenly commissioned to paint a work depicting the triumphal entry of Julius, another Cesare, into Rome, possibly as a gift from the marquis to the Borgian pope."

It was nearly a week after the return of Gian-Francesco Gonzaga to court before the customary celebratory dinner was held in the great hall to honor the return of the lord of Mantua.

The court dined on gold plates and ate lavishly and well of the best meat, and the finest fish and seafood and fruit imported from the south and east. The best wines were brought out and formal toasts raised to the marquis and to the one or two recent victories over the Turks. The toasts refrained from any mention of the major defeat at sea.

Niccolo noticed that the marquis seemed grim and reserved while the marquesa, her eyes reddened and puffy, wore a forced smile. She was robed in an exquisite gown of velvet with loops of gold woven into the pile.

On her breast was the Tears of the Madonna.

Lizette had told Niccolo of the letter from Laura de Gonzaga to the marquesa in which she revealed that Lucrezia Borgia had appeared in public only last month wearing the Tears. The dwarf had been prepared to dispatch this bit of information to the Cambio via the channels that Ser Agnolo had suggested, but now he was faced with the question of how the Tears could appear in two different cities on the breasts of two different women. Were there two sets of Tears in existence? Or was one authentic and the other a replica? If so, which was the real necklace? And did this mean that the necklace that disappeared with the Cambio courier had been recovered by either the marquesa or the Borgias? Was the appearance of the marquesa's Tears prompted, or perhaps necessitated, by the appearance of the Borgian necklace?

Niccolo secretly wished he could confide his mission to Leonardo, who had a way of unraveling even the most complicated puzzles, having prepared mind-twisting games for Il Moro during his years of service to the Moor.

Without the Maestro's help, Niccolo felt his ponderings couldn't untangle the mystery of the two necklaces. So, for the time, he told the Cambio nothing.

Ottaviano Cristani, seated at a table at the far end of the room during the "celebratory" feasting, had also been surprised by the sudden appearance of the Tears. He silently retreated to his rooms soon after the dinner and remained behind locked doors for several hours.

The morning following the feast Ottaviano appeared at the Maestro's workshop to discuss the completion of the requiem candles with Leonardo. He greeted the Maestro with both respect and dignity, and gestured to the servants who accompanied him to deposit the two boxes of candles, cradled in straw, on one of the worktables.

The Maestro withdrew one of the requiem candles from its nest, studied it, and passed it beneath his nose. Then he smiled and passed it to Niccolo who did the same. Each candle was black, quite thick and heavy, and when burned, they would give off the pleasant scent of lilies.

"They are magnificent," Leonardo told Ottaviano. "Much too beautiful to burn, Ser Ottaviano."

"Oh, many of the Magi Gifts are too precious in themselves," the chestnut-haired man replied softly. "They are very seldom used. More often they become part of the cherished treasures of the abbeys and the monasteries."

The Maestro studied the candles, imagining the images that might enhance them. "And the designs you wish me to put on the candles?"

"I was thinking of scenes depicting the passion and death of Our Lord," said the nobleman. Suddenly he began to cough, a deep, resonant cough that caused the man's entire body to shake. Small beads of perspiration formed on his brow.

"You are not well, my friend," the Maestro said, impulsively placing one huge hand on the man's forehead. "You have a fever."

"I cannot seem to stop this coughing," Ottaviano replied, gasping for air.

"Have you seen Maestro Bernardo, the court physician?"

"Several times," nodded Ottaviano. "He has suggested bleeding."

"Of course. Physicians prescribe bleeding for everything." Leonardo said in obvious disgust, and he remembered his ongoing war with the physician Ambrogio in Milan. "I have said it repeatedly: guardians of the sick must first understand what life is, what constitutes temperament and health, and how a balance and harmony of elements maintain all life!" He saw that his small lecture on well-being was doing little to alleviate Ottaviano's discomfort. "How long has this cough persisted, Ser Ottaviano?"

"Since late November," Ottaviano replied. "Or early December. Sometime within that period. I did not notice anything wrong with me, and then this damned cough began, and I began to weaken."

"Is it consistent?" Leonardo asked. "Do you cough more at one time than another?"

"More at night, or so it seems."

Leonardo nodded and crossed to the worktable where his parade of small glass jars and urns marched across the shelf. He opened one, scooped a bit of the dark substance onto the top layer of a sheaf of papers, added a portion of a lighter powder from another container, and then folded the paper into a small envelope and handed it to Ottaviano. "Add just a pinch of these herbs to your wine during the evening meal," the Maestro said softly. "But please do not report me to Maestro Bernardo, eh? The physicians and I do not always agree on the causes of illness. These herbs will, I believe, calm your blood and help you to rest. The body has remarkable powers of recovery if given the opportunity. Do not concern yourself with the candles. I will finish the project in time for the Magi Gifts."

Ottaviano accepted the folded paper. "Thank you, Maestro," he said. Then he quickly tucked the envelope into the sleeve of his tunic and put on his thick gloves.

Leonardo nodded and began to escort the nobleman to the door. "Remember," he said, "just a pinch at the evening meal."

Niccolo watched as Leonardo slowly closed the door behind Ottaviano. The Maestro crossed to where his notes were scattered over a tabletop and suddenly began to write. Niccolo stepped down from his stool and stood behind him. "What is it?" he asked. "What are you writing?"

"The man bore an unusual blue marking on the back of his right hand, situated between the thumb and forefinger. Didn't you notice it when he removed his gloves?"

"No." Niccolo glanced at the markings the Maestro had made on the edge of the parchment: two arcs separated by a straight line. "What does it mean?" he asked. "What is it?"

"I'm not sure," Leonardo replied slowly. "I remember seeing something similar on a brief visit to Venice with Il Moro."

"In Venice?" echoed Niccolo.

Leonardo looked up from his sketching. "In the Street of the Assassins," he said softly.

That same afternoon the Maestro hastily sketched cartoons of the required scenes for the requiem candles on thin strips of paper. Niccolo began to transfer the images in colored waxes to the candles themselves using a method called "spolverizzare" in which a bag of charcoal dust is dabbed against holes pricked in the paper, transferring the basic flat design to a cylindrical surface.

Suddenly the doors were flung open. The Marquis Gian-Francesco strode into the workroom unannounced. He was accompanied by Meneghina and two young officers with breastplates embossed with the Venetian lion. The marquis, elegant and erect and every inch a condottiere, briefly examined the room, the view from the windows, the chalk study of the Madonna and Saint Anne with the Christ child which the Maestro had mounted on an unframed canvas, the initial charcoal sketches that Leonardo had prepared for the marquesa's portrait, and the clay bust of the lady.

"I regret I was not here to welcome you formally upon your arrival," the marquis told Leonardo without smile or frown as he completed his examination. "Are you comfortable?"

"Yes. Thank you, Excellency."

"I tried to be here, but Venice is in a turmoil."

"Indeed?"

The marquis pretended to be interested in some texts, but it was apparent that he wanted to introduce a topic for discussion. "Are you acquainted with the city, Maestro?"

"I was there once, Excellency," Leonardo replied. "Briefly. In the company of the duke of Milan."

The mention of Il Moro creased the marquis' forehead. "Are you aware how difficult it would be to defend it?" he suddenly asked. "Especially from the north?"

"No," the Maestro replied softly.

"Look you!" snapped the marquis as he looked around quickly, seized a page of blank parchment, dipped the quill in the inkjar and began to sketch rapidly. "The republic is like, well, a sliver of land that reaches beyond the Largo di Garda to the eastern borders with Milan. To the south Venice shares a common border with my own marquisate and the duchy of Ferrara, and then it dips into the Adriatic. On the western shore of the Adriatic the republic controls the access to the sea, separating the kingdom of Hungary and the Ottoman empire from this waterway until it reaches as far south as the republic of Ragusa." He stepped back as Leonardo examined the drawing. "The city of Venice itself," the marquis then continued, again sketching along the edges of the parchment, "is little more than a collection of islands reaching into the lagoon and joined to the mainland by boat and a single bridge. You can walk from one end of the city to the other in an hour. The Grand Canal divides the city's heart into two sections." He made a quick, reversed "s" across one block of the drawing.

Leonardo nodded as he studied the sketch. "But the mountains, the Alps, the Dolomites here, and the lake areas at Trentino, these are natural defense barriers to the north, aren't they? The few passes could easily be defended. They are like great doors that can be opened to admit invaders and then closed behind them to trap them."

"Yes," nodded the marquis, "but once forced open, invaders could cut directly south to the Adriatic, hardly more than a day's ride, and follow the Adige all the way from Verona to the mouth of the Po, attacking the city from the north."

Leonardo ran his fingers through his thick beard and frowned at the sketch. "But why look to the land?" he said softly. "Venice is a city of water. In a sense, the Adriatic is only a Venetian lake, since Venice controls both banks. If you were to develop a plan whereby you could flood the Isonzo plain here, below Gorzia, you could prevent any attack from the north." He jabbed a finger at a point on the map.

The marquis watched intently. "Flood the plain?"

"Surely you have seen the results of water suddenly released," Leonardo continued. "The full force of the flood assaults and demolishes even the most heavily fortified areas. Villas, country residences, all must submit to the percussive force of a flood. Horses cannot stand against the striking power of water. Knights are thrown and drown in the weight of their own armor. Archers, lancers, nothing stands against the full impact of the force."

The marquis smiled. "Yes. I see." Suddenly he stood erect and turned to face Leonardo. "Maestro, I hereby commission you to prepare sketches and perhaps a model of how and where retaining walls might be built to control the flooding of the Isonzo plain! I would need this model and a detailed design before my return to Venice! I am certain the doge and the Council of Ten will reward you generously for this service. Will you accept?"

Niccolo could see that the Maestro was both intrigued and stunned by the proposal. It would be a project involving his two loves: engineering and mathematics. "Well, Excellency," he began, "I would probably have to visit the site, and then there is the pressing matter of the portrait for the marquesa . . . !"

"It can wait!" The marquis lowered his voice and spoke softly to the Maestro as if in strict confidence. "Our world is about to undergo incredible changes, Maestro Leonardo. A Geonese trader has established an overland route to the eastern shore of India, Ceylon, Sumatra and the Maldives. A navigator, Vasco de Gama, has organized a Portugese base at the port city of Calicut, and Lodovico di Varthema who recently returned from there reports that pepper, for example, can be purchased for as little as three ducats per hundredweight! Imagine! Three ducats a hundredweight! While in Venice the same amount sells for over eighty ducats!" His voice became a little louder, more emphatic. "Well, you can see how this will affect trade! Everything points to new routes, both by land and sea, to the spices and wonders of the east, and that means that Venice, once the center of all trade with the east, will lose its position of importance and become more vulnerable, unless we can maintain the appearance of stability, impregnability and prosperity."

The Maestro did not respond immediately. He seemed to be pondering the proposal, and he repeated, "The appearance of stability and prosperity?"

The marquis took the repetition for a form of acceptance, and he smiled at Leonardo. "You can be of great assistance to the republic in this matter, Maestro."

Leonardo finally nodded, and the marquis seemed as if a great weight had been lifted from his shoulders. He wheeled suddenly and almost collided with Niccolo. " 'Scuse!" he exclaimed. Then it seemed to the dwarf as if Gian-Francesco saw Niccolo for the first time. "Ah! The little man with the remarkable mind!" He dropped to one knee to shorten the distance between their two heads. "What do you think of our dwarf apartments, eh? Were you pleased? Impressed?"

Niccolo was surprised by the question, and he shrugged. "I have seen them only in passing, Excellency."

Again the marquis stood erect, glaring. "What? Here nearly two months and you have yet to be formally escorted through the dwarf apartments? What an appalling lack of manners! And the expense to design and build them!" He turned to face one of his subordinates. "See to it that Nanino comes to this young man immediately and personally introduces him to each of our small friends! Open the doors to him! Open all the doors!"

Niccolo chose not to mention his relationship with Lizette. He smiled and bowed smartly, which seemed to please the marquis who returned the salute with a quick nod as he swept from the workroom with his entourage.

"Just what I need," sighed the dwarf to Leonardo, "immediate access to rooms where small friends bite their thumbs at me."

That same afternoon, Leonardo and Niccolo were surprised by the sudden appearance of Johannes Vendramm and Madonna Maddalena in the workshop. The Belgian, now in the customary velvet tunic and hose of the court and with his face half-shadowed by a large-brimmed hat, bowed to the Maestro as Niccolo escorted the lady to the most comfortable chair in the workroom. Madonna Maddalena's glorious red hair was gathered and braided and woven around her ears and temples like a turban and then covered with a thin veil held in place by a jewelled comb, but her beauty was marred by an obvious air of anxiety.

"Forgive me for appearing without an invitation," the handsome young Belgian pleaded, "but I did not wish everyone in court to know I wanted to meet with you."

"You are welcome of course," said Leonardo. "You know my friend and associate, Ser Niccolo da Pavia?"

The couple glanced in Niccolo's general direction, but it was clear that their attention was focused upon Leonardo.

"Your hair, it is returning?" asked the Maestro quietly.

"Yes," nodded Johannes. It was evident he did not wish to discuss his humiliation as the Lord of the Revels. "I wondered," he whispered, "has anything unusual happened to you since your arrival at court, Maestro?"

"Unusual?"

"Were your rooms searched? Have you been followed?"

Leonardo and Niccolo exchanged quick glances, and the dwarf climbed up and perched on a stool beside the young woman whose attention remained focused on the Maestro. "I was not aware of any search or of being followed," Leonardo replied. "Why do you ask?"

"Because I think my own rooms were, what shall I say? Examined? And lately, especially when I have been walking with Madonna Maddalena, we have both sensed that someone was watching us."

"Yesterday," the lady said softly, "I distinctly heard something in the garden bushes, and when Johannes went to investigate, he found this."

She held a small, torn scrap of material toward Leonardo, but Niccolo took it from her and briefly examined it. Then he climbed down from the stool and handed it to Leonardo. "Gold braid," Niccolo commented. He looked at the Maestro. "From a uniform perhaps?"

"Perhaps," nodded Leonardo as he returned it to Niccolo and turned his attention to Vendramm. "Can you advance any reason for someone from the garrison to search your quarters or to spy upon you?"

"None."

"Though I cannot imagine someone from the court stealing from another, do you possess anything of value?"

"Nothing," said the Belgian. "I brought with me only copies of trade agreements for the marquis' signature, and several other official documents, but nothing of value. And I recently inventoried the papers, and nothing is missing."

"Trade agreements and other documents? What other documents?"

"A projection of the value of salt now that Il Moro's monopoly has been broken. A report that Vasco de Gama has sailed again, this time to establish trading posts at Hormuz and on the Malabar coast. A copy of the assessment of the marquesa's jewels . . ."

Niccolo was instantly alert. "The marquesa's jewels? An assessment of the marquesa's jewels?"

"Yes," said Johannes. "For some reason it was necessary four months past to have some of her jewels assessed and their value authenticated."

"All her jewels?" Niccolo tried to make it sound like a routine question. "I mean, well, for example, did this include the Tears of the Madonna?"

"Not all of the lady's jewels," Johannes said, puzzled both by the dwarf's intense interest and his knowledge of the necklace. "Although the Tears were included in the assessment."

"And . . . ?"

"What can I tell you?" shrugged the young Belgian. "They were authentic. I cannot tell you their value, because such matters are confidential, but I can say that the diamonds were genuine."

"Really?" Leonardo said softly. "And how was that determined?"

"The usual method I suppose. They cut glass. You see, a diamond is the hardest substance that . . ."

"Yes!" the Maestro stopped him. He noticed that the discussion was causing Madonna Maddalena even greater dismay although she struggled to hide it, her small hands clenched defiantly in her lap. "I know the qualities of a diamond, and the test of cutting glass is valid and trustworthy."

"You say this assessment was a copy?" Niccolo asked.

"Yes," Johannes replied, puzzled by this sudden inquisition. "The original was misplaced or lost, so a copy was requested. We had the assessor's full report in our office in Brussels, and a copy was made and included in the packet of papers I brought with me. I am to deliver the copy to the marquis tomorrow."

"The marquis?"

"Yes," the Belgian nodded. "He requested the copy."

Niccolo was about to press the matter further when he realized that Leonardo was studying him, his blue eyes flashing beneath the thick brows. Niccolo remembered that the contessa and the guildmaster of the Cambio had asked that the Maestro be kept ignorant of his assignment. "That, ah, that is very interesting," muttered the dwarf.

The tall man ran his fingers through his beard and turned his attention once more to Johannes. "May I inquire why you are here, Ser Johannes? In this court I mean."

The Belgian sighed. "Actually it is something of a business arrangement. Over the last ten years, my uncle, a past master of the Hanseatic Guild, has had several dealings with the courts of Ferrara and Mantua. You understand? Delegations of three to five persons at a time passed back and forth between Brussels and the Este and Gonzaga courts carrying agreements of trade, monopolies on certain commodities controlled by the duke and the marquis, appraisers and lawyers and traders, as I said: business arrangements."

"Yes," Leonardo repeated softly. "I understand. Business arrangements."

"Because of the increasing importance of the courts of Ferrara and Mantua, some say this marquisate will soon be elevated to that of a full duchy, my uncle felt it would be a bond between the German, Dutch, and Belgian merchants and the courts if I were sent here to absorb some of the teachings of the humanists in residence and to develop a certain 'polish' that would enable me to deal with the lords in other Italian and Spanish courts on behalf of my uncle and my family."

The Maestro turned to face Madonna Maddalena. "And you, Madonna? May I ask how you came to be in court?"

"Me?" She seemed startled by the question. "My reasons for being here are similar to those of Ser Johannes," the red-haired woman replied softly. "I am Venetian, from Murano. My father, apart from his profession, is an advisor to the doge, and the marquis was kind enough to offer me an education and a period as lady-in-waiting to the marquesa."

"From Murano? The famed world of glass?"

"Yes," the lady nodded.

"I see," smiled Leonardo. "You are here to be educated, and Ser Johannes is here to be, what was the term? Polished?" He again turned his attention to the Belgian. "And have you been sufficiently polished, Ser Johannes?"

The Belgian smiled too. "Well," he said, "I have been humiliated and embarrassed, mocked and mutilated, and now I believe I am being spied upon, so I suppose I have a better understanding of how matters are conducted in an Italian court. It is rather like being inducted into a guild, where naked applicants are shoved up chimneys, thrown in the cold waters of a river, or paraded around the piazzi while straddling a barrel. If you survive, you are considered strong enough to conduct business matters."

Niccolo was surprised to hear the Maestro actually laugh. The tall, bearded man placed one of his heavy hands on the young man's shoulder and mock-whispered, "These are princely arenas where unscrupulous and ruthless lords war with honest and genteel nobility in great games that affect the whole world."

He stood erect again. "That's why the playing field is called a court."

After the couple had departed, Niccolo fingered the piece of gold braid and tucked it under his belt. "Do you think they are being followed?"

"Quite possibly," Leonardo murmured.

"Why? Does someone suspect Ser Johannes of something?"

The Maestro peered at the dwarf for a moment from under his thick eyebrows and said softly, "Why do you assume it is Ser Johannes that is being shadowed? Why not the lady?"

"What could the lady have done to warrant being spied upon?"

"Ah!" smiled the Maestro. "Open *that* door, Niccolo, and you may have the answer to a number of interesting questions!"

The early January snows limited activity outside the palazzo. During the next four days Ser Ottaviano visited the workshop twice to oversee the decorating of the requiem candles, and Leonardo observed that the courtier's health did not seem to be improving, which puzzled him. The cough had diminished. That was plain. But the fever persisted, and the nobleman was growing visibly weaker. Niccolo watched with interest as Leonardo increased the potency of the herbal mixture he compiled from two or three of his small containers and gave the mixture to Ottaviano. He also noted that Ottaviano made no effort to disguise the strange markings on his right hand.

"It is very curious," sighed the Maestro. "The cough has diminished as I thought it would, but there is something else." His voice lowered. "I think, perhaps, that the man is dying, and he knows it, yet can do nothing to prevent or reverse it."

By the end of the second week, Leonardo had completed fourteen of the requiem candles which were then passed to the chamberlain to be dispatched with other artifacts as part of the Magi Gifts of the Gonzaga. Within an hour after the carts had departed, Ottaviano appeared in the workshop.

"I followed the general synopsis of the Stations of the Cross," Leonardo informed the dark man who seemed to have difficulty breathing. "The arrest and trial. The scourging. The crowning of thorns. Christ falling three times. Veronica's veil. The Cyrene helping. The crucifixion. The pieta. The entombment."

Ottaviano nodded. Niccolo saw the perspiration on the man's forehead and realized the fever had not broken.

"I assumed that is what you wished, Ser Ottaviano," Leonardo continued. "But the story only required fourteen of the candles." He gestured to another box resting on a workshop table. "There are seven remaining."

"Yes," Ottaviano whispered. "Well, I had to allow for accidents or mistakes in the molding or the decorating," the nobleman muttered. "I am certainly no artisan, as you could see. Where were the finished candles sent? Do you know?"

"I believe I heard the chamberlain say they were sent to San Zeno Maggiore in Verona. You know the church?"

"Yes, yes," Ottaviano managed to whisper. "Mantegna painted something for it a few years past,"

"Yes," smiled the Maestro. "A 'Madonna.' It hangs above the main altar."

"Yes," Ottaviano murmured. "I, ah, I wish to thank you for your work, Maestro. I have been honored." He struggled to rise. "Oh! Would you please be so kind as to send the remaining candles to my chambers? Perhaps I can use them next year, you see, for the Magi Gifts, and save myself a little work."

Leonardo smiled and nodded, but Niccolo knew that unless the man's health improved, he would not be among the living next year.

He kept his prognosis to himself.

"Of course. I'll have someone bring the remaining candles to you this evening," said the Maestro as he assisted the dark man to the doorway where two servants waited.

"You are a gentleman, Maestro." Niccolo was afraid the man might collapse, but the servants rushed forward and took Ottaviano's arms. Then the chestnut-haired man turned and murmured, "And that is rare in this court. Although there are a great many pretenders."

Despite his promise, Niccolo noticed that the box with the seven remaining candles was still on Leonardo's workshop table two days later. "The man is very very ill," frowned Leonardo when Niccolo brought the matter to his attention. "Maestro Bernardo, who has been treating him, says he does little but sleep. He has lost all appetite, and the fever persists. The candles will be safe enough here until the gentleman recovers."

Niccolo took one of the candles and reveled momentarily in the aromatic perfume of it. "Or dies," the dwarf said softly.

Leonardo looked up from his examination of an oddly-shaped stone he had found in the courtyard, "For your information, Niccolo, Ser Johannes' suspicion was correct. Our rooms, too, have been searched."

Niccolo replaced the candle in its nest. "They have? How do you know?"

Leonardo returned to his examination of the stone, tapping at it with a small hammer and picking at it with a curved metal instrument. "When I studied with Verrocchio, theft among the students was commonplace," he said. "Nothing of great value, you understand, because we had nothing of great value, but a brush was taken here perhaps, or newly ground pigment disappeared. Subsequently I learned a few tricks. I would place a towel through the handles of two drawers so a certain small mark on it might be visible. If the mark moved, it indicated someone had gone through my possessions. Brushes and books were arranged in a certain order. Any change in the location of these items indicated someone had gone through them, and a quick search soon determined what, if anything, had been taken." Suddenly a wave of melancholy seemed to sweep over him. "None of this spared me the constant thievery of Salai, of course." He paused as if the memory, which caused him so much pain, also brought him some pleasure. He gestured toward his brushes. "I noticed this morning that my brushes have been moved, and our books rearranged."

Niccolo climbed the stool and opened the first of the three books resting there: a text of Euclid. Then he thumbed through the Meditations of Marcus Aurelius and the Epictetus. "These books were moved?" he asked.

"Yes. The Euclid, which was in the middle, is now on top."

Niccolo quickly examined the books, leafing rapidly through their pages, and he shook his head. "Amazing," he said. "What do you suppose they were searching for?"

"Perhaps nothing," sighed the Maestro. "Nothing seems to be missing. It may have been curiosity." He suddenly looked up from his study of the stone. "Do you still have the red book in your possession?"

The red book, the record of what had transpired in the Castello Sforezco during the last days of Il Moro's reign, was seldom discussed. "I would never trust it to anyone else," Niccolo assured him.

"It's well hidden?"

"Absolutely."

"The book is the only thing we possess that could be of value to anyone. It could discredit Il Moro with his current benefactor, the emperor, if it was used for that purpose. At the same time it is our guarantee that Il Moro will not send agents against us. Make certain it is safe."

Niccolo smiled. "It is safe, Maestro," he said. "*That* I promise you."

True to his word, the marquis sent Nanino, the self-appointed overlord of the court's little people, to Niccolo with an invitation to tour the Dwarves' Wing. The invitation came nearly two weeks after Gian-Francesco's visit, near the month's end.

"I regret the delay in formally welcoming you, Ser Niccolo," said the black-bearded dwarf with a pretentious bow, "but affairs at court have been exhausting since the return of the marquis."

Niccolo smiled at the small man's pomposity. He wore a tunic of gold cloth, which was full-sleeved and emblazoned with an emerald star on one breast and a military decoration of some sort on the opposite. The dwarf's boots were made of some exotic leather that was speckled and scaled, and boasted ridiculously high heels and golden bows. His gauntlets, of the same leather as his boots, came nearly to his elbows, and a scaled-down sword in a jewelled scabbard was suspended by a sash from one shoulder. A soft velvet cap, also in gold with a huge plume that arced nearly to his shoulder, perched precariously on one side of Nanino's head. His dark hair had been curled and hung in ringlets.

"Shall we proceed?" he asked.

"Why not?" Niccolo replied with the air of a man totally bored with existence. "Let us open a few doors!" he cried in imitation of the marquis. Then he laughed and quickly added, "We have nearly two hours before dinner."

Later Niccolo had to admit to Leonardo that he was fascinated by the scaled-down size of the furnishings in the Dwarves' Wing. He didn't need a footstool to elevate himself to the height of a chair. Plates and utensils were his size and easily handled. He briefly sampled a bed and found he was cocooned in it instead of wallowing in a sea of sheets and blankets like a small ship caught in an ocean during a tempest. He did not have to stand on his toes to look through a window, and if he merely raised his hands over his head when he passed through a doorway, his fingers brushed the lintel.

He was introduced to the two other male dwarfs, Pico and Grimaldi, and to the female dwarf, Louise. Although Nanino formally introduced Niccolo to Lizette, the black-bearded dwarf made it apparent that he knew the two were acquainted, and he disapproved. Lizette welcomed the visitor with a deep curtsy, and Niccolo, in turn, kissed the lady's hand, or rather the lace glove upon her hand. He winked at her when the lady smiled at his attempt at courtly manners.

Nanino felt it necessary to point out that all of the marquis' dwarves were richly dressed in satins, brocades, and silks, in contrast to Niccolo's plain tunic and hose. "Our wardrobe, you see, is indicative of our importance in the court," Nanino insisted. "The history of dwarves has always been associated with nobility. In ancient Egypt, I have been told, it was the court dwarves who were entrusted with keeping the accounts and maintaining the inventories."

"That is true," Niccolo nodded, smiling at Lizette who now stood beside him. "And it was the same Egyptians who first dragged pygmy warriors into their courts where they were frequently attached to the thrones of the pharaohs with gold chains and jewelled collars." He glanced around at the others. "I see very little has changed, save for the removal of the chains. The collars apparently remain."

Niccolo saw that he had aroused the anger of the black-bearded dwarf. "Better a jewelled collar," snapped Nanino, "than the worn woolen neckpiece of a common peasant pretending to be the equal of a noble simply because he can read and write in Latin."

"Oh, I have no ambitions to be the equal of a noble," Niccolo replied quickly. "Why should I suppress my talents and intelligence to the level of a courtier whose principal concern every morning is whether to wear the red or the green slippers?" He sneaked a glance at Lizette who hid her smile behind the fan. "Besides," Niccolo continued, "your gold tunic looks a little threadbare itself, brother Nanino. If I am not mistaken, there is a snip of gold braid missing from the cuff of your left sleeve."

The embarrassed dwarf quickly examined the damage, and his face flushed. "It is of no consequence. If I so choose, I could wear a hundred different uniforms. I have the vestments of a bishop! Of a cardinal! Of a pope!"

"How fortunate for the Church that vestments do not make the man," Niccolo smiled. "The cardinalate is doubtless composed of several small-minded men, but small in stature. . . . !"

It was too much for Lizette who laughed quite audibly, and in a moment Nanino, livid, tore the fan from her grasp. His right fist was raised, ready to strike the lady who instinctively backed away, when Niccolo suddenly dropped into the crouched stance taught him by Rubini. In an instant his left leg swept in a wide circle, knocking both of Nanino's legs out from under him. The dwarf was sent sprawling.

"Did you feel that?" Niccolo cried, suddenly bending over the startled Nanino and offering him a hand. "Was that an earthquake, think you?" He glanced quickly at Lizette who stood, awed and open-mouthed, at the suddenness and efficacy of the attack. "Are you injured, Madonna?"

Nanino slapped Niccolo's hand to one side and got to his feet. In a moment Pico and Grimaldi had assembled themselves behind Nanino, and Louise had crossed to Lizette's side.

"You dared strike me?" Nanino screeched. "The marquesa shall hear of this!"

Niccolo took the torn piece of gold braid that Madonna

Maddalena had given him from under his belt and tossed it at Nanino's feet.

"Oh, I'm certain she will," he said. "Pet dogs may attract fleas and urinate on the carpets and salivate at table, but they always prove loyal to their lords and masters."

To Niccolo's surprise, there were no repercussions from the disagreeable confrontation. When Niccolo next met the dwarf lord in a corridor, Nanino nodded in stony salute as he passed and Niccolo responded in kind.

"It is rather strange," Niccolo told Leonardo that evening. "I would have expected some angry response from the marquesa, She indulges Nanino, but no one has said a word. It is as if an overseer had snapped a whip and commanded the dogs to stop barking!"

"That is not unusual," said the Maestro as he dabbed with chalk at his study of the marquesa. "What is unusual is that the dogs apparently *did*!"

During the snowy month Leonardo concentrated most of his energies and attentions on preparing the bust of the marquesa and a model of the Isonzo plains and Gorzia for the marquis.

Niccolo was left to his own devices. He spent much of the time in the company of Lizette which caused some sleepless nights when he thought of Ellie waiting and sighing for him in Cremona. Finally the lie that this association with Lizette was strictly business took precedence over his conscience, and he successfully placed his attraction to the French dwarf in one corner of his mind and his promises to Ellie in the other, the temporarily shaded, corner.

Lizette provided him with volumes of information on the court and the residents which served him in his role of bank- ers' spy. He had not forgotten his assignment for the Cambio, but he remained hopelessly confused as to what information he should send to Venice. Ser Agnolo had told him the necklace and the courier had disappeared. Then Lucrezia Borgia had appeared in Rome wearing the Tears, and the marquesa appeared with the necklace at her own throat. According to the Belgian the marquesa's necklace was authentic. What should he say? Yes, the Tears remain in the possession of the marquesa, which would imply that it was *her* agents who intercepted the courier and returned the necklace to its owner?

But he did not know that to be the truth. He remembered the principle drummed into him by the Maestro: "There is always another possibility."

All he knew was that Lucrezia Borgia wore the necklace on a singular occasion. Could the Borgian pontiff have sent agents to intercept the courier and then given the necklace to his daughter? Or was one authentic and the other some sort of replica? And if this were the case, which one? The Borgian necklace or the marquesa's? And who made it? And why? Ser Johannes had said the assessment proved the marquesa's Tears were genuine. Would the Borgias display a replica, knowing the information would soon be related to the Gonzaga court? And to what purpose?

Such mental probing produced the usual response in Niccolo.

It made him hungry.

Niccolo could easily have summoned a servant and requested food, but old habits refuse to die easily. The young man reverted to his former reputation, the terror of the Certosa, the kitchen thief, the bandit of the scullery, slipping through the shadowed corridors to investigate the delights tucked away in cabinets and barrels. Even common bread, when stolen, seemed more delicious and nourishing than all the offered loaves across the table.

He was returning through the Camera degli Sposi after his nocturnal raid with pastries of walnut and pecan and a dusty bottle of the local wine when he heard someone turning the handle of the door. He quickly realized he could never retreat fast enough to reach the door in the opposite wall, but his momentary panic triggered a memory, and he turned and scanned the painted walls.

Where was that panel? Flowers! Painted flowers on two-dimensional columns! But under the flickering light of the torches the painted figures, already life-like, seemed to move, which only added to his panic. The painted courtiers looking down from the nonexistent dome appeared to mock him and laugh at his dilemma.

There were several columns supporting flowered groups! Which one? He quickly patted the various bouquets as he heard the door begin to open. Suddenly the hidden panel was revealed, and Niccolo quickly darted into the narrow passage as the small door clicked shut behind him.

He found himself between the walls. Behind him was another small panel that he knew would admit him to the adjoining room. The panel before him provided a peephole into the Camera, and he was surprised how clearly he could hear the conversation between the two approaching figures. He nibbled one of the pastries as he put his eye to the peephole and saw the marquesa, mantled from throat to floor in a black velour robe, carrying a sheaf of papers. She was followed by a dull-eyed Meneghina, half-asleep, who carried a small panel containing a well for ink, a quill pen, and parchments.

Lizette had mentioned that the marquesa was known to walk and work late into the night and sometimes to the dawn's first light. The lady moved with energy and grace, pausing only now and again under the light of a torch to study a page and then to bark instructions to the chamberlain.

"I want it made quite clear to Maestro Luca Lombieni that I will not tolerate his inability to finish my commission in the time allotted. Either he presents the painting within four days or return the monies allotted him, or I will pass the matter into the hands of my kinsmen in Ferrara which will mean the termination of his career and possibly his life."

171

"You wish me to say that, Excellency? That you may have him killed?"

"If I say it, Andrea, then I certainly mean it. Write it as I told you. These artists feel they have every right to take advantage of their patrons, and it is about time that we enlightened them." She thumbed through some of the pages. "Prepare a letter for me to the Contessa Bergamini in Cremona."

Hearing the name of his friend and benefactor, Niccolo suddenly felt a cold wind brush against the back of his neck.

"To the contessa?"

"Tell her I have commissioned Maestro Leonardo to render a portrait of me, and I remember that he had performed this service for the contessa when she was in the service of the duke of Bari. Tell her I would like her to send me the portrait Leonardo did of her, so I can compare his previous work with the one in progress to determine that the Maestro is not rushing the assignment or doing inferior work."

"I understand."

"I doubt that the lady will comply, because she is no longer the sweet-faced young thing who graced Il Moro's bed, and I imagine the portrait serves to remind the lady that time has etched its passage upon that innocent face."

"Innocent?"

"That is what the Maestro painted. The harlot beneath is not visible in the work as I remember it. That is Maestro Leonardo's gift."

Again the marquesa rifled through the pages in her hand, then she gave a deep sigh and said, "My husband was furious to learn that Lucrezia Borgia was seen wearing a necklace that seemed identical to the Tears, for it raised doubts about our stability and posed questions concerning the authenticity of my own necklace. Fortunately Ser Johannes was able to provide a copy of the certificate of assessment, so he is temporarily satisfied that the necklace worn by the Borgian bitch was false, but I think it is now quite clear what happened at Montagnana, isn't it? The presence of this other necklace verifies that Ottaviano lied to me!"

"Yes, Excellency."

"And my suspicions, and my response, were correct?"

"Absolutely, Excellency. And effective. Maestro Bernardo says he believes it is only a matter of days before the gentleman will no longer be among us."

"Ah! You see?" cried the marquesa. "My little monkey is quite an accomplished assassin! Of what apparent cause will Ottaviano die, according to our illustrious Maestro Bernardo?"

"Officially, a general weakening which led to the malfunction of certain organs," the chamberlain replied coldly. "Unofficially, Maestro Bernardo feels the man has been methodically poisoned, and the process has been ongoing for some time. He says the poison, which he cannot identify, has already damaged some internal organs. There is no remedy. The procedure is irreparable."

Niccolo could hear the satisfaction in the marquesa's voice like the soft purring of a cat. "Isn't that too perfect? Aren't you impressed by my little monkey now, eh? And whom does Maestro Bernardo suspect of poisoning Ottaviano?"

The chamberlain drew closer to the marquesa, but from his hiding place in the wall of the Camera, Niccolo heard every whispered word.

"Maestro Bernardo believes it is Maestro Leonardo."

The marquesa and the chamberlain no sooner departed the Camera degli Sposi when Niccolo pushed the small button in the opposite wall that admitted him to the small adjoining chamber. He quickly and quietly made his way to the door leading to the arcade and found it empty and deep in shadow. With the bottle tucked under one arm he made a dash for the circular stairway that led to the workshop level, rounded the corner, and found himself face to face with Maestro Leonardo.

"Now, Niccolo," the tall painter said softly, "suppose you tell me everything you think I do not already know."

Niccolo, relieved at the exposure of his quiet commission, began his long recitation of the events that led to the night of spying. He told of the secret meeting with the master of the Cambio, of the commission given him concerning the Tears of the Madonna, of the contessa's history of the necklace and her advice concerning Lucrezia Borgia and Caterina Sforza, of his confusion over the appearance of two necklaces, and then everything he had overheard from his hiding place in the Camera degli Sposi.

The Maestro was obviously disturbed by the last statement, that someone believed he had been poisoning Ottaviano, and he quickly crossed to his shelf of jars and urns and dipped the tip of his little finger in each and touched it to the tip of his tongue. After his third experiment, the tall man sank dejectedly into a chair and murmured, "It's true. It is. Someone has laced my powders with poison. I cannot identify it, but it affects the taste of the herbs. There is not enough to kill instantly but over a matter of weeks or months." His voice dropped, and he seemed to sink deeper into the chair. "I thought I was helping the poor man, and I was actually assisting in his murder."

"But he was ill when he came to you."

"Yes. The poisoning must have begun earlier, and then the assassin saw the opportunity of continuing the murder of Ser Ottaviano and attaching the blame to me. Ottaviano must have told Maestro Bernardo that I was treating him with my herbs, and the physician, whom I obviously underestimated, had the intelligence to see that his patient was dying and the process was too far along to remedy. Naturally he attributed the poisoning to me."

"But who would do this? Who had the opportunity?"

"The same ones who searched our rooms. I see now why nothing was taken. The assassin was not stealing from me. He was *adding* something to my powders."

"Then it would have to be someone who wished not only to murder Ottaviano, but also to discredit you. If we can discern *why* Ottaviano is being murdered, then it may lead us to the assassin."

"I know why Ottaviano was marked for death. He lied, and his lying, formerly only suspected, was suddenly proven. I think it is also clear that his murder has something to do with your mission."

"With the Tears?"

Leonardo nodded. "I think everything that has happened at the court recently, the 'suicide' of the garrison captain, the humiliation of Johannes and the constant surveillance of Madonna Maddalena, the rage of the marquis on his return to court and the slow execution of Ottaviano, all these are related to the matter of the Tears. Remember, Ottaviano was away from the court when the courier disappeared. Shortly upon returning, a garrisoned officer is subjected to torture, and almost at once, another officer who had accompanied Ottaviano is found strangled. I suspect that the poor man under torture related something that pertained to Ottaviano's mission and our nobleman, fearing exposure, had his accomplice murdered before he could tell the truth."

"Why would Ottaviano murder his captain? What secret would be revealed?

"What was his mission?"

"To intercept the courier and return the Tears of the Madonna to the marquesa so the Cambio would have to absorb the loss. He certainly matches the description of the noble at the inn that night, according to two Franciscan friars who told me about it at the Certosa."

"Then why is he now being murdered?"

"He may have returned and informed the marquesa that he failed to find the necklace," shrugged Leonardo. "I think the tortured officer told a different story, that the necklace was recovered, but, for some reason, Ottaviano kept it."

"Why would he do that? He must have known that it would put his own life in jeopardy."

"The most simple explanation is that Ottaviano was sent by the marquesa to kill the courier and recover the necklace, letting the Cambio absorb the loss, but he became greedy and decided to keep the necklace for himself."

"And the other possibility?"

"Ottaviano's allegiance was split. Perhaps he served two masters, both of whom wanted the necklace. He told one that

he could not find it and gave it to the other. That would account for the fact that the stolen necklace, if it was indeed
recovered and kept by Ottaviano, was not found when Ottaviano's rooms were searched. He had already passed it on to his
other employer."

"How do you know Ottaviano's rooms were searched?"

"Because that seems to be a pattern of life here in Mantua,
doesn't it? Everyone, no matter how noble or how lowly,
seems to be subjected to quiet searches. Perhaps for simple
information or perhaps to incriminate, like the assassin who
appeared to search our workshop and actually planted the poison."

"But who is responsible? Who ordered these searches? Who
hired someone to plant the poisons in your jars?"

"It is obvious, isn't it, that the marquesa ordered the
searches and hired the assassin to poison Ottaviano."

"But if Ottaviano *did* serve two masters and gave the necklace to one, where is it now?"

"That is the primary question," Leonardo said as he stroked
his beard, "because instead of recovering a single missing
necklace, we now have two, both openly displayed. And, from
your description of this necklace, I now remember that the
marquesa was wearing it when she and the marquis entered
Milan with the French! I remember the refraction of the light,
and how I thought that the jewels distracted from the lady's
own beauty."

"But that's impossible!" said Niccolo. "The marquesa
would have to have been in possession of the Tears at the very
moment when the courier was intercepted!"

"Which would certainly support the theory that Ottaviano
told whomever sent him, the other master and not the marquesa, that he did not recover the necklace. Perhaps he *didn't*
find the necklace! Perhaps the marquesa never gave it to the
courier, and the entire confrontation and murder of the courier
was a sham."

"But the Cambio said they received a message from the courier that he had the Tears in his possession. So how could he

have the necklace at the same time the marquesa was wearing it in Milan?"

"I don't know," the Maestro smiled. "And what is even more curious, if you knew the Cambio suspected you of lying and having kept the necklace promised against their note, would you openly wear the Tears, especially after you told the bankers that the necklace was probably diverted to Il Moro by a turncoat courier? Isn't that a little foolish?"

"Yes!"

"Unless, of course, the marquesa has a second necklace, a false one, that she could prove to the Cambio was false, and that the authentic Tears was the one diverted to Il Moro."

"The marquesa had *two* necklaces?"

"Perhaps there are more than two! Perhaps there are three! Or four! That is always another possibility!"

"Three or four?!"

"Wonderful, isn't it? Who would ever have suspected that the Madonna had so many tears in her?"

Imola

In the encampment just outside of Imola, Cesare Borgia brushed his dark hair and smiled at his majordomo, Don Ramiro de Lorca. "I am going to leave you here to serve as my vice-governor. I do not think you will have any problem with the people. Since I disciplined the troops that ravaged their city, the people look upon me as their benefactor."

"And what of the Contessa Caterina?" asked the emaciated Florentine emissary, Niccolo Machiavelli, as he surveyed himself in a small hand mirror and brushed a forefinger over his smooth-shaven chin.

"Incredible, isn't she?" said Cesare as he quickly scrawled his signature on a parchment offered him by one of his subordinates. "Imagine! Riding out to greet me as if she were inviting me to tea, while planning to lower the portcullis of her fortress after I entered and so take me prisoner! What audacity! By God, if I had a dozen officers with that woman's courage and cunning, Niccolo, I'd have taken the Romagna in two months!"

Machiavelli moved the hand mirror aside. "Your Highness, I must be blunt and tell you: my superiors in Florence were appalled that you forced the lady to sleep with you following her surrender. They feel this was improper behavior for a duke of Valentinois and an obvious victor, and a gross insult to the lady and her family."

Cesare smiled at the emissary. "And how did you respond to your superiors in Florence, Niccolo?"

Machiavelli smiled, exposing a line of even white teeth. "I told them it was an act of incredible 'virtu' and 'terribilita', the stuff of great princes and overlords, something every Italian male with balls would understand and appreciate. Then I added that I have never known it to be necessary for you to use force to urge a woman to sleep with you."

Cesare gave a small laugh and adjusted his cloak around his shoulders. "A point well taken," he said. "But perhaps I was a little hasty in 'inviting' Madonna Caterina into my bed. I was curious. I wanted to personally experience a level of passion that actually killed a Medici before his time."

"And did you 'experience' it?"

Cesare placed the soft black cap on his dark curls and pinned a large diamond to the front of it. "As a gentleman, I cannot bring myself to defame the lady," he said. "But the point is moot since our illustrious French commander, Yves d'Alegre, has taken the woman under his own command and will not permit me near her." He pulled the black gauntlets on his hands. "I did not suspect the French of being so proper. After all, one doesn't acquire the French disease by eating bad fruit."

"The French call it the Neapolitan disease," Machiavelli replied with a laugh.

A junior officer entered the tent. "The command is ready, Excellency," he saluted Cesare.

"Fine," Cesare responded. "I will be there presently." He turned back to Machiavelli who was adjusting his fine cloak. "I have something else to discuss with you, as a Florentine. When I was in Milan, I had occasion to visit the workshops of Maestro Leonardo. Incredible. War machines with sword blades affixed to the hubs of chariot wheels! Flying wings and devices for walking on water! I saw drawings of possible war coaches that could move rapidly under the power of men pedaling and are nearly impossible to stop! I had no idea the painter was so deeply interested in warfare. Indeed, I was told that he called war a 'bestial madness.'"

"Maestro Leonardo has often said one thing and then re-

sponded in precisely the opposite manner. He has spoken
openly against war, but he came to Il Moro specifically to
invent war machines that would astound the world. He is an
enigma, unreliable. He has accepted commissions and never
completed them, because he became fascinated by some other
aspect of life, a mathematical problem involving the response
of structures to pressure exerted by water."

"Is he still in Mantua? Could you contact him for me? I
would like to talk with him."

"He is still in Mantua, I believe," Machiavelli said, turning
to leave the tent. "Painting a portrait of the marquesa."

"Why inflict us with another study of virago arrogance?"
sighed Cesare. "See if you can contact him, Niccolo. Tell him I
want to meet with him. As a gesture of goodwill I returned his
collection of herbs and powders that I found in his botteghe in
the Castello Sforezco, but my generosity was not acknowledged."

"If you really wish to impress the Maestro," said the diplomat, "I suggest you have *all* his personal belongings, his
books, his clothing and supplies crated and sent to him. Send
him everything that he left behind in Milan."

"To Mantua?"

"No," smiled Machiavelli, "to Florence. To his assistant,
Francesco Melzi."

"Florence?"

"Florence."

Cesare nodded and stepped into the bright sunlight. He
glanced over the ranks and files of mounted knights that
stretched the entire length of the encampment. He nodded to
the French commander at the head of the column who ignored
him and crossed to the grey jennet on which the Contessa
Caterina Sforza sat sidesaddle, unsmiling but erect in black
satin.

"Good morrow, Contessa," Cesare smiled. "Black satin?"

"I am in mourning," the lady replied softly.

"Surely not for your virtue," Cesare whispered.

"Nor yours," Caterina snapped. "I mourn for my poor people."

"Your 'poor people' are freed of your tyranny, Madonna, as all of the Romagna will soon be freed from the tyranny of the Sforza and the Varano and the Orsini."

The woman did not respond but turned her head. Cesare noticed the French commander glaring at him, so the Borgia stepped back from the lady's horse.

"Ah well," he sighed. "In any case, you appear contented today."

Caterina glared at him but did not speak. Instead she reached and opened her traveling cloak to reveal a necklace, a necklace of diamonds suspended from three strands of woven gold wire. The diamonds were shaped like tears and capped with a pattern of gold filigree resembling pointed thorns.

Caterina was pleased to see Cesare's smile vanish. She leaned from the saddle and whispered to him.

"Surprise!"

SURPRISES

February 1500

Mantua

Ottaviano Cristani died on the tenth day of February in the year of Our Lord fifteen hundred.

Warm winds blew across the Lombardy plains from the south and the west, and, almost overnight, the snow was gone. The day was noted in Leonardo's workbooks for other reasons as well. From his workshop windows the Maestro had observed flights of rondini, the ominous black birds whose presence precedes death according to many folk legends.

Ottaviano's body was wrapped in white linen saturated with aloe and crated with layers of salt, because a delegation from the Cristani family would be arriving at the Mantuan court to take the body back for burial in Venice. A certificate of death was signed by Maestro Bernardo although no cause of death was inscribed, nor was anything said to Leonardo or Niccolo concerning the slow poisoning. It was as if the marquis, relying on Leonardo's plans for flooding the Venetian lowlands, had simply ordered all rumors and speculations regarding the Maestro's involvement with the noble's death to end.

Leonardo and Niccolo watched from a courtyard loggia as two men in soft caps, wine-red tunics, and hose and heavy black cloaks came for the body. With a quiet efficiency they loaded the wooden crate onto the cart and covered it with a

185

canvas. The men seemed indifferent to their assignment, did not smile or speak, and the entire process took less than half an hour.

Leonardo noticed that it was the marquesa and not the marquis who stood watching with Lizette and Nanino from the steps of the palazzo as the coffin was loaded and covered. He noted that no crest marked the coach or the cloaks of the men, but over the heart of each of the tunics was a symbol with which the Maestro was now familiar.

Two arcs broken by a single line.

The "family" had come to claim its own.

That same afternoon Leonardo and Niccolo replaced the herbs that had been contaminated with poison.

"Whoever mixed the poison, possibly nightshade, with my herbs was thoroughly acquainted with both the herbs themselves and the potency of the poison," the Maestro observed to Niccolo. "The poison was mixed with the herbs they knew I would select to fight Ottaviano's fever and his cough, and in the exact proportions. No matter whether I increased or decreased the dosage, there would still be enough to kill the man. Further, the ground nightshade and the herbs I chose were of similar texture and coloring, which means the assassin was expert in poisons."

Niccolo checked the inventory as the Maestro opened jar after jar, examining the contents with finger and tongue and then replacing the receptacles on the long shelf.

"Was that Valerian root?" the dwarf asked.

"Yes," replied the Maestro, "and it is uncontaminated."

Niccolo made the appropriate notation in his book. The Maestro then proceeded to test and replace the jars containing ginseng, ginger and the "happiness plant," borage. He pointed out to Niccolo that the bark of the willow was a pain preventive.

"I discovered that in a book by Pedanius Dioscroides written more than thirteen hundred years ago," he told the young man. "I owe that to the Certosa who possessed a Latin translation." He poured some crushed petals into the palm of his hand, brushed a finger through them, and then returned them to the jar. "Did you know that the stamen hairs of the spider-wort change color when exposed to 'unclean' air, Niccolo?"

"No," Niccolo conceded. "And I doubt if I shall ever have cause to apply that information, Maestro."

"You would," Leonardo said grimly, "if you worked in mines or cesspits."

The Maestro then called out each ingredient as it was tested and replaced. Bloodroot. Goldenseal. Tansy. The saffron cro-cus. Thyme. Chervil. Garlic. Nasturtium. Chamomile. Angel-ica and woodruff. Foxglove and periwinkle. Larkspur and ver-bena.

"Yes," Leonardo sighed. "Whomever poisoned poor Ottavi-ano knew precisely what he was about. That shortens the list of possible killers at least."

"How?" asked Niccolo as he rolled the inventory and placed it in its leather sheath.

"The killer had to be trained for such an assassination. He knew poisons and herbs. He was obviously a professional, someone who could kill and never be recognized as an assas-sin. He had been employed only to murder Ottaviano, but he cleverly saw an opportunity to incriminate me at the same time. I doubt now that he had any motive for placing me in jeopardy, other than to focus attention away from himself."

"But who could that be?" Niccolo frowned.

"I don't know," said the Maestro, "But I imagine that when we *do* know, the identity will cause no little surprise!"

Encouraged by the warmth of the southern winds and eager to escape from the winter-imposed imprisonment in the palazzo and the grim spectre of death that had swept through the corri-dors in the past few months, the marquis and the marquesa lead groups of courtiers and their ladies on hawking and hunt-ing expeditions. The marquis announced to the court that in a

187

matter of weeks he would have to return to his duties in Venice and resume the war with the Turks. In the meantime it
was apparent that he intended to enjoy his privileges while he
could.

Leonardo did not enjoy such bloody amusements as hawking
and hunting, although he had occasionally joined the entourage of Il Moro to sketch the birds in flight or to study the
effect of light and shade on distant mountains. Now, with the
rest of the court, the Maestro also went gladly into the open air
and out of the confines of the palazzo. In the open he noted
that "every opaque body can be located between two pyramids, one dark and the other light, one seen and the other not,
and this only happens when the light enters through a window."

Later, when Niccolo reviewed the notation in the Maestro's
workbook, he saw that Leonardo had underscored the passage
"one dark and the other light, one seen and the other not." He
had scrawled a single word in the margin of the text.

The word was "assassins."

Two occurrences during the hawking and hunting outings also
merited notation in the Maestro's workbook.

The first was the elimination of a fine stallion from the list
of available horses offered to the members of the court. Pazzo,
Italian for "mad" or "crazy," was only four years old and huge,
nearly seventeen hands. The marquis had acquired the stallion
from an Arab trader who offered the animal at a ridiculously
low price for a purebred, because, as the trader explained, "the
animal has been mistreated. It was confined to a small pasture
where youths tormented it, throwing rocks at the unfortunate
beast and poking at it with long pointed sticks when they
summoned enough courage to actually enter the pasture with
it. Consequently poor Pazzo now becomes enraged at the merest sight of children, and he nearly killed a young boy in atten-

dance on the sheik. So he must be trained anew, and this will be a long, long process."

However, the marquis' trainers were noted as among the best in Italy, and Gino, the best of the best, had been working with the animal daily over a year's time, attempting to dispel the animal's fears and reassure it that humans could be friends and benefactors. The process was slow, as predicted, requiring patience on the part of the trainer and a focused attention on the part of the stallion. The animal was kept in a separate stall that enabled it to move about with some freedom and lie down if it wished. This stall opened into a narrow corridor about five times the stallion's length, and it could be closed off on both ends. Here Pazzo could be cross-tied, groomed, and shod when necessary.

The corridor led into the small indoor arena where Gino usually waited with lunge line and whip. The line was played out and the stallion was urged, at first, to run in circles, changing lead on the trainer's command. If he did well, he was rewarded with fruit and carrot. If he disobeyed, or was distracted, Gino would snap the whip to get his attention and begin the lesson again.

When the Maestro heard about the magnificence of the beast, he went to the stables with his workbook where he found Pazzo comparatively docile and at peace in his stall. He sketched the great horse seven times, from varying distances and near at hand, and then he wrote beside the sketches that "by the laws of linear perspective, every body at a distance loses those parts which are most thin. With Pazzo, the legs disappear first as I increase the distance between us, and then the neck, until one is left with only the torso, reshaped as an oval form, or rather translated into a cylinder, losing breath before length."

The Maestro's visit to the stallion was interrupted by the sudden appearance of Lizette who had come looking for Niccolo. At the sight of the dwarf, Pazzo became something from a nightmare, rearing and screaming in rage and slashing at the air and the stall with his forelegs and his hooves until Leonardo was afraid the animal might hurt himself. He quickly closed his workbook and ushered the young woman away.

The second item of interest evolving from the hunting forays of the court was the sudden unseating of Ser Johannes. Riding beside Madonna Maddalena, the young Belgian was mounted on Zanzara, a playful but gentled mare who acquired the name of "Mosquito," because she was given to swiftly darting away unless the rider maintained firm control by rein and stirrup.

According to reports received by the Maestro, and later affirmed by Ser Johannes himself, the hunting party had encircled a large wild boar in the wooden expanse. While the dogs and their handlers went about their work of flushing the beast from the thick underbrush, the Belgian amused his lady with stories of the mercantile world of Antwerp and Brussels.

Suddenly the massive boar, red-eyed and snorting in rage and frustration, broke loose of the entangling ferns and the heavy underbrush and started to dart back and forth across the clearing, slashing right and left with his great curved tusks. Startled, Zanzara reared and bolted. Johannes struggled to bring the mare under control, but it was useless, because the horse had taken the bit and was hurtling across the clearing and plummeting down the steep incline that led to the river. In an instant, too, the Belgian's saddle fell away leaving Johannes entangled by the right stirrup, and the rider was dragged for some distance before he slipped from his boot and lay moaning on the river's edge.

The item was worthy of note for the Maestro, because he later learned from the stablemaster that the cinch of Johannes' saddle appeared to have been cut half through. The rearing of the animal applied the necessary pressure to complete the severing, and the rider was unhorsed.

This second item of note in connection with this accident was inscribed in the Maestro's workbook and later transferred by Niccolo to the red book.

It read: "Initially Zanzara was to be Madonna Maddalena's mount, but the stablemaster said she exchanged the mare for Ser Johannes' chestnut gelding, because 'she liked the horse's eyes.'"

The Maestro also spent time working on the portrait of the marquesa. After a number of sittings and the creation of a clay bust, Leonardo completed a full-size cartoon of the portrait. His final decision was to paint the lady in half-length profile, looking off to her left. True to his convictions concerning beauty and adornment, the lady's hair was freed of snood or braid, falling gently down to her shoulder. She wore no jewels, no ermine headband, no gloves. Her right hand rested on her left, just below her bosom. The gown chosen by Leonardo was plain, cut low enough to suggest well-endowed breasts but revealing nothing. The dress was striped vertically with puffed sleeves from shoulder to wrist. True to life, the woman had a slightly double chin, a weak mouth, a prominent nose and a shortened neck.

But the eyes!

The Maestro painted them with heavy lids but focused intently on something out of the frame. She does not smile, and the eyes are penetrating, all-seeing. The eyes of a woman of intelligence and cunning.

A dangerous woman.

The winter became known as "the gift of the bull" in the chronicles of the courts of northern Italy, because the warm weather persisted throughout February and March and well into April. This was taken as a favorable omen for the Jubilee Year as proclaimed by the Borgian pope, whose emblem was the bull.

191

Leonardo, upset by the sight of Pazzo attempting to break from
his stall and attack Lizette, insisted that Niccolo go nowhere
near the stables. To keep him away from trouble, the Maestro
insisted on leading Niccolo into the sunny gardens for a lesson
on botany and the observation of trees and shrubbery. Niccolo,
who had a fascination for the games of the aristocrats, had
requested permission to ride with the others, but the Maestro
seemed determined to continue the dwarf's education that had
begun in the Certosa, and argued that "whatever exists in the
universe, either potentially or actually or in the imagination,
the artist has it first in his mind and then in his hands."

Astorre, the aged head gardener who was little more than a
bag of rags and tatters suspended from a bent frame of wheezes
and coughs, had a respect for Leonardo that bordered on adoration, and the old man insisted on joining the small class to
learn "everything" at the Maestro's elbow.

Astorre's assistant, Zecco, pretended to be turning the earth
in another part of the garden, when actually he was planning
to nap in a dry, cozy area behind a tall hedge.

Leonardo led Niccolo and the gardener along the pathway.
"Trees, as you can see, possess a wide assortment of green
hues and shades. Some tend toward blackness . . ."

"True!" Astorre said, his grey head bobbing up and down in
violent affirmation. "Firs and pines and laurels, all tend to be
dark. That's true, Maestro!"

Leonardo nodded and forced himself to smile. "Thank you.
Yes. While some tend to the darker hues, others tend toward
yellow . . ."

"Like chestnuts and oaks!" the gardener squealed.

Niccolo knew the endorsements of the aged man were beginning to annoy Leonardo, but he stifled a laugh and merely
said, "You have an enthusiastic pupil, Maestro."

"You can see that the branching of the elm, for example, is
wide and thin like a foreshadowed open hand, and . . . !"

Leonardo broke off his speech, and Niccolo turned to see
what had suddenly interrupted the lesson. The Maestro, brows

deep in a puzzled frown, was bent down studying a shrubbery. He ran his hand over the nearly bare branches, glanced quickly at the location of the sun, and then rubbed a bud between his fingers. He stood erect and began to turn slowly, scanning in all directions.

"What is it?" asked Niccolo.

"What is the matter, Maestro?" the old gardener wheezed.

"Why has this shrub been moved?" the Maestro asked quietly.

"Moved?" echoed Astorre. "Moved from where?"

Again Leonardo seemed to scan the surrounding plants and trees and then he pointed to a line of hedge. "From there, I would say."

The gardener looked to where the Maestro pointed and squinted in the light. "From there?"

"Surely you can see that the garden is completely symmetrical," Leonardo said. "Eight large polygons of grass bordered by these hedgings and shrubs and all oriented toward the large circular patch in the center and the fountain."

"Yes," Astorre nodded. "That is so. The fountain is the center."

"But look there," the Maestro commanded, again pointing to the hedging some distance away. "The border has been broken." He turned back to the shrubbery he had been examining. "And this single plant seems to be tacked on to the border of this section here. From the location of this moss and the stunted growth, it also has been plainly rotated. Anyone can see that it does not belong here. It destroys the symmetry. It unbalances the area."

Astorre began to nervously pace between the shrubbery and the place where Leonardo indicated it should be while at the same time bellowing as loudly as he could with his cracked voice, "Zecco! Zecco!"

The slovenly assistant appeared after a moment, reeking of manure and ambling slowly toward the master gardener in filthy work rags that seemed to be a colorful collection of the various fertilizers used throughout the gardens. "What is it now?" he groaned. "I was turning the earth for . . . !"

193

"Why was this shrub moved?" the old man screamed at his assistant.

Zecco stared at the gardener and then at the plant and then back at the gardener again. "How should I know?" he grumbled. "Who said it was moved anyway?"

"It is obvious!" the old gardener croaked at his assistant. "Look at the moss and the stunted growth, you moron! Look at the symmetry! It unbalances the entire area."

Zecco struggled to understand where the symmetry was destroyed. Finally he shrugged and muttered, "Maybe it moved by itself."

Astorre's pale and wrinkled face flushed with the disgrace of the moment. "By itself?" he shrieked. "By itself? What have we now? Frolicking firs? A parade of pines? Are you going to tell me, you spawn of a rancid she-goat, that this shrubbery danced over here? That it took it into its head to ramble ten braccia, because it liked the company of this hedging better?" He slapped a bony hand to his forehead. "What shall I do with such stupidity?" He pointed to the wayward plant and screeched, "Take it up! Take it up, you lazy pile of pigshit! Take it up now!"

Zecco mumbled something that could not be deciphered and began to grudgingly poke with his spade around the base of the shrub. The Maestro shook his head and led Niccolo and Astorre a little farther away. Here he fingered a branch of some hedging and said quietly, "Now see! Every branch of a plant that is not pulled down by its own weight curves toward the sky. And note that the twigs on the branches of these plants, those underneath, are bigger than those which are beginning to spout above."

Niccolo nodded, and continued to nod, through the brief enlightenment on branchings and the lustre of leaves and the response of trees to the wind's caress when suddenly Zecco gave a sharp cry that instantly drew the attention of all three to where he stood. The shrubbery had been uprooted and was lying on its side. As they approached him, the assistant seemed to be struggling against a foul odor for he continued to sweep his filthy hand back and forth before his face. As Niccolo and Leonardo came nearer, they caught the stench.

"What is it now, you baboon's backside?" Astorre railed at the ragged man as Zecco said nothing and pointed to the hole where the shrub had stood.

Astorre stared into the abyss and instantly backed away, blessing himself.

Niccolo reached Leonardo's side. "What is it?" he asked the Maestro.

Leonardo held a gloved hand to his nose and mouth, but the words were clear. "It is almost impossible to identify," he said quietly. "Some hair and a few folds of flesh are still attached to it, but the maggots and the worms have dined through the winter months on it."

Niccolo looked to where Zecco still stood pointing.

It was a human head, both eyes reduced to gelatinous masses, the lips all but severed and the teeth and jaws exposed!

The small swatches of hair that still clung to it were the color of autumn wheat.

Leonardo ordered Astorre to place the skull in a canvas bag, and then he carried it to the Camera and informed the marquis of the discovery.

"I don't understand," said Gian-Francesco. "The burial crypts for the Gonzaga family are on the grounds of Sant'Andrea, and our servants are usually interred in San Sebastiano. There has never been a battle fought here, and the records of Fra Bartolomeo, who has been in residence for nearly fifteen years, show no burials authorized here."

"Oh, I am certain it was not an authorized burial, Excellency," Leonardo said. "If it were a proper Christian burial, where is the body? The coffin? In addition, there were still some folds of flesh and strands of hair attached to the skull. I would determine that this head was interred no more than five or six months ago."

"My god," sighed the marquis as he melted into his chair. "What next?"

"With your permission, Excellency, I would like to take the skull to my workshop and examine it."

"Whatever for?"

"A general study of human anatomy, Excellency," Leonardo said. "About ten years past I was determined that the world could use a proper text on the human body. There is such ignorance on the subject. I have recently seen an Austrian text on the liver that is most certainly based on the liver of a baboon and not a human at all. I have been able to chart with some accuracy most of the vascular system and the placement of the principal organs." Leonardo noted that the marquis seemed distracted, so he dispensed with the remainder of his lesson on human anatomy. "Over the years I have made some sketches of human skulls that came into my possession from time to time, and I would like to make comparative measurements with this skull."

"To what end, Maestro?"

"Truth, Excellency."

Rome

Elisabetta da Gonzaga, kinswoman to Gian-Francesco and a former student with Isabella D'Este in the humanist school of da Feltre, arrived anonymously in Rome for the Holy Year. She had traveled with only a small entourage and arrived incognito in order to avoid the roving gangs of bandits and bravi who preyed upon travelers who might appear to have a little gold in their purses or an elegant wardrobe. She had come, as so many of the thousands that thronged the city, presumably to receive the plenary indulgences attached to the pilgrimage, but actually she was there to serve as a "silent emissary" for her kinsman, the marquis of Mantua.

The stately duchess of Urbino sat with infinite patience on a balcony overlooking the Via Alessandrina and watched as a small army of cardinals and civic functionaries inundated the Porta del Popolo to greet Cesare Borgia on his return to Rome. The duchess was visibly bored by the procession of a hundred mules mantled in black that preceded the actual parade of the Borgian family, although she joked with a retainer that the "similarity was striking." She nodded politely, returning the salutes from Cesare's brother, Jofre, and Lucrezia's present husband, Alfonso of Aragon, whom, she noticed, did not ride with his wife.

"Poor Alfonso," a lady-in-waiting whispered in her ear.

"The bird has already flown, and he has yet to recognize that the door of the cage is open."

The duchess stifled a laugh behind her fan, and then raised her eyes to heaven at the absurd allegory of the eleven chariots passing below her, each depicting events in the life of the "other Caesar," Julius.

The woman she had come to see, the Contessa Caterina Sforza, was not included in the procession, although Elisabetta knew that Cesare would have loved to have dragged the lady behind his horse in chains. The duchess reasoned that the absence of Caterina was probably due to the fact that the French had assumed responsibility for the prisoner following the reports of her outrageous and barbaric rape at the hands of Cesare.

"How frustrating it must be for the duke of Valentinois not to be able to parade the trophy of his boudoir victory," she whispered. "He wins so seldom."

Later, as she prepared to attend one of the endless festivals celebrating the Holy Year, one of her agents reported that "the contessa had been imprisoned in the Belvedere with twenty guards assigned to her, but the lady still managed to escape. Some say she seduced the captain of the guards, but it was to no avail. She was recaptured and is now in the deepest dungeons of the Castel Sant'Angelo where her warder is said to be Lucrezia Borgia herself."

Elisabetta smiled at the report as her ladies-in-waiting prepared her hair. An escape! And with twenty guards in attendance! She would expect nothing less of the woman who had proven herself a better diplomat and deceiver than Niccolo Machiavelli, a wife who had hurried to Forli to put down an uprising against her husband although she was in the latter stages of pregnancy, and a ruler who dragged another rebel ringleader through the streets by his hair.

"The woman is remarkable!" she said to her dressers. "I will never believe Caterina is dead until I see her body for myself, and even then I would wait three full days and expect a miracle."

Elisabetta surrendered herself unhappily to the next week of celebration which included an embarrassing race between Jews and old men fastened to the backs of donkeys and buffaloes. She attended and endured the bullfights in the Testaccio, but she was only visibly amused when two of the massive creatures escaped and sent the spectators racing for protection. She dozed behind her fan and veil at the Vatican ceremonies as the fat, hook-nosed pontiff elevated his bastard son to the rank of "captain-general and gonfalonier of the Church," investing him with the cloak and the crimson beretta and then handing him a standard bearing the Borgian arms, the keys of St. Peter, and the commander's baton of authority.

Finally, resigned to the fact that the contessa of Forli would probably never be released or arrange another escape from the Borgias, Elisabetta sat at her desk by the window looking out at the Castel Sant'Angelo and wrote Gian-Francesco.

"The story that the contessa appeared at Forli wearing a replica of the Tears of the Madonna was verified, cousin, by idle conversations I held with the French commander and one or two of his officers. Consequently, if another necklace similar to the Tears exists, you may be certain that it is now a part of the Vatican treasury, where, presumably, it has joined the third necklace worn earlier by Lucrezia Borgia, as reported by our cousin, Madonna Laura."

"I know you must find it disturbing, my dear Gian-Francesco," she wrote, "and I am at a loss to explain it, but in truth these necklaces seem to multiply faster than the bastard children to the Borgias."

Mantua

Leonardo barred the doors to the workshop and posted a notice that no one was to disturb him. He cleaned and scrubbed and bleached the skull until it was free of any tissue. He then mounted the skull on a framework of metal rods on a turning wheel. He worked with calipers and compasses and called out a long list of numerical measurements, which Niccolo was required to record. Then, to the dwarf's surprise, he began to recite a litany of comparative ratios. He took thin strips of wet clay and began to lay them in narrow, crisscross patterns on the skull, stopping after every addition to measure the depth with marked pegs. Within hours the skull seemed to suggest the merest outline of a human face with dozens and dozens of small white dowels driven into it at appropriate intervals.

Niccolo was then asked to repeat the ratios of facial proportions from the listings that Leonardo had prepared. To support him, he was given Leonardo's actual worksheets on the human face, and, as Niccolo called out each equation, the Maestro measured, added clay, removed some, smoothed others. The work sheets included a series of quick sketches detailing every degree of distance between eyes and cheek, nose and mouth, ears, eyebrows, lips and chin.

"The space between the slit of the mouth and the base of the nose is one-seventh of the face," Niccolo would read aloud, and Leonardo would trim and measure, add or delete some of

200

the wet clay. Then the dwarf would call out, "The space from the mouth to below the chin, that's marked 'cd' on your sketch, Maestro, is a quarter part of the face and similar to the width of the mouth."

Still the pattern of recital, addition, subtraction, measurement and adjusting continued. The space between the chin to below the base of the nose had to be precisely one-third of the face. The space between the midpoint of the nose and below the chin was exactly half the face. The distance from above to below the chin was one-sixth of the face and precisely one fifty-fourth of the man.

The forehead, cheeks, and nose began to form over the white bone.

Leonardo silently constructed the nose from two squares of clay, the width at the nostrils measuring exactly half the length between the tip of the nose and the start of the eyebrows.

The work continued throughout the long afternoon and deep into the night. Niccolo, while fascinated at the face slowly emerging from the clay, silently prayed that the Maestro might remember that humans also require nourishment and rest.

Long after midnight the work slowed. Finally Leonardo sighed, wet the clay, and covered it with a moist cloth.

"We will resume tomorrow morning," he said.

"Why?" Niccolo questioned him. "Are you trying to identify the man?"

"I already know who the unfortunate man was," the Maestro said softly as he cleansed his hands of the clinging pieces of clay. "Remember when you were trying to determine who was responsible for Madonna Maria's pregnancy in the Castello Sforezco? Remember that I said the identity would be obvious if . . . !"

"If I counted backward nine months!" Niccolo cried.

"Assume the skull is no more than four months buried," smiled Leonardo. "With what event does that date coincide?"

Niccolo reflected for a moment, and then his face brightened, and he said, "The disappearance of the courier from Venice!"

"Yes," sighed Leonardo. "At least now that much has been determined. The man *was* intercepted and murdered. His head was taken and buried in the gardens of the marquis in an attempt to hide his identity. Now I am attempting to reconstruct that face from the skull."

"But why?"

"Ah!" Leonardo nodded. "That is always the ultimate question."

Leonardo and Niccolo ate separately for the next few days, one person always staying with the clay bust. When the marquis came to talk to the Maestro concerning the model for the northern defenses of Venice, the bust remained covered, and the Maestro made no reference to it, simply informing Gian-Francesco that he was "making some comparative measurements."

When the doors had again been barred and the notice posted, Niccolo and Leonardo resumed their work on the skull. The width of the face was measured, and the eye sockets were placed so that the distance between the outer edge of each eye and the ear was exactly half the width. The width of the neck from the side was approximately the same distance from the chin to the jawbone, and the thickness of the neck was determined to be exactly one and three-quarters of the distance from the eyebrows to the nape of the neck.

Niccolo was stunned to see the face of a relatively young man slowly emerge from the wet clay. There were eyes and eyelids, eyebrows, cheeks and ears and a creased forehead. The chin was prominent, the neck relatively broad. The mouth was not wide, and the lips were thin and depicted as unsmiling.

"I know the man was blond from the few strands that were

still attached, but I have no way of knowing whether the eyebrows were thick or thin. The mouth," said Leonardo, "modeled precisely from the skull structure, will be fairly accurate."

"I am amazed," Niccolo said. "But if you feel this is the murdered courier, why go to all this trouble?"

"Aren't you curious?" said Leonardo as he removed and examined a peg and then replaced it as he adjusted the clay. "Wouldn't you like to see the resurrection of a murdered man? These lips might be able to speak volumes from the grave. They might even condemn his killer."

"How?"

"By confirming his identity first," the Maestro smiled, smoothing the finished product.

Leonardo took up a piece of parchment and quickly began to sketch the rebuilt skull. He then added highlights and dimension with chalk and tempera shading, a method known to Niccolo as "sfumato." In less than an hour, the face emerged from the parchment, a face with which neither the Maestro nor Niccolo were familiar, the face of a grim, purposeful, slightly frowning young man.

The face of Cecco.

When the sketching was completed, both profiles and a full-front view, the Maestro rolled up the parchments and began to scrape away the clay until the skull emerged again. Then he scrubbed and bleached it clean once more and had a servant take it, in the canvas bag, to Fra Bartolomeo for "proper burial."

"In a Catholic world," the painter instructed Niccolo, "always make small concessions to their rules of the game."

Ser Johannes abandoned the court, leaving under darkness and without a word to his host or hostess.

Madonna Maddalena "disappeared" with him.

Some said that the young Belgian had received a summons

from his uncle to return immediately, and secretly, to Antwerp. The young man, now madly in love with Madonna Maddalena, had persuaded the red-haired lady to accompany him. Others insisted that he saw the "accident" of the hunt as either a warning or a deliberate attempt on his life or that of the Madonna's, and he had wisely chosen to flee before the assassins completed their mission. Still others argued that the cut cinch was precisely that, a warning, and it succeeded in its purpose, which was to drive the Belgian and his paramour from the court.

Everyone agreed that the sudden departure was an ominous sign. There was a rise in activity of couriers racing to and from Venice, Milan, Verona, Ferrara, Padua, and Florence.

Something momentous was about to occur in northern Italy.

Two days later, Niccolo was relieved to see Lizette appear in the workshop. Elegantly gowned and smiling, she scolded him for ignoring her for nearly two weeks. He apologized and hinted that he and the Maestro were involved in a "grim business."

"Here!" the young man gloated as he handed Lizette the sketches. "Do you recognize this man?"

Lizette shook her curls. "No," she said quietly. "He's handsome enough. Do I know him?"

Niccolo was annoyed at the judgment of the dead man's "handsomeness," especially coming from a woman with whom he was beginning to form a personal relationship. "I suppose he's not totally hideous," Niccolo pouted. "But the point is moot, because the gentleman in question is dead. We uncovered a severed skull in the gardens. The Maestro applied his mathematical formulae, and now we have some idea what the man looked like."

"Well, I don't know him," said Lizette as she handed the sketches back to Niccolo. "He resembles a man who appeared in the court last autumn but it is difficult for me to say for certain, because the hair seems different and I cannot judge his height or weight. Furthermore, my own height does not always afford me an opportunity to study faces." Niccolo smiled, and Lizette gave a small laugh. "The gentleman in question was never formally introduced to us. I seem to recall he stayed only three or four days, appearing at all the meals and amusements, but then he was gone."

"Well," said Niccolo smugly, "then I have some startling news for you. That man was a courier from Venice, and the fact that his head has suddenly appeared in the garden ties his murder to *this* court."

The little woman frowned and began to fan herself quickly. "I prefer not to hear anymore," she pleaded. "Politics bores me. But if the game is information, I know something truly startling that was reported to the marquesa just an hour past."

The declaration didn't surprise Niccolo who had come to recognize the fact that the entire palazzo was honeycombed with the "dwarf panels" he uncovered in the Camera. He momentarily speculated as to whether there might be such panels in the walls of his own rooms, and whether the young woman might have been spying on him, perhaps as he readied himself for bed. The vision stimulated him, but he was not prepared for the pronouncement Lizette then made.

"There has been an uprising in Milan against the French," she whispered to him, "and the banished duke has returned with several legions of mercenaries supplied by the emperor. He was greeted in the streets by jubilant armorers and vast numbers of townspeople. The French mercenaries have thrown down their weapons and aligned themselves with the duke, as have some of the Gascon and Swiss mercenaries."

It took Niccolo a moment to realize the full importance of the news.

"That's right," Lizette said softly. "Il Moro once again rules Milan!"

The news of the return of Il Moro to power caused more than a ripple of anxiety throughout the palazzo and the garrison. The marquis quickly summoned his advisors and met secretly with envoys from Venice. Having only recently switched his allegiances to the Borgias, the question as to how the Mantuan court should respond to the return of the duke was the prime topic of conversation and dissension for three days. Most certainly the Borgias would rally the French forces and attempt to drive Il Moro back beyond the mountains, but it had become increasingly obvious that the townspeople of Milan and its fiefs had grown to hate the "invaders," hailed as "liberators" only four months earlier.

The fact that Il Moro had returned to Milan, and the recent flight of Ser Johannes and Madonna Maddalena, caused the marquesa to pace about Paradise in a constant cloud of fury. Her tirades fell not only on Meneghina but also on Nanino, who, in turn, made life miserable for the other dwarves. Isabella railed at her ladies-in-waiting, seeking to find out which one, if any, knew in advance of the defection of Madonna Maddalena. She reportedly threw a chamber pot at the garrison watch commander for permitting the two young people to ride away without so much as a challenge or a request for permission. Leonardo observed that these rages seemed "staged," and that the marquesa appeared "more genuinely disturbed" when she was informed by her husband that there would be no spring festival, because of the scarcity of funds, the pending departure of the marquis for Venice, and the uncertainty of the political picture.

The marquis also informed her that when he returned to Venice, Maestro Leonardo would accompany him, so that the painter-engineer could meet with the council and the doge and outline his plans for the defense of the city. She could not even protest, because the Maestro was now plainly in the employ of her husband.

What was even more unsettling for the marquesa were the reports from Nanino that the workshops and the private quarters of Niccolo and Leonardo had been thoroughly searched, and there was still no trace of the red book. In addition, the Maestro and his dwarf accomplice had been asking intriguing questions in the court concerning the Tears, had interviews with both Johannes and Madonna Maddalena before they fled from the court, and had uncovered a human skull in the gardens.

"Perhaps," she murmured to Meneghina that evening, "I have been ignoring our guests for too long a period. Tomorrow morning I would like you to summon the Maestro's dwarf to meet with me in the Camera."

"To what purpose, Excellency?" asked the chamberlain.

"To determine whether it might be necessary to take certain steps," she said quietly.

The next afternoon Meneghina appeared at the open door of the workshop and announced, "Ser Niccolo da Pavia! The Marquesa requests your presence immediately!"

The dwarf and the Maestro exchanged quick worried glances, and then Niccolo slipped from the bench to the footstool and crossed to the chamberlain.

"I am at her Excellency's service," he said with a false bravado.

"That's wise of you," smiled Meneghina.

The marquesa sat in an ornate high-backed chair placed on a dais at one end of the Camera degli Sposi and gestured for Niccolo to seat himself in the chair facing hers. Although they were alone in the room, the painted figures on the walls and ceiling made it seem as if the entire court had assembled to witness the interview. Niccolo also wondered if someone might not be listening in the dwarves' panel.

At first it seemed that the marquesa was simply inquiring after the happiness and comfort of the Maestro and the dwarf. She seemed relieved to hear that Leonardo had completed the cartoon for her portrait in chalk and charcoal and was transferring the image to canvas. She had heard that Niccolo had become "close friends" with Lizette, and she seemed to approve of the relationship. She questioned the young man about the skull in the garden, but Niccolo dispelled any concerns by telling the lady that it "appeared to have been interred for some time" and that Leonardo had made "comparative measurements" and then assigned it to Fra Bartolomeo for proper Christian burial.

She informed him of the cancellation of the spring festival and expressed her regret that the Maestro would no longer be required to "demonstrate his many talents" by designing the pageant sets and costumes.

"In a way, marquesa," the dwarf replied, "it might prove a blessing. After all, the festival would only amuse and entertain the members of the court. Think how much better it would be if your Excellency arranged an amusement that would benefit the townspeople as well."

"What do you mean?" Isabella asked.

"Something quite different and quite new," he replied. "I know your Excellency is fond of entertainments, and I think it would reflect favorably upon the court if you were one of the first to endorse the new peoples' theatre."

"Whatever in the world is the peoples' theatre?"

"It is called *commedia dell'arte*, and all who have witnessed it have found it to be amusing and exhilarating. I myself had the good fortune to travel with such a troupe for a brief period, and I can assure your Excellency that they are exceedingly droll and entertaining. Full of surprises."

"I think I have had my fill of surprises for one winter," the marquesa frowned. "Where are these montebanks now?"

"They have only recently returned to Lombardy and are playing nearby at Legnano."

"Ah, my friend," the lady sighed. "But you see I am afraid I cannot afford to pay for another amusement. That was why the marquis decided against the spring festival."

"You need not pay the commedians," Niccolo said. "They perform in the streets for whatever monies the people choose to give them."

"In the streets?" frowned the marquesa. "Are they some sort of vagabond or mummer?"

Niccolo said, "They improvise. They create their comedies from a simple idea, a sogetto. They have a number of these in repertory, but even when they perform the same piece every day, it is always different. Sometimes the sequences take a completely illogical course, depending upon the mood of the actors and the responses of the audience."

"But street performers!" said the marquesa. "Would it be proper to have such people play in the court?"

Niccolo played his final card. "They have played in the courts at Ferrara and Urbino. And they entertained at the festival celebrating the construction of the new palazzo of Sanseverino in Milan." He lowered his voice. "Il Moro was fascinated by them, and invited them to the court on two separate occasions."

He did not mention that the second invitation was because the steward reported a number of items missing after their initial performance.

The reference to Il Moro was not wasted on Isabella. The marquesa immediately attached a political profit to the proposition.

"Indeed?" she said. "What would be expected of me?"

"A simple invitation. Some small accommodations, although the players usually sleep in their own wagons. Meals. Nothing more."

The marquesa suddenly rose and offered her hand to Niccolo who took it gently and kissed it.

"I shall see to it!" she declared. "How are they called again?"

"I Comici Buffoni," Niccolo replied. "The company of clowns."

Near the end of the month Gian-Francesco Gonzaga prepared to depart for Venice and announced to his wife that "Maestro Leonardo will accompany me and stay in Venice for a week or two to detail the concept of flooding the northern plains to the doge and the council."

"But the Maestro was commissioned to do a portrait of me," she said softly. "These diversions, as vital as they may be for

209

the defense of Venice against the Turks, have prevented him from working at his assignment."

"It cannot be helped," the marquis informed her. "These are turbulent times, and his plan has possibilities. He is acknowledged as a master engineer as well as a painter, and I have even received an inquiry from Cesare Borgia as to the possibility of the Maestro being loaned to him for the purpose of designing war machines."

"Ridiculous!" snorted the marquesa. "I hope you refused."

"I have replied that this is not the time to honor the request because the Maestro is vital to the defense of Venice. I have attempted to soothe the refusal by saying it may become possible for the Maestro to meet and serve briefly with the duke of Valentinois after our return from Venice."

"I hardly think that will placate the Borgian bastard."

"It will suffice for the time. Cesare is bound to be involved with the French in recapturing Milan," the marquis said. "The Maestro would also like to have Ser Niccolo accompany him to Venice."

The marquesa seemed to pale. "Oh really, Gian-Francesco. You ask too much. Only recently the brilliant young man suggested an amusement to replace the spring festival that will cost us nothing and will entertain not only the court but the townspeople as well."

"An amusement?"

"A series of performances by a new type of montebank. One performance in the court and several in the piazzi for the townspeople. Ser Niccolo is the only one who has witnessed their comedies, and he is needed here to prepare the invitation to the troupe and to choose the selected places in the city where their wagons can be arranged. I absolutely cannot continue without him, Gian-Francesco!"

The marquis frowned, but he sighed and nodded. "Very well," he said. "I will inform the Maestro that Ser Niccolo is needed here. Their separation will be no more than a week at most, and that should provide you with enough time to plan and coordinate this little 'amusement.' "

She rose and kissed him lightly on the forehead. "Thank

you, my dear," she said. "I try so hard to maintain your court as a center of cultural activity."

"I forgive you," smiled the marquis.

That afternoon a handwritten note from the marquis informed Leonardo that Niccolo would be needed in the court to prepare for the performances of the *commedia* troupe. It was the first time that Leonardo had heard of I Comici Buffoni returning to Mantua, but the prospect seemed to please him.

"You realize, of course, the real reason my request for you to accompany me was refused?" asked the Maestro.

"I thought that was plain enough," the dwarf replied. "I am to coordinate the performances. You should be grateful, because it means you are freed of the burden of designing a festival for the spring."

"There is plenty of time to 'coordinate the performances,' as you put it," the Maestro informed him. "You could go to Venice with me and still perform your duties for the marquesa upon your return."

"Then why was your request denied?"

"Because the marquesa saw through my design. Once in Venice we could go anywhere we chose. There would be no way the marquesa could force us back to Mantua."

"Do you mean the marquesa is using me as some sort of hostage?" Niccolo asked. "To guarantee your return here?"

"Precisely."

"But why?"

"Because she refuses to let us both leave until she determines that we do not have what she is seeking."

"The red book?"

"Yes," the painter nodded. "That has become something of value again. It is even more important for her purposes now that Il Moro has returned to Milan."

"But our quarters have been searched a number of times," Niccolo said. "And the book remains where I placed it. This surely must have convinced the marquesa that it is not in our possession."

"Apparently not," the Maestro observed quietly, "because she intends to keep you here while I ride with the marquis to Venice. Her determination is impressive, but her plan is as transparent as . . . !"

"As what?"

"As glass."

GLASS

March 1500

Mantua

The Maestro and the marquis departed for Venice on the first day of March. Leonardo was permitted to ride in a light coach-and-four while Gian-Francesco and his four top officers rode on horseback in their gleaming armor. Behind the coach rode six mounted and armed mercenaries in metal helmets and hauberks of mail with shields bearing the lion crest of Venice.

Niccolo and Meneghina waved good-bye to the party from the steps of the palazzo, but the marquesa, watching from the windows of Paradise, did not salute her departing husband. Instead, as soon as the party had passed under the portcullis and rode on to the main road, she turned to the dwarf who sat upon her bed and said, "Now, little monkey, we have the time and the means."

Verona

The party traveled to Venice by a northeastern route that took them first to Verona. The Maestro spent most of the time exploring a text on the past popes and the achievements of their respective reigns. Then, as they passed over the Adige River, the marquis reined his horse alongside the coach and drew the Maestro's attention to certain buildings, delivering a commentary on each.

On every palazzo the sign of the ladder was prominently displayed and Gian-Francesco explained that this was the arms of the Della Scala family who controlled the region, although Verona was in Venetian territory and under the protection of the doge. The marquis pointed to the huge Roman arena in the heart of the city, and the Maestro shuddered, imagining the Christians and the gladiators who lost their lives in that bloody hollow of marble.

In the Piazza delle Erbe, the party paused long enough to water the horses and to purchase fresh fruit from the vendors who lined the piazza under enormous rectangular umbrellas that protected their wares from the sun and the rain.

The entourage continued past the Palazzo della Ragione at a walk, and the Maestro made a hurried sketch of the medieval tower and of the building opposite, the graceful arches of the Loggia del Consiglio bending like marble rainbows from column to column the entire length of the covered walkway. The route then took them past the Palazzo del Governo where they did not stop to pay their respects to the Della Scala, although the guns of the fortress saluted them, and mobs of townspeople, wondering who the visiting dignitaries might be, saw the lion impresa on the officers' breastplates and cheered.

The square by the Gothic church of Sant'Anastasia led into a shady roadway that paralleled the Adige and permitted a cool breeze to sweep into the musty coach and refresh the Maestro. The party crossed the Adige at the Ponte Pietra, and passed a huge construction project involving crenellated walls and towers, all prominently displaying the ladder standard. The marquis pointed out the church of San Zena Maggiore set down between two medieval bell towers. He volunteered the information that his court painter, Mantegna, had painted the Madonna that hung above the main altar. The Maestro requested that the party pause here, because he wanted to see Mantegna's work, and the marquis grudgingly agreed. The Maestro spent nearly half an hour in the church, and when he returned he was accompanied by two priests carrying a sealed carton, which they deposited inside the coach.

The attention of the Maestro was diverted, then, by a silent, brooding figure who stood gazing at the great rose window of the church. His hooded robe stretched from the top of his head to midcalf, but he was plainly no religious. He wore a sword and dagger prominently displayed, and his face was shadowed. What interested the Maestro most, however, was the emblem on the sleeve of the robe.

Two arcs divided by a straight line.

Vicenza

The marquis obviously thought Vicenza to be less interesting than Verona, because the party maintained a quick pace through the city, and Gian-Francesco rode at the head of the column. They galloped past a succession of palaces and churches, mostly in the Gothic style preferred by the Venetians, and through the Piazza dei Signori where the city's basilica towered.

There was a great deal of dust in the air, and Leonardo reasoned this was due to the vast construction of palazzi and villas along the route. He had not agreed to accompany the marquis simply to present the model and the plans for the northern defenses to the doge. Somewhere in Venice, he was certain, was the key that would open the final door to the truth about the Tears of the Madonna.

Padua

At Padua, the party slowed in an obvious attempt to attract attention as the marquis deliberately paraded his entourage through the Corso del Popolo and across the Bacchiglione River, past the Cappella Scrovegni, and through the marketplace of the Piazza della Regione where they were cheered lustily by the merchants and their customers. They continued at this pace past the basilica of Sant'Antonio, and the Maestro scanned Donatello's huge equestrian statue of Gattamelata, remembering his own clay model of the Milanese condottiere, he was suddenly swept under by a wave of regret and melancholy. He drew the damask curtains and refused to look out.

They spent the night in Padua at a comfortable inn chosen by the marquis. "One has to be careful of such choices," Gian-Francesco explained to the Maestro over a dinner of veal, fish in aspic, a minestra of vegetables, and slabs of ham. "The cities of the Venetian arc have established several legal brothels that pose as taverns, and food and comfort are not their principal offerings."

"The doge licenses brothels?" asked the Maestro.

"It is a matter of good business," the marquis shrugged as he sipped at his mulled wine. "Emissaries, especially the Germans, expect whores to be made available for them. Venice offers travelers and diplomats a catalogue of available prostitutes, their addresses and their prices, which range from two ducats for the conventional puttana to ten or twelve ecus for famous courtesans." He leaned closer and laughed as he said, "That is why, some say, it is called the Most Serene Republic."

As Leonardo merely smiled and did not join him in the laughter, Gian-Francesco drew back to his own side of the table. "Venetian whores do not operate with impunity, you understand," he added quickly. "They must wear special red caps as a sign of their profession, and soliciting from the gondolas is banned, as is wearing men's clothes. And, of course, we distinguish between the cortegiane, independent courtesans who own their own apartments, and the meretrici, women attached to the houses."

"I find this surprising," murmured Leonardo. "It was only three years ago that Venetian censors forced a publisher of Ovid's *Metamorphoses* to remove illustrations of naked women and phallic deities."

"True," nodded the marquis, momentarily flushed. "Throughout the arc, both Church and the Republic sponsor brothels, and profit rather handsomely from them."

"The Church also licenses brothels?"

"Why not?" the marquis replied with a shrug. "The cardinal himself has expressed the opinion that such sexual activity enhances the good, the piety and the honor of the whole commune."

"Indeed?" murmured Leonardo, his thick eyebrows arched in surprise.

"These licensed institutions cut the rate of illegitimacy and prevent the transmission of sexual disease," the marquis explained, and Leonardo realized that Gian-Francesco was actually defending his attendance in such places. He suddenly remembered Niccolo's report from the Contessa Bergamini that the marquis himself was secretly being treated for syphilis. "That is because the whores are subject to medical inspection by licensed midwives," he continued. "You must understand, Maestro, that Venice has a disproportionate number of influential unmarried men, some figures say as high as fifty percent."

"Why?"

"Because by not marrying, these men protect their family fortunes," the marquis smiled. "But they are normal males. They have appetites that must be satisfied, eh? And you must understand that Venice is constantly visited by peoples from both the east and the west, and their sexual customs, which can range from the conservative to the bizarre, cannot be ignored. Furthermore these licensed brothels keep prices low and divert young men from homosexual alliances."

The mention of sodomites made the Maestro plainly uncomfortable, remembering his own defense in the ecclesiastical trials in which he was charged anonymously.

"Of course," he said softly, and he finished the meal in silence.

Venice

The small contingent arrived in "the Most Serene Republic" the following day. The sight of the city built on water had first impressed Leonardo when he visited with Il Moro's court ten years earlier, but the image had remained with him, the overwhelming lagoon and the serpentine Grand Canal that served to bind the islands into a common city. The brooding sky, an immense canopy that stretched from horizon to horizon, was reflected in the waters, leaving the impression that the islands were afloat somewhere between heaven and earth. Leonardo remembered it to be an intimate city, crowded, crisscrossed by narrow walkways and bounded by numerous waterways so that it was impossible to walk from one point to another without meeting an acquaintance. It was this lack of privacy that had repelled Leonardo on his initial visit. He theorized that this also accounted for the typical Venetian attitude: gossipy, nitpicking, opinionated, and conservative. Those Venetians who preferred the vulgar tongue to Latin even spoke a regional Italian that initially surprised and confused visitors from any other city.

Still, he had also found the Venetians to be generous and fun-loving. Venetians were tolerant to the point of licentiousness, because tolerance is good business, and Venice was a city of a thousand businesses, the financial and mercantile center where Europe and the Ottoman Empire met to buy and sell.

Leonardo, surveying the city from his coach, promised himself that he would complete his own business and return to Mantua as soon as possible.

They arrived on the hour to the tolling bells in the campanile of San Marco. Their passage through the Cannaregio district was slowed and frequently halted by enormous masses of masked people dressed in fantastic costumes that ranged from the beautiful to the bizarre to near nakedness. The revelers thronged the narrow streets, singing and dancing to the music of flute, pipes, and drum, hurling strings of paper streamers and clouds of minute, glossy stars at one another.

The marquis passed the reins of his horse to a subordinate and took temporary refuge from the deluge of paper with Leonardo in the coach.

"Carnivale!" he said with a shrug. "Mimes, caperings, bedlam! It will be this way until Ash Wednesday and the beginning of Lent." He drew back as a false egg thrown by a laughing reveler smashed against the sill of the coach's window, and almost at once the interior was filled with a perfume that hinted at roses.

"I should have considered the carnival when I suggested you join me, Maestro," the marquis apologized. "It will be madness."

"I do not mind," Leonardo replied softly. No, he thought, crowded streets and the confusion of the revelry will serve my purposes very well.

"And tomorrow," the marquis sighed, "will be worse, because it will be the first of the four days of the Beggar Lords."

Leonardo was familiar with carnival, but the days of the Beggar Lords was an innovation that had developed in Rome and then spread north. During the four days the revelers paraded placards in the streets showing a giant crescent moon overwhelming a miniature and inverted earth, the world turned upside-down. Days in which the poor and the drudge could acquire enough wonderful memories to carry them through the next forty days of Lent and beyond. On these days, he knew, even the most modest and proper young women and the most dedicated young men studying for the priesthood would join with beggars and cutpurses and whores and bound into the palatial homes of the most prosperous merchants without being stopped, because the wealthy, especially these merchants who had amassed greater fortunes than the young nobles had inherited from their ancestors, were forbidden by custom to bar their doors to any of the revelers. Wearing grotesque masks they could gleefully and arrogantly rearrange or "borrow" the merchant's furniture, snatch food from his tables and his scullery, mock his art and add obscene and pornographic works to his collection, down barrels of his better wine and invade his cellars for the hidden best, and then, perhaps, make communal love in the downy softness of the master's private bed chamber.

As a student in Florence, Leonardo had heard stories of low-born revelers being joined by the mistress of the house who jubilantly stripped herself of the restraints of her position and her rich garments to frolic with the youthful invaders in an orgiastic communion of lust and licentiousness.

Now, watching the brazen women laughing and flirting with the bravi in the piazza, Leonardo leaned back into the upholstered seat, stroked his beard, and murmured, "*Spectatum veniunt, veniunt spectentur ut ipsae.*"

He was pleased with his Latin.

The escorted coach crossed the western bridge over the Grand Canal into the district of San Polo. Here the marquis decided they must abandon the coach, which was too wide for most of the narrow streets and passages. Leonardo was provided with one of the extra mounts, and the procession continued past the immense Gothic church of the Franciscans and the Scula di San Rocco. They worked their way through the larger piazza of the Campo San Polo, which was inundated with carnival revelers, and Leonardo was distracted momentarily by a toy being thrown by a small boy from the balcony overhead. It was a weighted box from which a corkscrew-shaped wing spiraled upward. When dropped, the wind would turn the wing and keep the toy in the air for a long time. As it slowly descended, Leonardo wondered if the principal might not work in reverse: men working a winch to turn the wing to lift the unit.

I must think on that, he reflected.

The procession passed through the massed and masked crowds to the Rialto where it crossed another bridge spanning the Grand Canal. Large gondolas filled with drunken revelers passed one another, exchanging wine by tossing the bottles back and forth and singing.

On the other side of the bridge was the San Marco district. Their horses cantered down the Street of the Beans and the Street of Wine, named for the products offered by the vendors who lined both sides of the thoroughfares. In the Piazza San Marco, throngs of people snake-danced around the square, sending the pigeons flying.

The party paused momentarily in the shadow of the basilica with its lunettes over the main doors depicting St. Mark's vision of angels. The towering church was known as "the temple of thieves," because thieves sent by the doge reportedly stole the body of Saint Mark the Evangelist from Islamic guards and snuck it into Venice among layers of pickled pork to its present resting place in the basilica. Among the items stolen by Venetian admirals after the fall of Constantinople were the four gilded bronze horses, rare marbles, and icons heavy with gems that now filled the cathedral.

That's all right, the Maestro thought to himself. A good thief is precisely what I may need to complete my work here.

The palace of the doge of Venice, a fantasy of white and pink marble, was set at one end of the Piazzeta San Marco. To the Maestro the building was a visible symbol of the spirit of carnival. It seemed to have been constructed upside-down with the heavy rooms of the upper floors resting on the thin colonnades of the lower.

They entered the palace grounds through the guarded Gate of the Card. Despite the traditions of carnival and the Beggar Lords, no one, reveler or emissary, would attempt to pass through this gate without the written permission of the doge himself. The marquis, once again at the head of the mounted escort, was immediately recognized, and the small caravan was admitted to the inner courtyard without challenge.

Leonardo stepped down and watched as a small covey of servants immediately fluttered down the expansive Staircase of the Giants to assist the arrivals with their horses and possessions, including the Maestro's model and the plans rolled tightly within leather cylinders. Leonardo gazed at the huge statues of Mars and Neptune that flanked the staircase and wondered what the late Florentine monk, Savonarola, would say to this display of pagan deities.

Once inside the palace, the marquis assumed an authority and an influence that rivaled that of his own marquisate. Guards snapped to attention as he led the Maestro down a maze of hallways, through large rooms, up monumental staircases, and into the Great Council Hall where the Doge of Venice and members of his Council of Ten were already gathered and waiting for them.

During his earlier visit with Il Moro, Leonardo had not been invited into the Great Hall, so he was eager to see it now. He noted the richly carved ceiling, the abundance of natural light, and the frieze of portraits of the past doges around the upper part of the walls. His attention was drawn to the void that should have been occupied by the portrait of Doge Marin Faller. He was pleased that he could read the Latin inscription beneath the hole that stated simply that Faller had been executed for treason one hundred and fifty years earlier.

Venetians, he thought, are unforgiving.

The doge himself was an old man, robed in scarlet and ermine and bent under the weight of several massive golden chains from which were suspended his medallions of authority. Leonardo had expected this. He understood that it was traditional for Venetians to choose an old man as their supreme civil authority, because he would not have time enough in his life-span to inflict any lasting damage on the Most Serene Republic.

The marquis snapped to attention in a smart salute which the doge, seated on his high-backed chair of state, acknowledged with a small nod.

"Magnificence," Gian-Francesco began, "and most illustrious and most revered lords, may I have the honor to present to you Maestro Leonardo di Ser Piero da Vinci, painter, sculptor, and engineer of Florence and late of Milan and Mantua. I believe he has a solution to our mutual problem to the north."

Leonardo's explanation of the model and the plans for flooding the plains was expedited by Jacopo de Barbari's "bird's eye" map of Venice, which showed nearly every house, byway, and piazza in the city. It was compared with Leonardo's sketches and with a map of Venice and the islands of the lagoon rendered by Francesco Rosselli thirty years earlier. The Maestro took the opportunity to not only use the maps to demonstrate his theory that restraining walls could be built and fortified, but he quickly scanned them to locate the three places in the city that interested him personally.

The palazzo of the Cambio. The island of Murano. And the Campo Sant'Angelo that led into the Street of the Assassins.

Following the explanation of his theory and the demonstration on the model, the doge said quietly, "We are also concerned, Maestro, that a Turkish attack on Cyprus would endanger our Famagusta. Are you familiar with that problem?"

"The marquis mentioned it in passing. It would appear to me that the best defense would be to keep the battlements free of ladders and grappling irons."

"It is a very long wall."

"I had in mind a battery of giant forks, each with seven

tines, that are attached to winches turned by oxen in underground compartments," said Leonardo.

"Giant forks?"

"As the basic unit is maneuvered along at the base of the
wall, they would sweep the battlements of invading ladders."

"Giant forks?" the doge repeated.

Leonardo nodded, but he could see that the idea seemed
ridiculous to the old man and the council members.

To their credit no one laughed.

Leonardo was quickly thanked for his attention and his dedication to the welfare of Venice, given a medallion of merit, and
informed that an armed escort would be made available for his
return to Mantua.

Leonardo pleaded to be allowed two more days in "your
magnificent city to visit the churches and to see the works of
the local artisans," and this seemed to unsettle both the marquis and the members of the council. The doge, however, took
the request as a compliment and assured the Maestro that he
would be provided with living quarters in the palace while he
stayed in Venice, and that the escort for his return to Mantua
would be "available whenever you so desire." His presence,
naturally, would be expected at the formal state dinner that
evening celebrating the return of the captain-general of the
Venetian armies and the arrival in court of a Florentine ambassador, Ser Niccolo Machiavelli.

The dinner that evening was lavish to the point of excess. The
doge and his lady sat at a separate and elevated table under a
canopy made of woven gold. A single line of armed lancers,
placed about six bracci apart, formed a boundary between the
aristocratic ruler and the two "guest tables" that were placed
in parallel and stretched nearly the entire width of the room.
At one of these tables Leonardo was placed between an elderly
woman, who persisted in speaking loudly and at length on the
"barbaric treatment" she had received on a recent visit to Flor-

ence, and a much younger and seemingly bored lady of the court. On the opposite side of this lady sat the Florentine ambassador Machiavelli, a clean shaven and exceptionally thin man whose eyes seemed focused on his companions, but whose attention was everywhere. From time to time he stroked his chin and ran a hand around the base of his neck to separate his long hair from the collar of his tunic, but he did not acknowledge Leonardo.

The conversation in general was less spirited, more subdued than in the court at Mantua, and Leonardo felt this may have been a result of the four massed choirs and musicians who maintained a constant flow of melody throughout the long evening. He smiled at the ostentatious placement beside each plate of not only a silver, three-tined fork depicting a half-naked pagan goddess, but also an ivory-handled knife whose blade was engraved with the words and music of the first few bars of the Benedicte. This combining of the sacred with the profane amused the Maestro who began to realize how carefully the Venetians trod the narrow line between the freedom demanded of art and the moral restrictions imposed by the Church.

The meal itself could have fed half the population of Mantua for a year.

There were such refinements as artichoke hearts, sweetbreads, frogs' legs, truffles, grated Parmesan, liver crepinettes, kidneys and cocks' combs, prugnoli mushrooms, songbirds roasted and served on spits, slabs of tongue, the customary soup of pigeons and almond paste, stuffed Lombard geese, venison shaped like lions, and pasties of pheasant.

But it was the gifts of the Adriatic Sea that were most abundant and painstakingly prepared. Salmon smoked and baked, roasted whale tongue served with orange sauce, fresh oysters, platters of crayfish and brill and herring, half fresh, half salted, fillets of carp and giant platters of broiled lobster nesting in seas of steamed mussels.

Leonardo, as usual, ate sparingly.

During one of the latter courses, a servant touched the Maestro lightly on one shoulder and handed him a small slip of paper indicating that it came from Machiavelli.

The message was curt and curious.

It read: "I must speak privately with you before you depart the court," and it was signed simply with an "M."

When the Maestro awoke the following day, he was greeted by a gaggle of servant women who brought him nourishment, prepared a bath for him, laid out his clothing for the day, and informed him that one of the council members wished to see him before he ventured out into the city.

The council member, Ser Antonio, had two surprises for the Maestro. The first was a young man, Giacomo Grottino, whom he labeled an "official guide."

"Ser Giacomo will see to it that no harm comes to you, Maestro," Antonio explained with a great deal of charm and a perpetual smile. "During carnival, the revelers occasionally turn rowdy, and there are small quarrels that erupt into fights and, occasionally, riots. Ser Giacomo is a native of the city and will prove to be acquainted, I'm sure, with every place you may wish to visit. He will suggest the best and least precarious way of reaching your destination. I am certain he will prove of value to you."

Leonardo thanked Ser Antonio and nodded to Ser Giacomo who was armed with two stilettoes and a sword. The Maestro knew perfectly well that this "guide" was an official spy who would report back to the Council of Ten where he went, to whom he spoke, and what he did. If he objected to having a spy trailing in his wake, the council would only point out that the "city is in a state of war with the Turks and security must be maintained."

The second surprise was a folded parchment sealed with wax that bore the impresa of the Florentine republic.

"There seems to be some turmoil in or around the republic

of Florence," Ser Antonio explained. "Ser Niccolo Machiavelli was suddenly and immediately called back. He had indicated that he wished to meet with you, but, being denied this honor by the demands of government, he left this document for you. He said it would explain all that he wished to make known to you."

Leonardo turned the parchment over in his hands trying to determine if Ser Antonio had opened and read it, but there were no signs of reheating or tampering.

The Maestro thanked Ser Antonio for his kindness, informed Giacomo that he would meet with him at the entrance to the palace, and then retired to his room where he opened and read the letter from Machiavelli.

Then, slinging one of the leather cylinders that held his sketches over one shoulder, the Maestro descended to the ground floor to meet Giacomo.

"Where would you like to go first, Maestro?" the young man inquired. "The basilica perhaps? Or the Bridge of Sighs? The Rialto?"

Leonardo's response surprised Giacomo.

"I would like to visit the costume shops on the Calle Boteghe and the Monodonovo," he said.

The Piazza San Marco was already filled with people in multicolored masks and outrageous costumes that ranged from a few carefully placed feathers to long flowing robes of silver and gold with wide sleeves and giant cuffs. Despite the early hour and the chill in the air, montebanks were swallowing fire and rope dancing, and mimes lining the piazza silently ridiculed the lordly nobility and the clergy. There were jugglers and acrobats and men with trained bears surrounded by circles of delighted women and children. Ragged beggars in half-masks and fishwives in dominoes linked hands and were dancing in a long chain to a saltarello being played on a flute. Leonardo saw a skeletal wraith of a man, who normally would appear crippled and barely able to crawl around the piazza on his wheeled begging board, suddenly rise and begin cavorting and gamboling on two very strong legs as he piped the revelers through the laughing and singing crowds.

"Carnival," Giacomo explained with a sigh.

On the Rialto, Leonardo purchased some sheets of music which he learned were newly printed with moveable type by Ottavio de Petrucci. He bought lithograph copies of Hieronymous Bosch's 'Ship of Fools' and Botticelli's 'Mystic Nativity,' hoping that if he provided his "guide" with enough things to carry, the young man would tire and abandon Leonardo to his own devices.

He was introduced to a uniformed gentleman whom, Giacomo explained, was one of the officials establishing the new and private "postal service" between Venice and Brussels by boat, horse and coach. Fascinated, Leonardo asked if he could make use of it, paying the customary fee of course, and the official, recognizing Giacomo as an agent of the Ten, quickly agreed. They stepped into a columned arcade where the Maestro was provided with paper and pen, and the letter, addressed to Ser Johannes Vendramm of the Hanseatic League, was quickly and officially sealed and placed in a pouch that would leave the city within an hour.

A mob of revelers surged by and around Leonardo and Giacomo as they stepped back into the street. The Maestro shook his head at the wild and raucous commotion. After dusk, Giacomo informed him, giant bonfires would glow. Inebriated men, liberated women and delighted children, who would normally be forbidden near fire, would weave and sing in human circles around the flames. Sometimes the more daring and self-confident would leap over the fires to show their strength and their courage, if not the state of their insobriety induced by consuming barrels of free beer and wine.

Leonardo and his guide discussed the carnival, Giacomo insisting these festivities were arranged by the nobility, because "they see that the common people need something to forget their despair."

Whatever the motive, Leonardo could see that these were obviously some of the happiest times of the year for the working people of the city. Everyone seemed to want to turn the world topsy-turvy, to make emperors of peasants and fools of kings. The lords served their servants. The grooms rode the mounts whose excrement they shoveled through the rest of the year. Beggars and cutpurses stormed into churches and emerged as bishops or cardinals, after forcing mythical and shocking confessions from the nuns. In the piazzas this afternoon, he was told, the revelers would enthusiastically help choose the Marquesa of Misrule and Duke Kick-Ass, and these mock nobility would then preside over the evening's festivities. The women, normally silenced and restricted, cavorted madly through the streets in masks, lifting their skirts upon request or for a few proffered coins. Some women, dressed as men, would pull ploughs or parade with phallic ornaments through the narrow streets and sing obscene lyrics to familiar hymns. Men, dressed as abnormally big-bosomed women, would strut and prance and occasionally flip their petticoats to moon the revelers.

Nothing was forbidden.

The palazzo of the Cambio was in the Dorsoduro district of Venice.

Leonardo and Giacomo made their way through the singing and dancing crowds snaking through the Campo Sant'Angelo, down the Street of the Spice Dealers and across the Accademia Bridge. They had to pick their way through the throngs of people who jostled one another outside the mask shops on the Calle Boteghe and the Monodonovo. These were the unfortunates who waited until the last moment to purchase carnival disguises and now would be charged ridiculously high prices.

Believing they would be less conspicuous, and therefore less vulnerable to insults and objects hurled by the revelers, Leonardo and Giacomo purchased costumes and masks.

Leonardo chose the dark robes of a necromancer for Giacomo, and he himself chose one of the more popular costumes offered by the shop: a long and heavy silver robe with huge sleeves, padded shoulders and a high collar that was worn with an elaborate wig of platinum ringlets and an overly large silver moon mask surrounded by a halo of stars on tiny flexible springs.

Leonardo and Giacomo had no sooner emerged into the Campo Santa Margherita and started across the piazza toward the five-story building set in the heart of the shopping area when Giacomo realized his error. Within that short distance, he encountered no less than three other "moon gods," became hopelessly confused, and obligingly followed the wrong one into the crowd that headed back over the Accademia Bridge.

Leonardo was free of the Council's spy.

The heavy bronze doors of the Cambio swung open in response to a bell cord, and the Maestro was admitted into the world of Venetian bankers.

The servant who admitted Leonardo asked for Leonardo's name and the name of the person he had come to see, and then instructed him to wait. From time to time he was quietly studied by passing men of obvious prosperity with heavy robes lined in fur at collar and hem and bearing the burden of heavy golden chains of authority. Leonardo had removed the moon mask and fastened it by its ribbons to his belt, but he still felt out of place.

Finally the servant reappeared and requested that Leonardo follow him. The pair journied through two long corridors, up two staircases and along a colonnaded arcade. The door at the end of this walkway was of dark wood and stretched from floor to ceiling. As if by magic, it swung open precisely as the visitor approached.

Ser Agnolo Marinoni rose from an imposing mahogany chair and crossed the carpeted floor to greet his guest. The man's portliness was well hidden under the folds of a long scarlet-and-gold robe, bound at the waist with a heavy leather belt studded with small jewels. One hand stroked his thin grey beard, and the other was extended to Leonardo who grasped it lightly and then let it fall.

"Maestro Leonardo!" Ser Agnolo greeted him. "How wonderful it is to see you again! Our introduction in Cremona was brief." He escorted Leonardo to a chair facing his own. "I see you have entered into the spirit of our carnival."

"For self-protection," Leonardo responded, and the banker laughed.

"I have ordered refreshments," Ser Agnolo smiled. The grand master of the bankers' guild seated himself, and Leonardo did the same. Ser Agnolo rested an elbow on the arm of his chair and focused his attention on the Maestro. "And how is your small companion, Ser Niccolo?"

"I thought perhaps you would be in a better position to answer that question since he has been in your employ for the past four months, Ser Agnolo."

The grand master showed no signs of emotion. "Ah!" he smiled. "So that little secret has been revealed, has it? Well, it is of little consequence. I was in favor of confiding Niccolo's commission to you at once in Cremona, but the contessa felt that the more people who know of a spy's existence, the more vulnerable the spy becomes. We were thinking only of your safety, Maestro."

"Of course."

"Have you brought a message for me? From Niccolo perhaps?"

"I think Niccolo knows as much as you do about what has happened," the Maestro replied.

Ser Agnolo frowned. "What has happened?"

"The marquesa still possesses a necklace that is reputedly the Tears of the Madonna," Leonardo explained. "But another

235

such necklace has surfaced in Rome in the possession of Madonna Lucrezia Borgia, and a third in Imola at the throat of the Contessa Caterina Sforza."

"Yes, yes," sighed the banker. "Our agents have reported the two necklaces in Rome and Imola, but our principal concern is not with those possible replicas, but with the specific necklace given to our courier. With it was an appraisal by a Dutch assessor, and we have copies of his notes verifying the authenticity of the missing Tears. They are the only Tears with which we are concerned."

They were interrupted by the sudden appearance of three servants pushing a two-tiered cart into the room. They placed it between the two men and removed the damask covering to reveal platters of pastries, candied castles, bowls of fresh strawberries and cream, chestnut tarts, marzipan balls, and a carafe of wine the color of pale gold. One of the servants poured the wine into goblets of exquisite glass and offered one to each. Then both bowed stiffly from the waist and backed from the room.

"I think I can enlighten you on the matter of the courier," Leonardo said as he watched Ser Agnolo select an empty plate and build a mountain of food upon it. "A man's head was found buried in the gardens of the marquis."

Ser Agnolo frowned. "A man's head? Just a head?"

Leonardo nodded and sipped the wine which carried a slight hint of pear with a texture approximating honey. "Probably taken and buried to prevent identification of the gentleman," he explained. "But I was able to reconstruct it using the proportionate formulae for human faces that we use in painting . . ."

"Proportionate what?"

"Formulae. Mathematical ratios. Nothing is true that cannot be proven by mathematics."

Ser Agnolo stared at Leonardo for a moment, and then murmured, "If you say so, Maestro."

"I sketched how the man probably looked in life." He reached down to the leather canister beside his chair, the only item he had refused to permit Giacomo to carry when they left the costume shops. He opened it and removed the sketches which he passed to the grand master. "Can you identify him?"

"My god!" Ser Agnolo cried. "It is him! It is Cecco! Our poor Cecco!"

"He is . . . ?"

Ser Agnolo leaned back in his chair, and pressed a thumb and forefinger to the bridge of his nose. "The courier. Our Cecco."

"Well," sighed the Maestro, recovering the sketches and replacing them in the canister, "now we know for certain that the courier was assassinated, and we can assume from its location who ordered the assassination. I can even say with some conviction who did the actual killing, and why. Now there is only one more question to be answered in Venice."

"What question is that, Maestro?" the banker asked.

"Was it necessary?"

Upon leaving the palazzo of the Cambio, the Maestro replaced his moon mask and mentally computed how to find his way to an island to the north, to Murano.

He started back the way they had come, across the Accademia Bridge and into the San Marco district. Here he avoided the major walkways and chose an indirect route that took him through a succession of narrow alleys and shadowed passages. As he passed through one of these dark walkways, Leonardo noticed a familiar mark carved into the sill of a closed door.

Two arcs separated by a straight line.

"What is this place called?" he asked a swarthy, pig-eyed and inebriated man lounging against a doorsill.

"Why in hell do you wanna know?" snarled the man.

Leonardo knew the quickest way to deal with such a person was to avoid telling him too much and to get directly to the matter of mutual interest. He slipped a small purse from the folds of his costume and dropped it at the man's feet.

The man quickly bent and recovered the purse. He undid the drawcords and glanced inside, and then he smiled at Leonardo and said, "This? Oh, this be the Street of the Assassins."

Leonardo was pleased that he had found his initial goal with a minimum of effort. "Why is it called that?" he asked.

"Possibly because men in that business, they frequent the taverns and inns here," the man murmured softly. "This street is also used for trainin' by the Janus."

"The Janus?"

The swarthy man frowned, looked in all directions and drew closer to the Maestro. His breath reeked of garlic and wine. "The less one knows of the Janus, the better. Men who knew too much have died from it, ye see."

"It has been my experience that more men die from a lack of knowledge than a surfeit of it," the Maestro responded sharply. He pulled the man to one side, and the inebriate was surprised by the strength of his hands. Leonardo drew him even closer as he whispered, "Now listen! I am not a fool. You are not dressed for carnival, so you are probably a resident of this area. Venice is small, and everyone probably knows everyone else's business. I know you know all there is to know about this Janus." He released the man. "If you answer a few questions for me, you could end this day far wealthier than when you started."

"Sure. It's your death," the man shrugged.

Leonardo nodded. "What is the Janus?"

"It's a school."

"A school?"

Again the man looked up and down the narrow street. "A very special and secretive school," he whispered. "It's located on a small island at the northern end of the lagoon called Burano. Nothing's on it, ye see, save the houses of some lacemakers and some old shacks of fishermen. But to one side of the Piazza Galuppi there are three buildings, all four stories tall and painted white as sepulchres. Above the door of each of these buildings is the impresa of the school."

Leonardo pointed to the mark carved in the doorsill. "Like this?"

"Somethin' like that," growled the man, obviously uncomfortable discussing the matter. "The impresa is a stiletto dividing two faces in profile, one facing left, one facing right. That is the sign of the Janus, the two-faced god, and it means that the graduates of the school will offer one face to the world and quite another to their clients. The stiletto is the symbol of their profession."

"Which is?"

"Assassination," he shrugged.

Having some compassion for the man who seemed very uncomfortable in the Street of the Assassins, the Maestro led him down the passage and into the Rio de Fava which led them north of the San Marco district. As they walked, dodging the snakes of carnival dancers, another gold coin persuaded the man to explain how the Janus school accepts only six students every half year. Each candidate, he explained, is "sponsored" by a rich and powerful family, and their training is tailored to the needs of that family. Each student stays at the Janus for two full years, mastering a hundred different skills and dozens of weapons, and upon graduation they take an oath never to disclose the methods of their training or the identities of their teachers or fellow students. Only in death would they be identified and honored. Upon graduation they join their sponsoring family who will use their talents as they see fit.

"What talents?" Leonardo pressed him. "Assassination is plain work."

"Oh, a Janusian is different," the man whispered. "They kill in a very special manner."

"What manner?"

"The assassination never appears to have been an assassination. The victim either seems to have died a natural death or as the result of some accident. If murder is suspected, the Janusian is always able to blame a third party without revealing his own identity."

They passed the hospice-reformatory of San Lazzaro, and the Arsenal, which was actually a shipbuilding community of nearly four thousand workers. The swarthy man, anxious to not answer any further questions concerning the Janus school, turned guide, pointing out the printing shop of Aldus Manutius which "has nearly five hundred proofreaders, illustrators, and translators, all living on the premises."

He showed Leonardo the Fondaco dei Tedeschi which were German warehouses and offices, the quay of the Schiavoni that catered to Slavs, the Greek church of San Giorgio, and the ghettoes, a Venetian word for the sections of the city inhabited mostly by Jews and largely composed of seven-story tenements.

"The Jews were deprived of a homeland, ye see," the man recited as they walked, "because of the Crusades and by the Muslim occupation of the Levant; but the buggers have a flair for languages and good business sense, and Venice is a city of business."

"Yes, I can see that," Leonardo responded softly. "In addition, the existence and tolerance of the Jewish ghettoes must annoy Rome and maintain the independence of Venice from the Borgian papacy."

"And them Jews, they seem to like to live among their own where they can live by their crazy practices, so Venice has the ghettoes."

By this time they had reached the Fondamente Nuove where boats were available to transport visitors to the islands of San Michele, Murano, Burano, and Torcello at the far end of the lagoon.

"One last question concerning the Janus," Leonardo murmured to his unwilling guide as they waited for a boat.

"Oh please," begged the man.

"What do you know of the sponsorships? For example, did the marquis of Mantua, the Gonzaga, sponsor a candidate for the Janus school?"

The guide frowned. "How in hell would you expect me to know that?" The man shrugged. "I know the marquesa's family, the Este, they sponsored one. I know that, because he was brought back here by members of the family for burial recently."

The Maestro was about to ask the identity of the Este assassin when his attention was shattered like the shell of the egg that struck him in the back of the head and drenched him in perfume. He wheeled to see a young woman, naked to the waist and draped in paper streamers, laughing at him from the pedestal of a column before a building. She cupped her hands around her mouth and yelled, "Old man in the moon! Do you want me?"

Leonardo shook his head, and the dark-eyed woman laughed and leapt from the pedestal into the arms of a waiting man in the mask of a leopard. The groping wind lifted her skirt, revealing strong and well-formed legs; and the Maestro and the new "guide" turned away from the laughter as Leonardo stepped down into the boat that would take him up the lagoon.

But before the boat departed the Maestro resumed his interrogation. "You say you know the Este had a Janusian assassin who was buried up there, presumably on the island. Do you know his name?"

It took the man some time to remember, then he yelled out, "Cristani! Ottaviano Cristani!"

Only four of the seven passengers embarked on the landing dock at Murano. Three women instantly went to the left, and the Maestro was directed to the right and up the embankment to the buildings that housed the guild of glaziers, the makers of the world-famous glass.

A burly man in a white smock that reached almost to midcalf responded to the signal of the bell, and he smiled as he gestured the visitor into a small antechamber and introduced himself. "I am Giovanni d'Oggiono, grand master of the glaziers' guild."

The Maestro introduced himself and was invited to sit on an

upholstered high-backed bench bearing the impresa of the guild.

"I am acquainted with your work and your reputation," the glazier said. "I am honored to have you visit us."

"Your name is familiar to me, too, Ser Giovanni," said the Maestro. "I had the pleasure of being introduced to a young lady in the Mantuan court who told me she was from Murano, Madonna Maddalena d'Oggiono."

"My niece!" bellowed the glassmaker.

"Ah! You know, of course, that she is no longer at the court?" said Leonardo.

"Yes." The smile vanished, and it was a moment before Giovanni resumed the conversation. "To tell you the truth, Maestro, we were relieved. We thought she might just take it into her head to marry one of those prancing simps whose only wealth is a centuries-old name, but now she is more or less betrothed to a young guildsman with a growing fortune and a promising future!"

The Maestro nodded and smiled. "Did she say why she left the court?"

"Some nasty business there," growled Giovanni. "She sent a courier to us with a letter in which she said she feared for her life, so her father, her other uncles and I made some special and secretive arrangements for her and this betrothed of hers. She is now safe in Brussels under the protection of a wealthy Belgian merchant and his wife and discussing marriage with the young man from the lowlands who fled the court with her. He is, I believe, the Brussels representative for the Hanseatic League. Even now her father and the young man's father are negotiating a marriage contract and discussing a dowry."

"Indeed?"

"Wouldn't you love to be present at those meetings, eh?" laughed the burly man. "Such haggling, eh? Imagine! A Belgian and an Italian! In the end the Belgian must win, of course, because they are better businessmen, but with offers and counteroffers, the bride may be fifty years old before the matter is settled!"

"Was Madonna Maddalena a frequent visitor to your glass-works?" asked the Maestro.

Leonardo was aware of the sudden shift in tone and attitude. "Why do you ask?"

The Maestro nodded, trying to put the man at ease. "I thought that something she had learned, perhaps here, may have been the cause of that, how did you put it? That 'nasty business' at court?"

Giovanni studied the tall man seated before him. Again the moon mask was fastened at his waist, and the glazier noted the long beard and hair streaked with silver, heavy brows, and the thick nose and lips. Finally he decided that it was the face of a man who might be trusted, and he said softly, "She was here frequently." He forced a smile. "Come, come, Maestro, she was the daughter of a glass-blower and had four uncles in the business! We all live on Murano! That was one of the provisions of our guild. Each of us and our families live and work on Murano. It is our own little world. Here we have our supplies of soda and lime brought to us on barges. You understand that is how glass is made? Soda and lime and sand. Heated to a very high degree until it is like a gelatin. Then we dip our rods into it, wind it like honey around one glowing end and we blow and turn." He threw up his hands. "Naturally she learned a few of our secrets but I doubt if anyone in the court at Mantua would want to kill her because she was acquainted with the making of Murano glass. I am of the opinion that the nobility is more concerned with the beauty and commercial value of fine glass than in the process of making it."

The Maestro took a long pause before he posed the pressing question. "Would she know the secret of bonding diamante?"

Now there was a definite chill in the air. Giovanni almost rose from his chair, and the Maestro could see his fingers tighten the arms. "What do you know of bonding diamond dust to glass?"

"Nothing," the Maestro shrugged. "That is why I asked."

"Well, there is nothing secret to the process really," the burly man murmured halfheartedly. "Diamond dust is produced when the cutters facet and polish diamonds. We purchase it from their guild, and during the final stages of the forming of certain crystalline glass containing lead, we can bond a thin veneer of the dust to the glass. It is a matter of some skill."

"To what end?"

"Why to simulate a genuine diamond, of course! Such a crystal will cut other glass, and the only way you can discern the difference between the genuine and the false is in the way it refracts light, and by its the weight, of course."

The Maestro smiled and stroked his beard. "Can anyone make these lead crystals? Can you?"

"No," Giovanni shook his head. "It's not my specialty. Color, that's my art. I can make a vase that would rival your palette, Maestro." He seemed to relax a little, apparently satisfied with the conversation's path. "No," he repeated. "There are only three Murano men who mastered the bonding of diamante dust, and one of them is dead."

The Maestro leaned forward. "Did they keep records? I mean, is there any way of knowing for whom they may have been commissioned to produce these false crystals?"

This time the glassmaker was on his feet. "Now please, Maestro. I admire you and your work, and Maddalena says you were very kind to her at Mantua. However, although I have only the highest regard for you, I would never reveal a commission!"

Leonardo also stood. "Then there *were* records kept? As far back as thirty-five or forty years ago?"

"Be reasonable, Maestro!" grumbled Giovanni. "We are men of business. Of course we keep records. What kind of a business can succeed without accurate records?"

"May I see them?"

Giovanni wheeled to face him. "Never! That is a scandalous suggestion, Maestro! Would you ask a priest to violate his vow and reveal the secrets of the confessional?"

"That seems like quite a different matter."

"Well, it's not!" he bellowed. "Business is the guildsman's religion! We have our rituals, our secrets, our hierarchy, same as the Church! We may have slightly more than ten commandments, but most assuredly the principal rule is no one outside the guild must ever have access to our records! Some of our clients do not wish to be identified! Many of them do not wish to be identified! To betray their trust would be as scandalous as coughing up the host at communion and trampling it into the floor!"

And then, without another word, he stormed from the room.

Leonardo returned to the palazzo of the Cambio where he demanded an immediate audience with Ser Agnolo. He related what had happened at Murano and requested the banker's help.

"What is it, specifically, that you wish to know?"

"I would like to affirm a commission made approximately thirty-five years ago, probably in Rome."

"To what purpose?"

"It will clarify some of the mystery surrounding the Tears as well as the assassination of your courier."

"Wait here please, Maestro."

It was nearly an hour before Ser Agnolo again approached them in the antechamber. "The grand master of the glaziers' guild was reticent at first, but there is a bond between bankers and artisans that remains mutually profitable. He has agreed that he personally will answer one question, only one, concerning this commission. Think carefully how you will word it, and you will have the answer in two or three days."

Leonardo quickly inscribed something on the paper provided. Ser Agnolo took it and read it.

"Well articulated, Maestro. I will send this by special courier to the grand master."

"Thank you."

"You say this question relates to our mutual problem concerning the Tears of the Madonna?"

"I believe it does."

"You'll have your answer the day after tomorrow."

The answer, when it came, was one word.

"Yes."

Suddenly Leonardo recalled the contessa's argument against subsidies for artists, that every commission carries with it a set of restrictions that circumscribe the art. In this matter he imagined that the restrictions included a promise of complete secrecy, which he had violated.

"Now," smiled Leonardo in his rooms in the doge's palace, "it is time for enlightenment."

ENLIGHTENMENT

April 1500

Venice

Leonardo had planned to depart Venice on the first day of April in a coach drawn by four horses and a full escort of eight mounted lancers, but he was required to stay longer than he intended. The Council of Ten was "disturbed" that he had managed to lose their spy almost immediately, and there were several "inquiries" as to where he went and what he did on that day. They were also curious about the one-word message he received from the grand master of the glaziers' guild, and it took some sessions with the Council and the marquis to assure everyone that Leonardo had not been doing anything that might harm the Most Serene Republic. In point of fact, his extra days in Venice were put to use showing where the retaining walls for the flood project could be constructed.

When he was finally permitted to leave, he took with him the books and music he had purchased on the Rialto, the crate from the church in Verona, and a small book in which he had inscribed what he learned at Murano and all the information he had managed to pry from the man in the Street of the Assassins.

Montagnana

It surprised and annoyed the officer in command of the escort when the Maestro requested an alternate route. Rather than travel the better road from Padua to Vicenza to Verona and then south to Mantua, Leonardo suggested the party turn south at Padua and take the much less-traveled road through Abano Terme, Montegrotto Terme, and then west to Montagnana.

The officer was further distressed when the Maestro insisted that the party rest at a small inn called the Olive Tree, an establishment obviously incapable of accommodating the lancers, coachman, footman, and Leonardo. As was to be expected, the food was poor and served cold and the wine was aptly described by one of the lancers as "concentrated horse piss."

The Maestro did not eat or drink at Montagnana. Instead he spent the entire hour in deep discussion with the innkeeper who was plainly uncomfortable with the conversation. He then disappeared briefly up the narrow staircase to another room with the proprietor, and, after a matter of some minutes, he returned to the common room and announced that he was ready to resume the journey.

There is no record of what the innkeeper of the Olive Tree and the Maestro discussed, but when the entourage departed, the Maestro was seen to place a thin gold wire in the pages of his notebook, and from Legnago to Mantua, he slept the peaceful sleep of a child.

Mantua

Leonardo was welcomed by Meneghina on behalf of the marquesa who was again "indisposed." The chamberlain, overdressed and opulent as usual, ordered the servants to carry the books, the crate, and other purchases into the palazzo, simultaneously gushing over how much Leonardo had been missed.

"We were worried about you, Maestro," said Meneghina as he galloped to keep pace with Leonardo's long stride down the corridors and arcades. "There were no reports of your coach having passed through Verona or Vicenza, and with the trouble to the north . . . !"

The statement caused the Maestro to pause. "Trouble to the north? What trouble?"

"You haven't heard? The French returned to Milan in force and drove the German mercenaries away. Il Moro fled. He was captured, they say, at Novara, and then immediately sent to a prison in France. His imprisonment, and the imprisonment of the Contessa Caterina, spells the end of the Sforza power in northern Italy."

Leonardo sighed deeply and ran a hand across his forehead as if the information pained him. He now knew what pressing matters had drawn Niccolo Machiavelli back to Florence after a single day in Venice.

"The poor duke has lost his state and his property," the

Maestro said softly, "and none of my works were ever completed for him."

Leonardo's reunion with Niccolo was warm but brief. The Maestro displayed the texts he had purchased and the music printed with moveable type. He did not draw attention to the crate or to the small receptacle that held his Venetian costume, but he described life at the court of the doge.

"I was not permitted access to all the secrets of the palazzo, you understand," Leonardo explained as he drew back in his chair and seemed to relax. "I understand that the entire place is honeycombed with secret passages, some of which lead directly to the Piombi prison and the torture chambers. Indeed, near the east wing, and not far from the Pozzi prison where the hardened criminals are kept, there is a bridge called the Bridge of Sighs, because of the sighs of those being led away to rot in the eighteen dank dungeons of the prison."

Leonardo delineated the madness of carnival, of the eggs filled with perfume and the Days of the Beggars. He mentioned only in passing that he had visited the glassworks at Murano, and he remained silent about what he had learned of the Janus school for assassins and what he had uncovered through his brief interrogation of the innkeeper of the Olive Tree.

Niccolo described how the days were spent while the Maestro was away. He skirted any discussion of his deepening relationship with Lizette, but he detailed an exchange of insults with Nanino that would surely have led to physical conflict had not Meneghina intervened. He said that he found himself in the company of the marquesa for longer periods of time as they planned for the arrival of the *commedia* troupe in three days. The marquesa had the young man explain to the entire court how the players worked through improvisation, how the characters, such as the Capitano, Harlequin, Scapino, and Pantalone, were traditional and possibly derived from the Roman theatre. He told how the men wore half-masks, but the women and the male lover were obliged only to wear dominoes. He warned the courtiers that some of the material might

252

seem vulgar in the extreme and may mock some of the con-
ventions of nobility and religion that the court might hold
dear, and he demonstrated how the players would create a
piece from a simple idea or outline called a sogetto.

Then he casually mentioned to Leonardo that their rooms
had apparently been searched again, this time quite openly and
thoroughly, but the red book was still intact. With the fall of Il
Moro the information was no longer of value to anyone.

"Well," smiled Leonardo. "I am impressed. Since it has lost
its value, suppose you tell me where you hid the red book?

Niccolo crossed to the three books still lying on the worktable: a text of Euclid, the Meditations of Marcus Aurelius, and
the Epictetus. He picked up the copy of the Meditations and
brought it to the Maestro. "Look," he said simply.

The Maestro opened the book to the title page and thumbed
through the first section before he realized that the text had
been altered. Beyond the title page and the first ten pages of
the Meditations, he was reading the red book!

"The Meditations and the red book were identical in size,"
Niccolo informed him with just a touch of arrogance. "I removed the text of the red book from its cover, slit the binding
of the Meditations, removed most of the inner pages, and replaced them with the pages of the red book." The Maestro
gave a small laugh, and Niccolo pressed on. "I knew the
searchers were looking specifically for a book with a red cover.
They were also not inclined to page through something that
seemed as dull as the Meditations of Marcus Aurelius."

"Clever," the Maestro nodded. "And I am pleased it was the
Meditations you chose to deface and not the Euclid. I would
never have forgiven you for that." He put the book to one side
and stood. "Now," he said, "while on the subject of hidden
objects, let us carry the supposition of hiding-in-plain-sight to
the ultimate."

He crossed to the workbench, bent, and picked up the box
containing the unused requiem candles of Ottaviano Cristani.
He then placed the crate he brought from Verona beside it,
opened it, and removed one of the ornately decorated candles
that had been Ottaviano's Magi Gift. He placed one of the

candles on the workbench, and Niccolo thought he might light it. Instead the Maestro chose a small hammer that was pointed at one end, and with one swift blow he brought it down and shattered the candle.

As he brushed away the larger portions, an object caught the light, an object about the length of a man's thumb, tear-shaped with a gold cap that suggested a crown of thorns.

One of the Tears of the Madonna.

The Maestro passed the diamond to Niccolo. "There is one hidden in each of the candles," he said quietly. "I wondered why Ottaviano made so many, when there are only fourteen sequences in the story of the passion and death of Our Lord. We had seven remaining and the other fourteen had been sent to Verona. That's twenty-one, precisely the number of tears in the necklace."

Niccolo fondled the diamond, cleaning away some of the wax until the light bounced between the table and the facets of the gem and sent small rainbows around the room. "But how . . . ?"

"The facts all point to it, as plainly as one and one are two," the Maestro replied, seating himself again. "The sketches I made of the reconstructed skull found buried in the garden enabled the grand master of the Cambio in Venice to identify the dead man as the courier. So *that* much of the puzzle could be verified and was no longer a supposition: the courier was intercepted and murdered, and the assassin was in this court. It is highly unlikely that an assassin from, say Milan, would travel all the way to Mantua to bury a head in the garden. In Venice I was able to learn that Ottaviano Cristani was a graduate of the Janus school of assassins, a rather unpleasant institution, and he was 'attached' to his sponsoring family, the Este. Presumably he came to the Gonzaga court at the request of the marquesa who is an Este. I was able to link Ottaviano with the Janus because of the marking on his hand, a corruption of the Janus impresa: two faces severed by a stiletto. So! This much can be verified: the courier was intercepted and murdered and the assassin was Ottaviano."

"That doesn't tell us much," said Niccolo. "Even the Cambio assumed the courier had been murdered."

"But now they can be certain," Leonardo said. "And on my return from Venice I stopped and had a brief discussion with the innkeeper of the Olive Tree, the last place the courier was seen. I could see that the man was frightened, and he insisted that the courier had departed the following morning, which was the story he had told the Cambio agents. I assured him that the man who had threatened him was dead, and after some persuasion, and two Venetian ducats, he admitted that Ottaviano had returned to the inn in the middle of the night with some armed mercenaries. That much, of course, had been told me by the two Franciscan monks at the Certosa. The proprietor told me that when the mercenaries departed, they carried something, presumably the courier's body, wrapped in a bloody blanket. He said the room had been splattered with blood and vandalized, as though the mercenaries had been looking for something hidden away, but the only thing the innkeeper found that was unusual was this."

He crossed and picked up one of the books that he had brought from Venice. He extracted the section of gold wire and handed it to Niccolo who passed the diamond to the Maestro. "What is it?" asked the dwarf.

"A section of wire from the necklace," the Maestro replied as he chose a glass jar from his herbal collection. "We have been looking for an intact necklace when the actual necklace had been broken down into its components. After all, it is the diamonds that possess the real value, and it is much easier to hide the individual Tears than the entire necklace."

He made one quick movement down the side of the jar, and the diamond etched a line in the glass.

"I began to consider the number of diamonds in the necklace," he continued, "and that immediately corresponded with the number of candles that Ottaviano had given us. Twenty-one!"

He placed the diamond on his small scales and began to read and adjust the measuring rod. He stopped now and then to make a quick numerical notation in his workbook, and then he resumed his weighing of the diamond.

"I was now able to reconstruct what must have happened that fateful night," he said as he continued his measurements. "The courier, on his way to Venice with the necklace, was followed by Ottaviano Cristani who had been instructed to intercept the courier, kill him, and recover the necklace, possibly by Isabella d'Este who would be unhappy at the prospect of forfeiting her jewels to pay a loan for which Il Moro should be responsible. The plan was that the marquesa would circulate the story that the debt had been honored, and that the courier probably turned thief and ran off with the valuable necklace, leaving the bankers' guild to absorb the loss. But something went wrong. Apparently Ottaviano reported that he could not find the Tears of the Madonna, despite the fact that a search was conducted of the courier's room and his clothing, and the fact that the poor man was apparently tortured to reveal the hiding place."

The Maestro frowned, removed the weights from the scale, and then began the entire operation again.

"Instructed to destroy all trace of the courier," he said softly, "and to prevent any future identification, the body was beheaded, and the head was buried in the marquis' gardens."

The Maestro emitted a low growl and readjusted the scales.

"But there is always another possibility." Niccolo smiled but remained silent. "There is the curious matter of the death of Captain D'Angennes."

The Maestro turned to look directly at Niccolo. "Suppose the courier did not have time to hide the Tears, and suppose Cristani arrived with his captain, Captain D'Angennes, and recovered them immediately. Suppose, however, that Cristani had no intention of returning the Tears to Isabella. Suppose he was in the employ of someone else, the Borgias perhaps or the Sforzas, as we discussed before. He would then have killed the courier at once and attempted to make it appear that the man was tortured to reveal a hiding place. This would support his story that he made every effort to recover the Tears, but they could not be found. Then Ottaviano hid the necklace on his own person, in the presence of Captain D'Angennes, and summoned the mercenaries to search the room, confident they, too, would then verify that every attempt was made to find the hiding place."

The Maestro picked up the diamond from the scales with small tongs and slowly moved it back and forth before a candle flame. The light splintered into flowing ribbons of red and green.

"On returning to Mantua," he continued, "Ottaviano reported he could not find the necklace. Isabella was distressed but there was little she could do about it. She continued with her plan, however, so she could have a story for the Venetian bankers. In the meantime Ottaviano pondered where to hide the diamonds and how to get them from the palazzo without arousing suspicion. Knowing the court's traditions, he molded candles, hiding one diamond in each of the twenty-one. He knew these would be given to some religious organization following the tradition of the Gonzaga court. Then he would visit that monastery or the convent and buy the candles back, knowing that they were too beautiful to be used in the meantime. This is precisely what I did as we passed through Verona."

"But his companion, Captain D'Angennes, was not satisfied with his share. He had been drinking heavily, and Ottaviano was afraid he might divulge the truth. When one of the captain's drinking companions was actually taken to the dungeons to be interrogated, Ottaviano knew it would only be a matter of time before they would come for Captain D'Angennes himself, and he would be exposed. So he murdered Captain D'Angennes to silence him. As befitting a graduate of the Janus, it appeared to be an accident."

The Maestro placed the diamond back on the scales once more and adjusted the weights.

"But when reports of two more necklaces appeared in Imola and Rome, Isabella immediately assumed that Ottaviano had lied, that he had found the Tears, and had sent the jewels to another employer, either the Borgias or the Sforzas."

"Who *was* Ottaviano's other employer?" asked Niccolo. "The Borgia or the Sforza?"

"It doesn't matter," sighed the Maestro as he placed the diamond on his worktable. "The theory is just as valid if Cristani did not have another employer. Suppose it was simple greed that moved him to keep the jewels for himself. That is also another possibility. Although, from what I have learned concerning the Janus assassins, their loyalty to their sponsoring families is absolute. It is possible, of course, that something the marquesa did or said offended Ottaviano, and he kept the jewels to avenge his honor. Terrabilita is a characteristic of all Italian males, remember. It is most likely that Ottaviano turned against the marquesa for something she did, something she forced him to do, such as to use an armed force to intercept and kill a courier when sole assassination was Ottaviano's specialty. Armed mercenaries and witnesses were not his style, and it reflected on his honor as a Janusian."

"Pride can be deadly," Niccolo said. "Epictetus says . . . !"

Suddenly the Maestro picked up the heavy mallet he used in sculpting and brought it down hard on the diamond, which instantly shattered into a thousand pieces.

"What are you doing?" screamed Niccolo.

"Exploring an alternate possibility," Leonardo said quietly.

The Maestro sighed and smiled at Niccolo. "Lead crystal," he said. "Heavy, but it does not refract light as a diamond would."

"Then the necklace that Ottaviano took from the courier was a *replica*! All those lives were sacrificed for lead crystal!"

"But a unique blending of lead, soda, lime, and sand," Leonardo commented. "It would take a genuine artisan to make such copies. And a question now rises: did Ottaviano know the necklace was false? Did the marquesa?"

Niccolo and the Maestro then removed the crystals from the remaining candles and subjected them to the same measurements. Each of the false diamonds could cut glass, which would seem to verify their authenticity, but they did not correspond in weight or in the refraction of light as a true diamond of that size should.

"Illumination partakes of light," the Maestro explained. "And lustre is the reflection of this light. Light striking the faceted surfaces of opaque bodies, dense materials, is immobile, whereas the lustre on these same bodies will be in as many locations as there are places to which the eye is moved." He opened his workbook and began to hastily sketch a series of pyramids and angles. "Every light which falls on opaque or dense bodies produces the first degree of brightness, and these sections will be darker which receives the light by less equal angles." He began to initial the crossing lines and shaded areas. "Light and shade, by the way, both function by means of pyramids."

"Please, Maestro," Niccolo pleaded. "Spare me the explanation and just tell me what all this means. I saw with my own eyes that the diamonds, false or not, cut glass."

"Yes," the Maestro sighed as he returned to his chair. "It is an art and a secret of the glaziers of Murano, the ability to meld actual diamond dust with crystal. The result is that each single Tear, although only glass itself, can cut other glass. Only in weight and refraction of light does the false differ from the real." He opened a book and began to make notations. "Remember I told you that whomever was following Ser Johannes and Madonna Maddalena may have been more concerned with the woman than the man?"

"With Madonna Maddalena?"

Leonardo nodded. "All the humiliations, the small 'accidents' were contrived to drive the lady and her lover from the court."

Niccolo frowned. "Then the marquesa wanted Maddalena driven from the court because . . . ?"

"Because the lady was raised by Venetian glaziers. The artisans of Murano all live on the island with their families. Madonna Maddalena was familiar with some of their secrets, including the bonding of diamond dust to crystal. She knew that the fact that the Tears cut glass did not indicate they were real diamonds."

"Which reaffirms my conviction that the marquesa knew the Tears she sent to Venice were false," Leonardo said. "That was her real motive in having the courier murdered and the necklace recovered. Not because the Tears were valuable and she wanted them back, but because she knew the Cambio would test the necklace, discover it to be a replica, and she would be humiliated. By passing the necklace to the courier before witnesses, and then have both the Tears and the courier disappear, she would no longer be liable for the debt, and no one would realize that she attempted to defraud the Cambio."

A smile creased Niccolo's face. "Imagine the lady's state when she was told the Tears was not recovered from the courier! It was still out there somewhere, ready to condemn her!"

"Exactly," said Leonardo. "She was in a state of hysteria. She saw a hundred potential enemies about her. Her problems were compounded, you see, when her husband learned that the Tears had suddenly appeared at the throat of Lucrezia Borgia. He suspected a plot of some sort by Cesare. He demanded proof that Isabella possessed the genuine article. She was unable to show him the Dutch assessor's appraisal which had been taken from the courier with the necklace but had been destroyed by Ottaviano as another piece of incriminating evidence, but she *did* have the copy that Ser Johannes brought from Brussels and that seemed to calm the marquis."

"Then the necklace the marquesa wore in Milan when you saw her in the procession, and at the dinner, that was the genuine Tears!" Niccolo cried.

Leonardo shook his head. "No," he said quietly. "That was a fake too."

"The marquesa had *two* fake necklaces? How is that possible?"

"Ah," sighed Leonardo, "to explain *that* we must begin at the beginning." He rose and handed a Tear to Niccolo. "Look," he commanded. "These replicas are remarkable. Look at the filigree caps. A master goldsmith would have to be employed to make these." He began to pace between the worktables. "Let's test that wonderful memory of yours. Where did the Tears originate, according to the Contessa Bergamini?"

"The necklace first appeared as part of the wealth of Senor Juan Domingo de Borja, a Spanish grandee, and was then transported to Spain's Italian fief, Naples, by Juan's son, Alonso de Borja, the bishop of Valencia and later Pope Calixtus III."

"Very good! That ability of yours to re-create a conversation word for word always astounds me!" He stroked his beard. "Now that information about Calixtus is most interesting."

"Why?"

He stopped and looked at the dwarf. "What do you remember of Calixtus?"

The dwarf shrugged. "Nothing!"

"Well," the Maestro smiled at him, "on occasion, *what* one reads is even more important than *if* one reads, my friend. Consider that!" He resumed his chair. "I, for one, took the time to leaf through a history of the papacy on my trip to Venice."

"So?" Niccolo frowned.

"I read that Calixtus took a solemn oath upon becoming pontiff that he personally would fund the crusades to save Christendom from the threat of Islam. He saw this as his divine mission."

"I knew that."

"To do that he needed money. Did you remember that he was the pope who ordered all the gold and silver bindings of the Vatican library stripped and melted down? Did you remember that he sold Vatican art works, including silver salt cellars and gold plate from his table. Or that, when a great marble sarcophagus was discovered under Santa Petronilla's containing two coffins lined with silver and two bodies wrapped in gold brocade and bearing ornaments of solid gold, he did not hesitate to order all the gold and silver melted down to fund his cause?"

"No," Niccolo replied softly. "I didn't know that."

"Calixtus sent solicitors throughout Europe to preach the crusade, and if any of the noble families refused to contribute, they were subjected first to ecclesiastical penalties, and then secular authority."

"What is the point?"

261

"It is a matter of record that Calixtus, in order to raise more cash, sold a vast amount of the Vatican jewels to King Alfonso of Naples. Listed among them, I found this in the history of the papacy, was the Tears of the Madonna."

"The pope sold the Tears to Alfonso of Naples?"

"I didn't say that."

"You said . . . !"

"I said listed among the jewels listed as sold to Alfonso was the Tears of the Madonna," Leonardo said. "That shows what errors can be compounded when one hears only what is said and not what is implied."

Niccolo threw up his hands. "I do not choose to play games with you, Maestro," he snapped. "Did the pope sell the Tears to Alfonso, or didn't he?"

"I'll tell you," smiled Leonardo, savoring his moment of triumph over the dwarf. "The pope had a nephew whom he had elevated to the cardinalate, Rodrigo Borgia, a man of cunning and deception. A man can change his clothing, you pointed that out to Nanino, but he cannot change his character to correspond with his costume."

"What has the nephew to do with this?"

"Whether it was Rodrigo's idea or whether it was a misguided sense of morality on the part of the pontiff, we cannot be certain. Certainly it is a terrible thing when a man has to do the wrong thing for the right reason. But evidence indicates that Calixtus put the success of the crusades above personal integrity. A plan evolved: he would sell Alfonso *false* Tears, keeping the valuable original and still raising the needed money."

"The pope sold Alfonso a *fake* Tears?"

"Apparently," Leonardo nodded. "This was the primary question I had to consider: if there are two or more magnificent replicas of the Tears, replicas so well crafted that they could pass a test of diamonds for cutting glass, who would have the means to have them made? That was the *primary* question! Remember? I told you always consider the primary question and not the subordinate questions that might arise from it! "

"I remember," Niccolo replied sullenly.

"Such perfect fakes, and you can see that they are exceptional, would require superb craftsmanship, genuine artisans in glass and gold."

"So?"

"So who would have the means to have such replicas made?"

He paused for effect, and Niccolo found himself growing impatient. "Well, who?" he roared.

"Why, the pope, of course!" Leonardo smiled. "The pontiff had all the artists and smiths of Europe at his command! So let us assume that Pope Calixtus, possibly at the suggestion of his nephew, had three copies made of the Tears."

"*Three*? Why three?"

"Because we know of four necklaces: one worn by Caterina at Imola when she was a prisoner of Cesare Borgia; another worn by Lucrezia Borgia and reported to the marquesa; the one worn by the marquesa on the return of her husband, and the fourth set into candles by Ottaviano. Only one of the four can be authentic; so there were probably three replicas."

"I see," said Niccolo. "Obvious."

"Besides, it works mathematically," Leonardo added. "The Church thinks in threes. Its theology centers around a trinity of three distinct personalities in one divinity. The papal tiara has three crowns. Christ was in the tomb three days. The 'Mea Culpa' is recited three times at the Mass, and the breast is struck three times. There were twelve apostles, a number divisible by three. Even the number of diamonds in the necklace, twenty-one, added together is three. It goes on and on."

"I find that questionable."

"It is mathematics!" railed the Maestro.

"It is games with numbers!" Niccolo snapped back. "But I will accept your explanation for now!"

"Furthermore when I was in Venice," the Maestro said sharply, "I inquired of the Murano glaziers after a specific commission. I was given permission to ask one question. I asked 'Did the Murano make three replicas of the Tears of the Madonna for Pope Calixtus?' The response was 'Yes.'"

"You should have said that first," sighed Niccolo. "All right. Let's say that Pope Calixtus *did* make three replicas of the original, what then?"

"He sells one of those copies to King Alfonso who does not question their authenticity. Who would question the integrity of a pope? Especially one of the Borgia family? In any case, the first replica, staying with the parallel of the trinity we shall call this the Father replica, falls into the hands of the king of Naples."

"The Father replica?"

"It makes the explanation less confusing. Calixtus sells the Father replica to Alfonso. But now we have evidence that Alfonso discovered the Tears sold him were false."

"What evidence?"

"Church history. Within two years the king of Naples and the pope are sworn enemies. Indeed, they say the papal bull, *In Coena Domini*, was aimed directly at Alfonso."

"So Alfonso discovered the deception and protested?"

"Yes. But Calixtus still needed Alfonso's help in the crusades, so what does *he* do? He apologizes to the king, says there was some unfortunate mixup, and he promises to send the original Tears. He even agrees to have the necklace authenticated by an assessor chosen by the king."

"And *then* he sends the real Tears to Alfonso!"

"Of course not! Who carries these Tears to Naples? The nephew, Rodrigo Borgia. But what he carries is not the original but the *second* replica, the Son, and following the examination which assures the king of the authenticity, that the diamonds cut glass, Alfonso now has *two* fake Tears, the Father and the Son replicas."

"Incredible!" Niccolo said. "It is understandable that a man can be deceived once, but twice!"

"Precisely! It is a humiliation, and when the king ultimately finds out, which he was bound to, sooner or later, he does the prudent thing: he says nothing and quietly works against the pope until his own death a few years later. *That*, too, is a matter of history."

"And then?"

"Then both copies, Father and Son, fall into the hands of Alfonso's widow, Ippolita Sforza, *who is told that only one is false, to spare the king humiliation,* and she in turn wills them to her niece, Caterina, upon her death."

"Then it was one of the replicas, either the Father or the Son, that Caterina was wearing at Imola!" Niccolo said.

"Yes," Leonardo nodded. "But there is more to it. Years pass. Caterina has to borrow nearly thirty thousand ducats from Il Moro. She offers the Tears as collateral, but, like the pope, she cannot bear to part with the one necklace she believes is authentic: the Father replica. Like the deception with the king, she sends the Son replica of the Tears which now passes into the hands of Il Moro. She keeps the Father replica, thinking it to be authentic."

"So that was the Father replica she wore at Imola?"

"Yes. And the Son replica passes to Il Moro and eventually to his wife, Beatrice, who also believes *her* necklace is authentic. She, in turn, presents the Son replica as a gift to her sister, Isabella d'Este, upon the birth of the marquesa's son."

"Those are the ones the marquesa wore at the return of her husband!"

"Yes. But the marquesa is not quite as gullible as Alfonso of Naples had been. Through her brother, Cardinal Ippolito, she discovers that the necklace is a replica, and she suspects that the original Tears is with the current Borgian pope, Alexander. She threatens to expose the whole affair before the crowned heads of Europe who want to be rid of Alexander anyway, forcing a schism in the Church, so the marquesa demands that Rodrigo send her the *original.*"

"But we know now that both sets that the marquesa had were false!"

"Of course! So what does that indicate?"

"This pope didn't send the original either!"

"That's right! He repeats the process that worked twice before, and the marquesa ends up with the *third* replica, the Holy Spirit, which she believes to be authentic."

"So she has two false necklaces, the Son and the Holy Spirit, and she believes one is authentic!"

"Yes!" the Maestro said. "And she didn't know both were false until the Dutch appraisal. Naturally she cannot permit the truth to leak from the court, so the Dutch assessor is bribed to certify to the authenticity of the Tears on a single factor: the diamonds appear to be cut glass. The marquesa still has to deliver a necklace to the Cambio, so she hands the courier the Son replica and the certificate of authenticity."

"And then she has him murdered in transit, specifying that he be beheaded, so the courier cannot be identified!" Niccolo cried.

"Precisely! She expects the false necklace to be returned to her so there would be no scandal if the Cambio tested the jewels, which they would. Then she tells the Cambio that the courier probably defected to Il Moro with the Tears."

Niccolo was on his feet. "Let me see if I understand it from that point," he cries. "The marquesa sends Ottaviano on this mission despite his protest that he is a professional and would prefer to work in his own fashion rather than just barge in with a band of mercenaries. But Isabella doesn't trust anyone, and she wants others there when Ottaviano confronts the courier. Angry, Ottaviano develops a plan of his own. He intends to report that he could not find the Tears and keep the necklace for himself. The courier did not have time to hide the necklace, so only the first two men in that room at the inn in Montagnana, Ottaviano and his aide, Captain D'Angennes, know the truth which is . . ."

"*That Ottaviano already has the necklace in his possession,*" said Leonardo.

Niccolo grinned. "He then orders the mercenaries to search for it, destroying the room and making it appear that a search was held and nothing found. But he completes the rest of his assignment. He has the head brought back to Mantua where it is buried in the marquis' garden and a bush transferred from one area to hide the burial location."

"Very good!" Leonardo nodded. "Of course, Ottaviano's report that he could not find the necklace sends Isabella into even further hysteria. She knows the necklace she sent to the

Cambio is false. She depended on the return of that necklace. If the replica falls into unfriendly hands, she could be disgraced."

"Yes!" Niccolo says.

"When Ottaviano returns," Leonardo continued, "he knows he cannot keep the necklace intact, because Isabella is certain to send her dwarves to search his room, as they do for all guests at the court. He quickly separates the strands and deposits one diamond in each of the twenty-one candle molds. The black wax is not translucent and will not reveal them. He intends to pass all twenty-one to a selected monastery, and then buy them back with cash, which the monastery would probably prefer."

Niccolo excitedly broke in. "But when he tells you he wishes the candles decorated with scenes from the passion and death of Our Lord, you can only account for fourteen episodes, those depicted in the ritual of the Stations of the Cross. "

"So I prepare only fourteen and place the others aside. Now the marquesa has that other Janusian in the court, the unidentified one, murder Ottaviano. That assassin, looking around for someone to be blamed if the poisoning is revealed, finds it convenient to substitute a poison for my herbs."

"Convenient?"

The Maestro rose and crossed to Niccolo. He placed one huge hand on the dwarf's shoulder and said softly, "Yes. You showed her everything. She had complete access to this workshop because of her relationship with you."

Niccolo felt a cold hand on his heart. "Do you mean Lizette?"

"Lizette."

"I can't believe it."

"Remember her history? She went to a school in Venice. There she was taken into the employ of the Este who took her to Ferrara, and then she became a member of the Gonzaga court through the marquesa. Remember how the marquesa referred to her assassin? 'My little monkey'?" He stopped and saw the effect that this disclosure was having on his friend. "It can be verified," he said softly. "Every graduate of the Janus carries a small blue mark between the thumb and forefinger on their right hand, two arcs and a straight line. If you can coax your diminutive friend to ever abandon the lace gloves she always wears, I'll warrant you'll find the mark of the Janus."

Niccolo collapsed into a chair. "My god."

"Amusing, isn't it?" the Maestro looked down at him. "Especially because the Contessa Bergamini wanted your spying kept secret from me, because *I* did not understand women."

"Lizette . . . !" muttered Niccolo.

The Maestro nodded and returned to his chair. "In any case, the marquesa now believes that no one will ever discover where the missing necklace is. Ottaviano is dead. Obviously the marquesa doesn't care if the Son replica remains lost. She still has the Holy Spirit replica, which she can easily prove false if the Cambio questions her, *or* authentic, to satisfy her husband, by use of the copy of the appraisal which Johannes brought."

"So Caterina Sforza had the Father replica," Niccolo said, counting the copies on his fingers. "The marquesa has the Holy Spirit replica, and we discover the false diamonds from the Son replica hidden in the candles, which means . . . !"

"Yes! The necklace Madonna Laura reported seeing at the throat of Lucrezia Borgia must be the authentic Tears. *They never left the Vatican since Calixtus brought them to Rome from Spain! Never! The Borgias do not willingly surrender anything!*"

"Then what shall I tell the Cambio?" Niccolo asked.

"The truth. If they want the real Tears, they must go to Rome! There they not only have the real Tears, but the Father replica which, I imagine, has now been removed from the Contessa Sforza and resides in the Vatican treasury. The other two replicas, one dismantled, are here in Mantua." The Maestro squatted beside the young man. "But what was your assignment, Niccolo? To determine if the Tears had found their way back to the marquesa. Now you can report that they didn't. The marquesa, I assure you, will never tell the truth."

The young man turned his head and stared at Leonardo. "But the marquesa had everyone involved in this matter murdered! She tried to discredit you! Surely such a woman will not let us live knowing what we know!"

The Maestro shook his head and stood erect. "You're right. I assume that once the palazzo is cleared of guests, we will disappear."

"Like the courier disappeared?"

"Perhaps."

"Well, what are we to do?"

Leonardo turned and smiled. "We change," he said.

Nanino, listening at a niche in the wall, hastened through the next room, down the corridors and into Paradise. Breathlessly he informed the marquesa of everything he had overheard.

The marquesa sat brushing her hair and heard the report in silence. Then she sighed and turned to Nanino. "Well," she said. "If the Maestro expects me to have him and his obnoxious little friend murdered, I must not disappoint him."

She resumed brushing her hair. "But it must appear to be an accident," she said softly.

Nanino smiled and nodded. "I'll tell Lizette," he said.

Neither Leonardo nor Niccolo were surprised to find more guards posted along the colonnade outside the entrance to the workshop and their quarters, nor was it unexpected when additional "servants" suddenly appeared at every turn "to assist" them.

Fortunately, within two days, the courtyard of the palazzo rang with the trumpets, the pipes and the tambourines as I Comici Buffoni arrived, and the oppressive atmosphere lessened somewhat. Leonardo and Niccolo watched from the windows of the workshop as Rubini walked on his hands and performed a series of cartwheels that dazzled the servants. Piero Tebaldo, with his pillow-belly and the red half-mask of the Capitano, sat on the driver's seat of the colorful wagon that could be transformed into a stage. Marco Torri, in the dark robes and soft cap of Doctor Graziano of Bologna, sat beside him and spouted gibberish that was supposed to be some obscure and ancient language that only he knew. Simone Corio in the diamond suit of Arlecchino juggled six colored balls and two sharp blades, and Turio of Verona, the Pantalone of the group, pretended to throw a leather purse to the spectators, but it was attached to a string and pulled away before anyone could snatch it. Prudenza of Siena, whose theatrical character was Colombina, drove the smaller cart behind the great wagon while the two lovers, Francesco and Isabella Corteze, danced together. Anna Ponti, the Lesbino of the troupe, sang.

> "Wine and wit and women and war,
> Apart from these there is nothing more
> that tightens the throat and enlivens the heart
> save one, the explosive relief of a fart!"

"Well," smiled Leonardo, "at least *they* haven't changed."

Niccolo was soon reunited with his friends and exchanged pleasantries even as he advised the actors to not steal the silver plate as they had done in Milan.

"The marquesa will pay you well enough," he explained. "And the food and wine will be good and plentiful. You need not steal."

"Of course we don't *have* to steal!" Prudenza exclaimed. "It's a matter of principle and tradition. With actors and gypsies, one always expects a little thievery!"

When the troupe met with the marquesa in the Camera degli Sposi, the players were awed by the paintings that fooled the eye and suggested that courtiers were watching them from false rooms and the overhead dome.

"If we could paint a curtain like that," murmured Anna. "We could carry an audience with us."

The marquesa was radiant and alert and projected the image she cultivated, a woman of culture and refinement and wealth. Nanino, in his gold uniform, stood beside the chair of authority and glared at Niccolo.

It took some little effort on Niccolo's part to make the lady understand that the players could not possibly tell her in advance what the performance would contain. "There is no manuscript," the dwarf sighed. "It is not like a play at court that is written down. The gift of these players is that they can improvise an entire work on only a single word."

"Indeed?" sniffed the marquesa. "And what word shall we give them?"

"Oh, deception, perhaps?" Niccolo asked.

The marquesa's frown spoke volumes. "I think not," she snapped. "Perhaps arrogance?"

"I have it!" Niccolo cried. "Greed!"

The choice of the word was commended by the troupe who immediately began to consider possible sequences that could incorporate their own specialty bits of business, which they called "lazzi." The theme of greed immediately cast Turio as Pantalone as the central character, because his was the traditional role of the miser. Niccolo, invited to attend the planning session, suggested a sogetto in which Pantalone might have a valuable jewel. His daughter, Isabella, is about to marry Francesco who is the son of the Capitano. The bride's dowry requires that Pantalone surrender the jewel, but in his greed, he substitutes a piece of worthless crystal for the jewel. Unfortunately Doctor Graziano, a specialist in everything, easily spots the fake, and together with Arlecchino and Prudenza they so confuse the old man that he cannot tell the real from the false and ends up bestowing the authentic jewel on the Capitano.

"A strange sogetto," murmured Turio. "Where do you get such ideas?"

The performance was scheduled for the Camera that evening and would follow a banquet to honor the players. Niccolo had argued against this, because the capacity of the commedia woman for wine was legendary, and he was afraid that they might go well beyond the bounds of taste under the influence and shock the court. Nevertheless, the marquesa insisted on honoring the players with a feast, and Niccolo had no choice but to watch.

As the performance time neared, Meneghina appeared with a folded and sealed letter for Niccolo. He opened it at the table and read, "I know there have been some malicious lies told about me, and I have cause to believe that even the Maestro, a man I admire and deeply respect, may believe these untruths. I plead with you to consider our friendship and permit me an opportunity to show you that these stories rise from the jealousy of Nanino, who is the real assassin. Please, please meet with me in the indoor arena when the players begin their performance. That way no one will see us and report it to Nanino or the marquesa. I believe our past relationship permits me to ask this of you, and I am certain that when I explain everything, you will be satisfied that I remain your most devoted, Lizette."

The diners moved to the Camera for the performance, and Arlecchino appeared and announced the theme of the work and set the story in motion.

When Pantalone entered with an absurdly large diamond as big as a man's fist, Niccolo laughed and slid from his chair. Using his old skills as the kitchen thief he was able to avoid the guards that lined the corridors, and in a matter of minutes he was in the garden and headed for the stables.

Lizette waited and watched from the front row of seats of the viewing area at the far end of the arena. From this position she could see the door through which Niccolo would have to enter at the opposite end. Pazzo, already in the closed corridor that led to the arena, was plainly confused and restless. The great stallion pawed at the earth of the corridor and snorted and threw his head around so that the long mane whipped around his eyes and ears.

The horse had been placed there by the groom under instructions from the marquesa, although he protested that "surely no one intends to groom Pazzo so late at night?" Nevertheless the horse was in position, the corridor darkened and separated from the well-lit arena by only a single panel. The rope that could raise this panel was in Lizette's hand.

The plan was obvious. As Niccolo entered, Lizette would call to him, and the young man would start across the arena. Behind him, a woodcutter trusted by the marquesa would slam the door and bar it from the outside. Lizette would open the door to Pazzo's corridor, and the stallion, enraged at the sight of someone of Niccolo's short stature, would stomp the dwarf to death.

In the Camera, Pantalone was extolling his unbridled devotion to his jewel.

"Oh, my beloved, my dazzler, my snatcher of light, I do adore you!" He began to waltz with the jewel pressed against his cheek as the laughter began. "Oh, friend of my youth and protector of my old age, I worship and honor you and promise you that never, never shall we parted by the lascivious hands of someone like that arrogant Capitano! No! Never! Our love is eternal! It is immortal! It will survive Armageddon!"

That comment obviously disturbed the miser who stopped, thought about it, and then cried, "Well, if I can't take you with me, I'm not going!"

There was a full moon as Niccolo crossed the gardens and headed for the arena. He was devoted to the Maestro, but even the contessa had said that the man knew nothing about women. Surely Lizette *could* have been maligned. Nanino was more likely an assassin than poor Lizette. He knew her well enough to be sure she wasn't a trained assassin.

His confidence in Lizette rose with every thought. His walk became a trot as he spied the light spilling from the door of the stable, and he knew she was inside.

"I'm coming!" he murmured to the moon.

Then the reflexes and the antic spirit of the scullery thief arose in him. He scanned the open door, the night, the arena, and he laughed to himself.

"I'm coming," he repeated softly.

In the Camera the Capitano was specifying the conditions of the dowry that would enable his daughter to marry Francesco. "I will accept four of your full-blooded horses, six thousand ducats of gold, and the jewel you mentioned when we first discussed the arrangement."

"What?" shrieked Pantalone. "Four horses, six thousand ducats, and my beloved jewel? What am I buying for this? Is your daughter some sort of magnificent creature that her worth surpasses that of a palazzo? Has she balconies? A garden on her backside? It's a ridiculous proposition! I will bestow a dowry of no more than two horses, whose bloodlines, by the way, are better than your daughter's, and five thousand ducats!"

"But the jewel! You promised the jewel would be part of the dowry!"

On the dais at one end of the Camera, the marquesa frowned and began to fidget in her chair.

"I was in a momentary fit," shrilled Pantalone. "I was not myself. I would sooner cut off my right arm than part with my beloved, my true and faithful jewel!"

Suddenly Capitano drew his absurdly long sword and growled, "That can be arranged."

Lizette waited near the edge of the viewing area of the arena and focused her attention on the door at the far end. She was exhilarated, filled with a passion that rivalled any experience in her life. These were the moments for which she lived, for which she had been trained at the Janus, the cunning, the deception, the moment before the killing.

In the Camera Arlecchino had placed the jewel under one of three large cups aligned on the table. "You see?" he said to Pantalone. "It is all a matter of chance. Lift one."

Pantalone chose the cup on the far right end, and when he lifted it, there was the jewel! "Magnificent!" he cried. "My beloved called to me!"

Arlecchino laughed and raised the cup beside the jewel. Under it was another jewel that was an exact duplicate of the original. "Really?" the comic servant said. "Then what did this one call to you?"

Pantalone was plainly confused, and when Arlecchino lifted the final cup to reveal yet another copy of the jewel, the old man began to sputter and shriek.

And the marquesa's hands tightened on the arms of her chair until the knuckles were white.

Come on! Come on! Lizette mentally summoned Niccolo. Her total attention was centered on the door at the far end of the arena, and the rope that would open the panel of Pazzo's corridor was clenched tightly in her hand.

"Do you know there is another entry to this arena from the roof?" came the laughing voice behind her, jubilant that he had surprised the lady.

Lizette whirled, stunned to see Niccolo smiling at her from the top row of the viewing area. As he approached her in his pride at being the successful master of the shadows, she instinctively backed away. The low railing of the stands struck her at the small of her back, and her movement caused her to momentarily lose her balance. She teetered for a moment, frightened and confused, and then she fell over the railing and into the arena. As she did, still clutching the rope in her hand, it grew taut and the door to Pazzo's corridor swung open. In an instant the great stallion was in the soft earth of the arena and had spotted the lady dwarf scrambling to her feet. The horse's ears went back, and his nostrils flared. His lips drew back over his upper teeth, and he emitted such a piercing cry that Lizette, now on her feet, bolted for the open door at the far end of the arena.

The rapid movement excited Pazzo even more. In an instant he was on the lady, hooves flailing the life from her as she screamed and became embedded in the bloody earth of the arena.

Suddenly watching from the open door was Leonardo and the woodcutter who was to bar the portal behind Niccolo. The woodcutter, shocked at the sight of his confederate trampled to death, turned and ran to inform the marquesa. Without a word Leonardo closed and barred the door and leaned against it, drawing deep breaths of the night air. He had a package under one arm, and after a moment he was soon joined by a shocked and anguished Niccolo who climbed back over the roof entry and down the side of the building.

"It is time," said the Maestro gently.

Following the performance, the marquesa stormed into Paradise, Nanino waddling behind her. "Insulting!" she roared. "That was what it was! Insulting!" She turned to face the dwarf. "I want the guards doubled on the Maestro! By now Lizette has attended to that hideous little man! I want these players removed from the palazzo now! *Now*, do you hear? *Now*! This very moment! After they have departed, I will handle the problem of the Maestro myself. I still have the secret report from Maestro Bernardo that Ottaviano was killed by a continual application of poison from the Maestro! What do you think that will do for his reputation?"

"I will see to it immediately," said Nanino as he bowed.

The players, who assumed they would remain as guests for the evening, were surprised and confused when a contingent of mercenaries from the garrison suddenly appeared at the Camera, gathered them together and ordered them to leave immediately, still in costume and makeup!

"I didn't think I was all that bad," snarled Prudenza.

The players were escorted in their costumes and masks to their wagons in the courtyard, and then Piero shrugged and said, "Well, maybe we'll do better in Verona."

It was only a matter of minutes after the woodcutter gave his report that the body of Lizette was found in the arena and removed to the palazzo. "Look for that dwarf!" cried the marquesa. "I want that arrogant little man on his knees before me! I want him beheaded and buried in the arena! I want the bastard dead!"

As the wagon and the cart of the commedia troupe wound its way through the Piazza Sordello and down the narrow streets through the gates of the walled city, inside the wagon the ladies were helping Niccolo from his Capitano costume and were unbelting the stilts with which he had appeared to be of normal height.

"The Maestro?" he asked.

"On the cart," said Isabella. "Isn't it fortunate that the guards did not think to ask why we had two Capitanos and a moon god?"

And, indeed, on the seat of the cart beside Turio, Leonardo, in silver robes, was removing the large Venetian moon-mask. "The guards were too confused to even wonder how many there were of us, and why one seemed to be playing the moon in the evening's entertainment!" laughed Turio.

The Maestro laughed too. "Niccolo?" he asked.

"In the wagon," said Turio. "He was never in any trouble. After all, they were looking for a dwarf, not for a tall mockery of a military man!"

The Maestro laughed again as Anna began a little song, and the wagon and the cart turned south and away from Mantua.

In Paradise, the marquesa was handed the letter by her chamberlain. "It was in the workshop and addressed to you," Meneghina explained.

"The Maestro and the dwarf?"

"We cannot locate them," shrugged the chamberlain. "But they are somewhere in the palazzo. Where could Niccolo hide? In the dwarves' apartments? We'll find him!"

Isabella opened the letter. It read: "My most illustrious and revered marquesa, your secrets concerning the Tears of the Madonna will remain locked in my heart forever. By the time you read this, I, and Niccolo, will be far from Mantua, but if you should choose to send men after us, I will be forced to reveal all. You see, while I was in Venice I took advantage of the newly organized service for the transmittal of letters between Venice and Brussels. I sent a packet to Ser Johannes in which I detailed all your crimes and all your deceptions, and I included my sketch of the courier's head. This information, however, was contained within a sealed letter with an accompanying outer message that the seal should be broken only if Johannes hears of my death or disappearance. I am certain our young Belgian friend will honor my request. If Gian-Francesco learns of your deception, Excellency, I imagine his honor would force him to put you away, possibly to a convent, a fate far worse than death for someone of your breeding and vitality, something that could have you, Madonna, shedding genuine tears for the rest of your life."

The marquesa sat with the letter in her hand for some time, then she forced a smile of ice, shook her head, and said to Meneghina, "There is no point in further search. Let them be."

Meneghina seemed surprised. "But how . . . ?"

"With that old man," the marquesa said softly, "I have no doubt that they turned themselves into birds and flew away."